THE
NoMO
KILLER

by

Joseph B. Hodgkins

COPYRIGHT

The NoMO Killer

Copyright © 2022 by Joseph B. Hodgkins

All Rights Reserved

ISBN (paperback): 978-1-7363849-4-7

ISBN (e-book): 978-1-7363849-5-4

ALSO AVAILABLE

by

JOSEPH B. HODGKINS

The Reverend Elizabeth Williamson & Church Gagne

Crime Drama Series

Murder in the Apothecary

Lizzy's Jazz Joint

IN MEMORY

of my friend and Masonic brother

WB Rocco A. Lania

On April 29, 2020, "Rocky" was called to the Lodge on High.

PROLOGUE

After graduation from university, Bridgette Dubois had joined France's National Police Force, formerly called the Sûreté. She had worked her way up the ranks and was now an *inspecteur*. Well regarded as a detective, she had also developed a niche role as a profiler even though she wasn't attached to a Behavioral Analysis Unit. Bridgette looked at her watch—five thirty in the afternoon. Eight thirty in the morning in San Francisco.

Ellen will be at her desk in police headquarters by now. Not too early to call, Bridgette thought.

She was calling Dr. Ellen Sandler, a senior profiler attached to the Serious Crimes Unit who'd been working for the San Francisco PD after her retirement from the FBI in 2000. She'd had a successful twenty-five-year career in their Behavioral Analysis Unit, where she'd been a lead profiler. After retirement, Ellen had returned to her roots in San Francisco.

Bridgette and Ellen had met at a conference in Montreal in 1999. And even though Bridgette, then twenty-five, was twenty-four years younger than Ellen, they'd easily become friends. They had kept in touch, and Bridgette had consulted with Dr. Sandler during the winter of 2011 when Bridgette was on training leave at the Sûreté du Québec, Montreal. She had helped the San Francisco police in a high-profile international investigation called the Warehouse Murders. The women had much in common, especially their unconventional approach to profiling. Both thought traditional analysis was inflexible, tending to look merely at the obvious. So, if characteristics such as weapons, sex, age, type of victim, occupation, location, date, and so forth didn't lead anywhere, then it was necessary to go beyond appearances and deal with core subconscious motivations—psychological characteristics. Determining these unconscious motives was difficult, and the process wasn't always understood or appreciated by their colleagues.

But more important, Bridgette trusted Ellen, and that was the reason for her call this afternoon. She needed a friend who didn't think she was nuts. Today's overzealous teasing by her colleagues about the NoMO Killer had been over the top, and Bridgette was upset. She was routinely teased about her search for the NoMO Killer, as her colleagues had named him. The fact that the NoMO Killer seemed like he'd been inactive for the last few years didn't help her case. But Bridgette was sticking to her guns.

Years ago, she'd become suspicious that there was a highly successful, professional killer operating in the EU. She wasn't certain what had triggered her thought process, but she wondered if this killer had escaped detection because he had never used the same modus operandi twice. Each crime appeared to be singular, never showing up in any search for similar crimes. Obviously, her thesis presented lots of problems, but she was convinced that the lack of an MO could be an MO. And Dr. Sandler got it—they thought alike.

"Bridgette, good to hear from you. It's been a while! Is everything all right?"

"Well, yes and no." Then Bridgette told her about the teasing. "I needed cheering up."

"We've talked about this before. I think you're onto something, and because he has gone to ground doesn't mean anything. He could be working far afield where you couldn't gather any intelligence. And don't overlook the obvious. Perhaps something went wrong on a job, or he's had a life change. Maybe he got married and had a baby?" Ellen joked.

"You always make me feel better!" Bridgette responded. "I have happy news, though; I'm with someone now—finally."

"That's wonderful. Tell me."

"His name is Nando Medina. He's a year older than me and never married either. Nando is a partner in an upscale boutique art gallery and teaches art history at the Sorbonne. That's where I met him when I took a class on the Impressionist painters. He's an interesting man. He graduated from Princeton with a degree in art history. Then, incongruously, he went to work for the CIA, but he won't talk about it. I gather he left after a rumpus over the way he'd handled an assignment. That was about eight years ago. But it couldn't have been so bad, because they gave him a sizable buyout and pensioned him off. Then he came over here, obtained an advanced degree at the Sorbonne, and bought in to an art gallery, La Galerie, with the CIA's money."

"So it's serious?"

"Yes. I'm in the process of moving in."

"Best of luck. And don't forget to send me an invitation to your wedding. I'll fly over."

"Okay, but before you go, did you ever apprehend Denis Rodolphe? When we spoke last, your detectives were convinced he was hiding in Montreal."

"Nothing much is new with the Warehouse Murders case. We still think Rodolphe is in Montreal, and the body count is still four women and another if you include his accomplice, Zack. But there's good news for the detectives, Joe Cancio and Gabi Müller. Their long-serving captain of detectives retired this spring. So their captain was promoted to that spot, Joe to captain, and Gabi to lieutenant. However, every six months they still review that case themselves."

"Well, let's hope something turns up. Thanks for listening; I'm better now. I'll let you know when we have any definite plans."

CHAPTER ONE

Wednesday, August 20, 2014
CIA Headquarters, McLean, Virginia

The director stood at his window overlooking the campus. The senior analyst attached to the clandestine Special Operations Group that reported to him and the president had left. That group didn't exist; it never appeared as a line item in any congressional budget, and if you had to describe it, *blacker than black ops* would be an appropriate sobriquet. The director had known the analyst Jay Jaeger for many years, dating back to the director's tenure as homeland security adviser to the president. Jay wasn't an alarmist and was detailed to the point of exasperation. That was why their meeting had alarmed the director.

Earlier this morning, his secretary had come in and said that Jaeger needed to see him immediately—alone. Curious about such an unusual request, he'd said, "Have him come up now," thinking, *What the hell is this all about? Completely out of character!*

The director listened intently for ten minutes, not interrupting. Finally, when Jay had finished, he stood, walked over to his window, clasped his hands behind his back, and thought. At last, he returned to his desk.

"Okay, if it were anyone besides you who came in here with such a vague, imprecise analysis, I'd throw their ass out. But we go back a long way; I trust your judgment.

"So you've been picking up all sorts of unusual chatter about a threat of the highest national security happening before year end—here in the homeland. And it seems like there may be as many as six or seven actors involved from various sectors such as energy, construction, finance and banking, big tech, and industry, as well as, possibly, one foreign country."

"Yes, sir."

"Who are your sources?"

"General EU chatter and an anonymous stateside one."

"Any idea who that is?"

"No."

"You're confident that this alliance is the real deal?"

"Yes."

"And you're convinced there is no greater risk to our country other than a nuclear attack?"

"Yes."

"I'm only thinking of one thing."

"Yes, sir."

"All right, but don't mention this to anyone. We'll talk again.

The director had been standing at his window since Jay left. *What the fuck! I gotta tell him now—shit.*

He went back to his desk, buzzed his secretary, and said, "Get me the president—pronto!"

***

Nando and Bridgette were on a ten-day auto tour and were sitting Wednesday afternoon in a quiet bistro overlooking Honfleur's Vieux Bassin. They were spending three days in this picturesque harbor, located near where the Seine met the English Channel. The area was a favorite of Impressionist painters like Monet. Later, they would explore Normandy's countryside and coast and eventually make their way to the American Cemetery and Memorial in Colleville-sur-Mer and then to Pointe du Hoc, where Allied forces had landed on D-day, June 6, 1944. Afterward, they would return to Paris through Tours and Chartres.

Bridgette had been out of sorts before leaving last Friday. However, Nando was still adjusting to and learning about their deepening relationship, so he had let it pass. *Perhaps she'll tell me when she feels more comfortable,* he'd thought. But whatever it was, it seemed like it still weighed on her. Finally, he decided to broach the subject. "Bridgette, you seem like you're bothered about something," Nando said. "Did I do anything?"

"Oh no, I didn't think it showed—sorry if I've been pouty. I had a bad day last Wednesday. I even called my friend Ellen in San Francisco for moral support. She made me feel better, but I guess it's still nettling me."

"She's the profiler with SFPD, right?"

"Yes."

"You can talk to me. I'm a good listener."

"I know, but I don't like to bring my work home, and a lot of what I do is confidential."

"I understand. But we're going to be living together when we return; you might try it. I still have my top secret clearance from my CIA days if it makes you feel better."

"Really. It never occurred to me you still had your clearance. Huh, after all these years," Bridgette said, and they sat silently. *I guess I could tell him. It's not like it's an active investigation. But I'm going to be hurt if he laughs at me. Maybe I should, though; maybe it's part of taking the next step?* she reflected.

"All right. Here goes." Bridgette began telling him about her niche as a profiler. And quickly moved on to her theory of an assassin who had been operating in Europe for years but hadn't been detected because he didn't use the same MO twice. She told Nando how her colleagues had dubbed him the NoMO Killer and at times teased her. Last Wednesday they'd been unfair, describing her as having a disorder, an obsession. She had started tearing up and left her desk. Then after washing her face with cold water, she'd returned and called Ellen.

"I know I'm right, and Ellen agrees with me. And she was the FBI's top profiler for twenty-five years. We both think that physical attributes such as type of victim, operational methods, weapons of choice, those sorts of things are less important than underlying psychological characteristics, traits, et cetera. The problem is, I can't develop enough information to take my analysis further. Each one of the killings that I think is a possibility bears no similarity to any other one—don't laugh at me!"

"I'm not laughing at all. I understand, and I think it makes sense. After all, you have an excellent authority on your side with Ellen."

"Also, if he exists, he seems to have gone to ground for the last several years," Bridgette finished.

Nando squeezed her hand and ordered more wine. *Son of a bitch! She's been tracking me! Jesus, how the hell did Bridgette ever get onto me? Most of the killings are mine—a few I don't recognize. I've been fuckin' lucky! At least I haven't heard from Satie or the CIA in a few years. Fat chance the CIA would have my six if the shit hits the fan, especially in this administration. Dammit!*

They started talking about the rest of their trip, and Bridgette seemed happier. But although Nando wasn't happy, he managed not to show his disquietude. The rest of the trip was pleasant enough, and they returned to Paris on August 25.

***

Early Tuesday morning the twenty-sixth, the president's secretary buzzed the Oval.

"Mr. President, the director of the CIA is here."

"Send him in," the president said, and rose from his desk to greet him as he entered. The director had called earlier requesting an emergency meeting—just the two of them.

"We've developed additional credible intelligence about what I reported to you last Wednesday. We still haven't been able to identify the conspirators or unearth why, but we now know they've reached out to Satie, and the price is a hundred and fifty million plus expenses."

"Jesus, that's well above market."

"Yes."

"Was that from the EU or stateside?"

"The EU. I think our next step ought to be putting eyes on Satie."

"Is he still in Munich? Do we have anyone there?" the president asked.

"Yes to both questions, but I would prefer to go in another direction. I don't have a high level of confidence about leaks. This is too serious to fuck around with. We have an officer from our Special Operations Group in Berlin finishing up an assignment. He'll be heading to Paris for R & R, but I can divert him to Munich."

"Who?"

"Church Gagne. He and Satie have never crossed paths. He should be invisible," the director said.

"Excellent idea. He's the best, right?"

"Yes, I trust him completely. But he's only a stopgap measure; we need around-the-clock electronic monitoring of who's going in and out of Satie's office."

"A bug inside?"

"Maybe. We'll watch the surveillance for a week or so and see if Satie is routinely sweeping his office. I don't want to risk having our listening devices found—it would tip him off. I think I'll use a team from our Langley group for this—less chance of a leak."

"Let's do it," the president responded, concluding their meeting.

***

Later, Church received his orders for Munich. *Now Paris is all screwed up. I've been looking forward to five days of relaxing, sightseeing, and visiting art museums—especially the d'Orsay*, Church thought. Instead he canceled his flight, exchanging it for an early Thursday morning one to Munich. The director had assured him the assignment wouldn't be long although he hadn't committed to a specific period. However, the director had said he could take a full week in Paris when he finished with Munich. It was a simple surveillance of the business premises of a man called Satie whose office was in the old city, near the Marienplatz. *Sounds boring but not difficult.*

***

Bridgette was taking two weeks off, so she still had the rest of the week. Their plan was that on Tuesday, Nando would help pack her belongings into his car and drive them to his apartment. Afterward, they would unload everything. The following day, Nando would return to work, but Bridgette would set about unpacking and reorganizing their apartment. He was suspicious that he wouldn't recognize it by Friday. But it was okay with him if Bridgette was living there. Nando was confident that he'd gotten the better part of the deal. It seemed like their vacation and her enthusiasm over moving to his place had pushed her concerns about the NoMO Killer teasing to the back of her mind. Nando was beginning to get his head around it also. *After all, she has absolutely no idea she's searching for me. I'll have to keep it that way*, he thought.

Wednesday morning after breakfast, Nando left their apartment west of the Rue de Rennes in the sixth arrondissement. It was a comfortable day for August, so he walked along the Rue de Rennes and Rue Bonaparte to La Galerie. It was located on the Rue Bonaparte near Ladurée, about halfway between the Boulevard Saint-Germain and the Quai Malaquais. The sixth arr. was wonderful to live and work in. From their apartment, the Sorbonne, the d'Orsay, the Louvre, and La Galerie were all within a semicircle of less than two miles—easy walking.

He had bought into this boutique art gallery in 2007 after leaving the CIA in 2006 and completing a master's degree in art history at the Sorbonne. The seller was Madame Bertrand; she and her husband had owned La Galerie for many years. It had developed an excellent reputation for handling local, undiscovered painters. Her husband had recently passed away, and she'd been forced to sell La Galerie to cover profligate undisclosed gambling debts he had left behind. She'd had no idea about the debts, and the gamblers had been unwilling to wait for payment, hence a distressed sale.

Nando had done his homework. He knew what La Galerie was worth compared to other galleries that were also for sale. It was easily the most valuable and being offered at half the market price. This piqued his interest. So he made an appointment and called on Madame Bertrand, a lovely, sophisticated woman who looked like she was in her late thirties. Much later, Nando would learn she was over fifty. They chatted; she knew art, and they got on well. She showed him the books, and he was correct. The gallery was worth double what she was asking, and Nando had the money to pay market price.

Finally, he closed the books and said, "You're selling at a distress price. Why?"

"I have commitments I must honor, Monsieur."

"Look, I'm not putting out all this money without a sensible answer. Tell me."

He could see her beginning to tear up. "I can't tell you, and I can't lower the price." Then, as Nando looked at her folded hands resting on the table, she said softly, "Monsieur, I will do anything you ask if you'll meet my price. But I won't tell you. Please—I'm desperate." Then she raised her head and looked him squarely in the eyes.

Nando hadn't expected this turn of events. Here was this gracious lady willing to prostitute herself to avoid disclosing her secrets, but more extraordinary was her absolute self-assurance in her desirability. Surprisingly without a blush, she put what she had left on the table. Years later, when he learned her age, he found this even more remarkable. Although Madame didn't need to regain her composure, they looked at each other for a bit before he said, "Madame, your offer is unnecessary.

"I'll buy into your business, but I have conditions, nonnegotiable conditions. Here's what I'm willing to do. I'll purchase fifty-one percent, but for all intents and purposes, you'll continue to be the owner with an appropriate salary. I will be your new assistant, and we'll work out acceptable hours. Is that agreeable?"

"And you'll meet my price, Monsieur?"

"No, Madame, it's out of the question." Nando wrote a number on a piece of paper and handed it to her. "You'll have to decide now."

Hesitantly, she opened the paper and stared for a moment. Then she burst into tears, jumped up, ran around the table, and started hugging him, kissing him on the cheek.

"Oh, thank you, Monsieur! Thank you, thank you . . ."

Nando had written an amount almost two times her asking price; he was convinced he had made a fair deal. He never saw any reason to change the gallery's name. They called each other Madame and Monsieur. Eventually she told him about her husband's debts. And later, after a successful opening for a new artist, when they were celebrating in the office and she'd had a little too much champagne, she giggled. "I'm sorry you didn't accept my full offer when you bought in to the business."

"I may have made a mistake, Madame."

"Oh yes, Monsieur, I'm sure you did!" And they both laughed.

***

Nando wasn't enjoying his walk home as much as he had enjoyed his walk to work this morning. The day had gone well, with several profitable sales. Madame had come in at three o'clock in the afternoon and would stay until closing at seven, so he'd left early after calling Bridgette and suggesting a bistro for dinner that evening. Bridgette had thought it was a great idea.

Unfortunately, after he had called Bridgette, he'd received a coded text from Satie, who wanted to see him in Munich on either Thursday or Friday. Nando hadn't heard from him or the CIA in two years, so he'd thought that part of his life had drifted into oblivion. *I guess not! Don't need this shit on top of what Bridgette told me.*

He spoke to Madame, and she could cover for him. Nando would leave in the early afternoon tomorrow, spend the night in Munich, and return Friday on an early-morning train. He preferred trains because of lighter security and less CCTV monitoring than at airports. *Old habits die hard, and I don't have to get to the station three hours early. But Bridgette isn't going to be happy about this. I'll wait until after dinner or when we go to bed to tell her. I'll say it's a last-minute meeting with an important new artist.*

So on Thursday the twenty-eighth, Nando left from Gare de l'Est at two p.m. and arrived at Munich's Central Station before eight o'clock. He walked to Satie's office near the Marienplatz; the office's entrance was from the street at a polished brass plaque that read ANDRÉ SATIE, LAWYER & CONSULTANT. In the growing twilight, Nando hadn't noticed Church Gagne, who was already in place.

CHAPTER TWO

Thursday, August 28, 2014
Munich

By early afternoon, Church had checked into a small hotel and found a suitable place to observe Satie's office near the Marienplatz. The surveillance was easier than expected because the suite, which occupied the entire street level, had only one entrance and exit. Using his phone, Church photographed Satie's few visitors before texting them to Langley. Nothing looked unusual, and there hadn't been any clients since six p.m. Now it was after eight o'clock, and soon the twilight would be too deep for photographs. Church was about to return to his hotel near Munich's Central Station when a man, who seemed familiar, approached from that direction. He stepped back into the abandoned garage entranceway he'd been using for cover. He took several pictures as the man entered Satie's. Then Church boosted the light on his phone before reviewing them. *Son of a bitch! I know him*, he thought, and dialed the director.

"Our analyst tells me your photos have been coming through," the director said. "What's going on?"

"I was packing up because it's getting dark over here. But Satie had a last visitor a few minutes ago. The photos should be coming through by now. I know him—Nando Medina. He was from our Special Operations Group. We went to Princeton together and joined the company at about the same time. There was a dustup eight years ago and he left.

The last I heard, Nando was a part owner of a Paris art gallery and teaching at the Sorbonne."

"I don't recognize his name. Stay with him and call me when you have additional information. I'll pick up, no matter how late. This is important!"

Nando left in about thirty minutes. Church followed him to a small hotel not far from his own. He saw Nando talking with the reception clerk, who nodded yes. Nando checked in, took a key, and went to the elevator. For five euros, Church learned that Nando had requested a wake-up call for four forty-five so he could catch the first train to Paris in the morning.

When Church called the director, he said, "Keep following Medina. Here's his phone number and both home and business addresses. Check back with me when you arrive in Paris. I'll probably have you make contact, but I'm not certain yet. I need to talk to him, but I can't read you in on this now; it's too sensitive."

The next morning Church followed Nando and boarded the train a few cars behind him.

***

During the six-hour trip to Paris, Nando pondered his situation. What Satie wanted alarmed him, and he had only a few days to respond. That had been their normal procedure. Satie's ask had complicated his life, especially with Bridgette, turning it topsy-turvy and putting him in danger. Although their conversation had been subtle, there was no ambiguity about what Satie's clients wanted. Of course, Nando could say no. But sooner or later the clients would conclude that his knowledge was a pointless risk they didn't have to take. Nando had no misapprehensions about his safety after that; they would act swiftly and appropriately. And based on the payment offered, $150 million plus $50 million in expenses, they had the resources.

Stay calm; think your way through this. There must be a way out. I'm too happy now to chuck it all and go to ground! Damned if I will— screw them!

Nando kept ruminating, thinking back to his childhood. His life had been straightforward in Hagerstown, Maryland, and later at Princeton—a variant on the classic American dream. Nando was the only son of Hernan and Alicia Medina. As migrant workers, they had trekked north from Mexico, where Nando's father was an out-of-work auto mechanic. Their first year they'd moved along the Gulf Coast before joining a band of illegal migrants heading up the East Coast. They made it as far as the farms south of Princeton, New Jersey. That was where Hernan first heard of Princeton University. The second year, in 1973, when Alicia was pregnant with Nando, they connected with a legal crew out of Florida. The crew's boss provided them with H-2 temporary work visas, issued under the Immigration and Naturalization Act. But more important, they acquired social security numbers. Then, after the harvest, when their crew headed south, they jumped off the truck in Maryland and walked the seventy miles or so to Hagerstown. It seemed far enough off the beaten path for them to safely overstay their visas. Hernan found a job in his vocation, and after Nando was born, Alicia worked as a part-time waitress.

Then, before he was even a teenager, Nando spent weekends tramping through Maryland's Hagerstown Valley woods with his father, rifles in hand, hunting or target shooting. *That's when my friggin' talent first reared its ugly head. I wish I'd never become such a crack shot, especially at long distances. It's the root of all my problems!*

Later, at Hagerstown High School, Nando excelled in academics and lettered in football and baseball. He was accepted at Princeton with combined athletic and academic scholarships that paid all his expenses. Nando chuckled. *It wasn't as if I had a choice to go anywhere else. Princeton was all Dad ever talked about.*

So after graduation, he worked locally for a year. His father had never understood his degree in art history, and Nando finally accepted that his father had been correct. There weren't many jobs for art history majors, especially in the western panhandle of Maryland. Eventually, in 1996, Nando joined the CIA—it seemed cool. The CIA was glad to have him. Having been born in Maryland, he was a US citizen, but he spoke Spanish with native proficiency and was fluent in French because of a minor at Princeton. His father, who had been impatient to have Nando get a real job, was happy now. A bonus was that the CIA also appealed to his father's assimilated patriotism. Before reporting for duty, Nando visited his buddy Church Gagne, who was living in Paris for a year. They'd both graduated from Princeton with degrees in art history. When Nando told him about the CIA, Church thought it sounded neat. So not long after Nando returned home, Church followed, joining the CIA as well. They both ended up in the same twenty-five-man blacker-than-black-ops Special Operations Group that reported to the director and the president. They were required to undergo Navy SEAL training before beginning at the CIA.

That's when my talent took over my life!

When the CIA discovered Nando had scored the best shot ever recorded during SEAL sniper training, his future was set. After 2001, Nando did multiple deployments in the Mideast, usually attached to military units who were clearing urban areas. Typically, using a McMillan TAC-50, Nando would take positions on rooftops and clear the way for the soldiers below, who were going building to building. The only kill that ever bothered Nando was in 2002 when he took out a Taliban leader. The man was home, in the backyard, celebrating his thirteen-year-old son's birthday. The kill was right in front of the boy—twenty-five hundred yards—dead bang.

Still can't get that one out of my head.

Gradually, Nando discovered snipers were different—a breed apart. The troops loved how they protected them in the field but were distant in their off-duty relationships. So eventually, Nando obtained reassignment to a traditional, clandestine role within his group. Then in 2006, he'd been assigned to meet a CIA officer from Kandahar at Berlin's Tegel Airport. The Kandahar officer was escorting two Afghans fleeing persecution for having helped the US. Nando's mission was to accompany them the rest of the way to Langley; it seemed simple enough. But as the officer and the Afghans cleared passport control, two Taliban militants, who were waiting in the terminal, opened fire. Nando was also an expert with a handgun and fired two shots, each round hitting a militant in the forehead. Unfortunately, the Kandahar operations officer earned a star carved into the white Alabama marble wall at CIA headquarters. The Afghans fled into the airport, and Nando was arrested on weapons charges. It took the president's intercession with Germany's chancellor to have the charges dropped, and Nando returned home. Almost immediately, Nando was pensioned out of the CIA. The director hadn't even done it himself—a deputy director drew that duty.

Fuck them!

Nando received benefits as if he had retired after twenty years. And in return for signing a nondisclosure agreement, he received a mid-six-figure buyout. But in it, Nando waived his right to sue for wrongful termination. It hadn't been too bad once his ego healed. So it was off to Paris for an advanced degree in art history at the Sorbonne.

But then an unexpected event occurred. One day, when Nando was returning from classes along the Rue de Vaugirard, a limousine with tinted windows pulled up to the curb. The rear door opened and the general who had taken over as the director of the CIA at the end of May said, "Medina, do you know who I am?"

Nando recognized him and nodded.

"Do you have a few minutes to talk?" the general said, and slid over; Nando got in, and the car started moving immediately. "Excellent. I'll be direct. I've been getting up to speed and saw your file. I think you got a bum deal. Financially, you've done all right, and I imagine your hurt feelings will eventually heal. But it has been a blow to your reputation, and I don't think a retraction buried deep within a newspaper will help. I don't know what else can be done. So let's make it work for both of us."

Twenty minutes later when Nando was dropped off at his apartment, Bridgette's NoMO Killer had been created.

The train was nearing Paris now. *How am I going to explain all this to Bridgette? I hope she can process it. Maybe recognizing that she has been correct all along will give her solace—hope so!*

***

On Friday, August 29, at eight a.m. in the Oval Office, the director met with the president. "We have additional intelligence. I spoke with Officer Gagne last evening. He sent a photo of Satie's last visitor, and he knows the man, Nando Medina. We've confirmed his identity from the photo. Nando was on a train back to Paris early this morning, and Gagne is following him. Medina has a history with us."

"What do you mean, 'a history'?"

"I pulled his file first thing this morning; it's interesting—before my time. He joined us in 1996 a year after he graduated from Princeton. Medina and Gagne were friends there, and Medina was the one who interested Gagne in us. They both ended up in our Special Operations Group. When we discovered Medina's sniping prowess, we brought him aboard as a sniper. He had a terrific record with multiple deployments to the Mideast. It's vague, but Nando seems to have wanted out of sniping— a bad experience. So we accommodated him. Now the file becomes vaguer. On a routine mission in Berlin, Medina was involved in a shoot-out at Tegel Airport." The director explained the circumstances. "In the end, he was arrested on weapons charges, and the president had to intercede with the chancellor to get his ass out of jail and home. Then we busted him out with benefits. He has been in Paris since."

"It doesn't sound like Medina did anything wrong. Why did we bust him?"

"I don't know, but here's where it becomes curiouser. I've had to piece this together. Remember, I'm the fourth director since he was released. His kerfuffle in Berlin was in the early spring of 2006. We had a new director in May that year who went to Paris and hired him as an independent contractor—a mercenary."

"Jesus, it makes no sense. We probably paid more for his services than if we'd kept him on staff?"

"I don't think we can look at it in a linear way. A couple of things came into play. First, the new director thought Medina got the shit end of the stick, and secondly, it played into an op we were trying to set up in Europe. Portraying Medina like a disgruntled former employee fit in with our plans. It involved our old friend Satie."

"How so?"

"Again, unclear—but I suspect Nando's termination might have been orchestrated to take advantage of the situation. Simply put, Satie had started popping up on our radar with his clandestine gunrunning, assassination brokerage, sex trafficking, and the like. You name it, he was into it. Satie worked out of Munich, as he still does, under the guise of a lawyer and consultant. Originally, there had been no specific plan other than to have someone inside and close to Satie. The new director saw an opportunity. So we leaked that a disgruntled Medina was a gun for hire. It wasn't long before Satie made contact. We used Medina to take care of people where we needed a few degrees of separation."

"It sounds very *Mission: Impossible*: 'Should you be caught or killed, the director will disavow all knowledge of your actions,'"[1] the president bantered.

"Yes, sir." The director chuckled before continuing. "It was easy. We had different deep-cover operatives use Satie as a broker, requesting Medina because of his reputation. So that he could vet the legitimacy of each kill, we set up a verification procedure for him. I can't prove it, but it seems like we verified every job Satie offered him even if it wasn't one of ours. Apparently, that was done to keep Medina in tight with Satie."

"How many kills altogether?"

"It looks like nine, with six being legit. With all the personnel changes here, Medina seems to have fallen through the cracks, plus this is Satie's first contact in a few years."

"How much did we pay him?"

"About four hundred thousand dollars, in addition to whatever he received for the three bogus kills."

"Jesus! And Medina didn't have a clue about the bogus ones?" the president asked rhetorically. "Is it time to bring him in from the cold?"

"Yes," the director answered. "Obviously, we can't verify this job for Medina, and if he turns Satie down, how long do you think the collaborators will let him live? They know that any professional with a grain of sense will immediately figure out who the contract is on."

"Because of the price?" the president asked.

"Yes."

"All right, let's recall Medina. If he isn't doing the job, he's probably the best suited to track down the son of a bitch who is. Talk with Gagne; he knows him. See what's the best approach."

"My thoughts as well, sir."

***

Later, Church followed Nando from the train to La Galerie and stayed out of sight until closing at seven o'clock. Nando walked home, and then he and his girl went to a bistro for dinner. Church shadowed them there and waited across the street. When Nando and Bridgette finished dinner, they walked home, holding hands, looking happy. When Church was satisfied they were settled for the night, he went in search of a small hotel. From there he intended to call the director, report, and discuss what his approach to Nando ought to be. While Church looked for lodgings, Bridgette and Nando went to bed. She slid over, snuggling. "I'm glad you're back. I don't like to be apart even for one night."

"Neither do I."

Bridgette reached for him, but Nando said, "We need to talk about something first."

"Okay . . . but did I do anything? You seem so serious."

"No, it isn't you; it's me. This is going to take a while. I honestly thought this was all behind me. But when you told me about your conversation with Ellen, I realized it wasn't. Add in why I went to Munich, and I simply can't put this off any longer. I hope you'll still want to stay with me after you hear me out."

"Nando . . . don't say that. It can't be that bad!"

"Well, it might be. You see, you don't know me at all. All you know is what I try to be. What I thought I'd become."

Bridgette was still close but started sniffling, sensing this might become a watershed moment. Nando began—it took him over an hour. It all came out, including Satie reappearing after several years. And finally, what Satie wanted: the killing of the president of the United States for $150 million.

Bridgette was sobbing now and moved over to her side of the bed. Nando wished she hadn't but understood. *It's a natural reaction to finding out you've been intimate with a killer.*

She got up, putting on her robe. "Nando, I'm going to the couch . . . at least for a while. I love you, but I need to get my head around this. How can you dump all this stuff on me at once? I can't believe it's happening . . . dammit!" Bridgette left, and Nando fell into a disturbed sleep. Then, around four o'clock, Bridgette came back to bed and put her arms around him.

"Are you all right?" Nando asked.

"Not now. We'll talk in the morning . . . just hold me."

Nando was relieved. *She's staying.*

The next morning, Saturday, they slept in and had a late breakfast. Nando wasn't going to the gallery until three in the afternoon, so they took their time. Knowing she would have her say, he didn't press. He could wait. Finally, Bridgette began.

"Well, I'm mad as hell at you. You could have told me about this, at least some of it. You said you had a top secret clearance and did clandestine stuff for the CIA. But *this* . . . I didn't realize. I didn't see it coming . . . Jesus. And have you told me more than you ought to?"

"Some."

"All right . . . I understand . . . I'll keep your secrets." Bridgette sighed. "Here's what bothers me the most. A sniper is a necessary part of war and legal. Honestly, if I ever thought about it before, it was as an abstraction. But it isn't one. There're human beings at both ends of the kill. And I'm guessing it is not always twenty-five hundred yards away like the Taliban leader you did in front of his son."

"No, sometimes it's up close."

"Well, that sure as hell takes any sense of adventure out of it. I understand *why* when you were on the job—it was for God and country. But I'm having trouble with your transition to a civilian mercenary. You weren't really CIA anymore, and you didn't get a direct order from the president or the director. It doesn't seem to be the same—it doesn't seem to be justified. If it were, why not use CIA or other licit snipers? And do you think they would've had your back?

"You had changed along the way, so you opted out of sniping. Why did you return to it?"

"I've thought a lot about that. I'm not certain, but I was still mad as hell at the CIA for busting me out. Maybe I had something to prove to them?" Nando said.

"Or to yourself?"

"Perhaps."

They were quiet for a while. At length, Bridgette said, "There's something else upsetting me; you hinted at it last night. If you say no to Satie, will you be safe?"

"I could say yes, yet there's no avoiding that I know too much."

"*Exactement*! How long do you think you'd have?"

"Not long."

"You need to contact the CIA, but first we need to come up with a plan. We can think about it for the next couple of days before you report back to Satie. We need to control this as much as possible. I'm not convinced the CIA will have your back."

Nando stifled a smile, thinking, *I like that it's "we." Bridgette is smart and understands the predicament I'm in . . . we're in. She's part of the solution now, not part of the problem—thank God!*

CHAPTER THREE

Saturday, August 30, 2014

Paris

Nando arrived at La Galerie before three that afternoon while Madame was busy with a customer. He did paperwork in the office until another couple came in and began to discuss a painting they liked, thinking it was ideal for their new apartment. The couple was driving a hard bargain when Church walked in, smiled, and waved. Even though Nando responded suitably, he was alarmed. *Shit— the CIA on top of Satie!*

Madame completed her sale and approached Church. They talked briefly before Madame broke away and came over to Nando, saying, "I can finish up here. Why don't you take your friend to the office?"

In the privacy of the office, Nando chatted casually with his old Princeton buddy for a few minutes. Finally, Church said, "Let me make this easy; I have no idea why I'm here. I was finishing up an op in Berlin— about to come here for R & R—when the director rerouted me to Munich to surveil a guy named Satie. That was Thursday. I photographed Satie's visitors and texted the photos to Langley. You were my last photo that evening, and I recognized you. So I called the director. He told me to stick with you and stand by. All I know is that the director wants you back at Langley, pronto!"

Jesus, can this be any more fucked up? Nando thought before answering. "I still have my clearance, so I guess we can talk."

"What I told you is all I know."

"Fine, but you can listen. Will you keep what I tell you confidential until the director reads you in?"

"I won't if it compromises the company or me," Church replied.

"Fair enough. I've already decided to contact the director. But this is a mess, and I need to put a plan in place. I'll be at odds with what the director's priorities will be, because my security won't be his top concern. I need to level the playing field." And then Nando filled Church in on everything: Bridgette, the CIA, Satie, and the NoMO Killer. Finally, Nando told Church why he had gone to Munich . . . and why Satie wanted to hire him.

Church thought for a bit. "I assume if you say no, they'll come after you?"

"Yes, that's the problem—and you know what it means. I'm not convinced the company will have my six. And I can't enter the Federal Witness Protection Program or anything like that. I'm too happy with Bridgette and my life now!"

"Jesus, I don't have a bright idea," Church said, and they sat silently for a while.

"I have a suggestion," Nando said. "If Bridgette can put dinner together for tonight—on short notice—would you come and talk? I don't want to do it at a restaurant. If you don't like what you hear, you can leave."

Church met Nando at La Galerie at seven o'clock, and they walked to the apartment. When they entered, it smelled wonderful. Church looked at Nando with a smile. Bridgette caught on. "You guys were fortunate. I was already making a *daube de boeuf* when you called; I only ran out for bread, wine, and cheese for after dinner."

"You're a lucky guy."

"He certainly is," Bridgette teased.

This is good—she's moving on.

After dinner, they sat and talked. Finally, Bridgette said, "I'm confident that the CIA thinks that if Nando isn't going to make the hit, he's the best person to prevent it. Nando wants to give the CIA any assistance he can, either here or in the US, yet we need to protect him."

"That may be a tall order," Nando continued. "I don't think a fake ID or beard will do it."

"No," Bridgette admitted. "Satie and his customers are too powerful."

Church looked at her carefully, smiled, and said, "I think you have an idea."

"Well, yes . . . but not me. Graham Greene. Have you ever seen *The Third Man*?"

Now both Church and Nando were smiling. "How the hell are we going to orchestrate a fatal accident, not to mention a corpse?"[2] Nando asked.

"Why bother with all that mess?" Bridgette said. "I have friends at the Associated Press who can place an appropriate story in the papers along with the radio and internet. We scratch each other's backs. I think an urn filled with sand is all that's required at your funeral. We'll probably need to have Madame involved. She may even enjoy it, but in any event, we can't let her think you've been killed!"

"I like it," Church said. "It keeps Nando's future in our hands, not the CIA's. And it gives them what they want. Count me in. What the director doesn't know won't hurt him! We'll tell him after it's done."

"Don't forget at least one small bouquet of flowers," Nando said, feigning dismay.

***

On Sunday morning, August 31, Bridgette called Madame and invited her to lunch after church. They had an enjoyable time, but when they were nearly finished, Madame said, "This is lovely, but why do I feel like there's another purpose besides a pleasant lunch?"

"You're correct," Nando said. "We need to tell you about things that are going to happen and ask for your help."

"Please, tell me," she responded.

"I'm going back to the States—probably for three months. I'll be leaving early Tuesday afternoon."

"Does this have to do with your previous employment with the CIA?"

"Yes. I know this is short notice, so please hire a part-timer if you need help. I won't be drawing a salary while I'm away, so it shouldn't be a burden."

"Oh, I don't think that will be necessary. I'll miss you, though. How do you feel about this, Bridgette?"

"There's more. My feelings are secondary."

Madame looked perplexed and redirected her attention to Nando. He told her it was a matter of national security for the US, omitting the assassination attempt, and filled her in on the rest of the plan.

"After midnight on Wednesday morning, I'm going to be run over and killed by a hit-and-run driver while I'm crossing the Boulevard Saint-Germain. By then I'll be in the US. Will you help Bridgette organize a small memorial service?"

"Of course. So your life is in danger."

"Yes. You can't mention this to anyone."

"I understand." But Madame started to tear up. "Is this going to work out all right? I couldn't stand losing you, Monsieur—we're family."

"I think so if we all do our parts."

"Okay . . . I know the rector at Saint-Sulpice well. It's my parish. Bridgette and I will give you a fine send-off."

"Excellent. There's something else. A man called André Satie from Munich may call you when he hears about my death. Act upset and confirm my demise. If Satie asks about the arrangements, tell him. I wouldn't be surprised if he attends."

"Is this the man you visited Thursday?"

"Yes."

***

On Tuesday, September 2, at ten a.m. in Munich, Satie received a call from Nando. They were using burner phones, as had been their procedure in the past.

"'Morning," Satie said. "Have you decided?"

"An interesting project. Here's what I'll need to make a final decision. I need to see his calendar for the next three months, including any classified events. And, as we go along, I'll need it weekly. Also, tell me how I'll obtain ordnance in the US, because I can't bring it with me."

"I'll call you later this week about the calendar. Don't worry about the ordnance—it's my primary business."

"A high-end sniper rifle if it's the way I decide to go—okay?"

"Yes."

"Call me."

***

At three o'clock that afternoon in Paris, Church called the director and gave him the fake identity Nando was traveling under.

"He'll land at Dulles at five thirty. I told him you were expecting him first thing Wednesday morning."

"Terrific. Is Medina with the program?"

"I think so."

"He's airborne now—correct?"

"Yes."

"Fine, you can stand down. Enjoy your R & R."

***

On Wednesday morning, September 3, in Paris and all over Europe, an early print edition of *Le Monde* as well as its internet edition carried the story of the hit-and-run death of Nando Medina. He had been a well-regarded art instructor at the Sorbonne and part owner in a distinguished boutique gallery. The authorities had no clues about the driver's identity. A memorial service would be held on Saturday at Saint-Sulpice. Several radio stations picked up the story as well. No one seemed to notice that the prominence of the story was disproportionate to its significance.

On the same day at eight in the morning at CIA headquarters, Nando was escorted into the director's office.

"Glad you're on board," the director said. "The president is too. If you'll proceed as you normally would, we think it's our best opportunity at heading this off. Study the situation; figure out where, when, and how is best; then we'll nab the bastard!"

"It makes sense. I assume I'll have all the support I'll need?"

"Yes."

"Including unrestricted access to his calendar?"

"Yes. This administration considers it public information, so it is readily available online except for classified or secret meetings. You'll have those too."

"Fine. Have someone show me where I can hang my hat when I'm in the office. I need a ten-millimeter semiautomatic also."

The director buzzed his secretary and asked her to escort Nando to his desk. "Do you have any idea who'll be your stand-in now that you've turned Satie down?"

"Probably Defarge. A few years back he was becoming my competition. Oh, and regarding telling Satie, I never had a chance. About midnight this morning while crossing the Boulevard Saint-Germain, a hit-and-run driver killed me. It should be in the news already. My memorial service will be at Saint-Sulpice on Saturday."

"That wasn't in the plan," the director snapped.

Nando shrugged his shoulders as he left. "It is now."

Son of a bitch—goddammit—Medina doesn't need us now! the director thought as he dialed the president.

***

On Thursday morning, September 4, the director met with the president in the Oval Office and updated him on Nando's arrival.

"That son of a bitch faked his own death before leaving Paris. A hit-and-run accident. His memorial service is Saturday at Saint-Sulpice."

The president started laughing.

"What's so fuckin' funny?"

"Well, in addition to protecting himself from Satie and his employers, he sure as hell slipped out from under your thumb!"

"I don't think it's so funny."

"Well, maybe not. Is Medina going to cooperate?" the president continued.

"Yes."

"Let's not worry about it, then—no harm, no foul. What else?"

"We have our surveillance camera in place covering Satie's entrance; there's only one. The photos have started streaming. It's nifty—a high-resolution tiny close-up rig across the street. It's motion activated by movement at the upper corner of the door as it's opened. It photographs whoever enters or leaves from the waist up but isn't activated by passing foot traffic."

"Unless they're very tall," the president quipped. "How are they transmitted?"

"Real time to one of our satellites, then to our analysis unit."

"Anything interesting?"

"Not yet. We're running facial recognition software. I'll let you know."

***

At three o'clock that afternoon, in Paris's eighth arrondissement, Church found the nondescript pawnshop Nando had recommended. The owner, Jean, in addition to running a legitimate business, sold and modified all manner of miniature spyware, which was his main source of income. If he couldn't locate or create what you wanted, it wasn't available. Jean dealt in cash, wasn't fussy about his clients, kept their names in his head, and never disclosed them to anyone. Even law enforcement found him too valuable to meddle with. Church told him what he needed.

"Monsieur, normally on such short notice, I wouldn't be able to accommodate you. But as a courtesy to Nando's memory, I will. It won't be cheap, because I'll have to pay top dollar for my supplies."

They negotiated a price, and Church paid the amount Jean requested in advance.

"I guarantee I'll have it by eight o'clock Saturday morning. I know the memorial service is at eleven, but it's the best I can do. When you come to pick it up, bring me a ring that fits the lady comfortably. I'll adjust the new one with a ring guard if required. Also, bring her smartphone. I need thirty minutes of your time. Tell her to wear a suit to the service."

"Thank you, Jean," Church said, and left.

***

At the same time in La Galerie, Madame received a phone call. When she answered, the caller said he was André Satie. "Madame Bertrand, I'm so sorry for your loss. I'd been trying to reach Nando, and finally I saw the story in this morning's *Le Monde*. If you have no objection, I would like to attend his memorial service?"

"Of course. We would be pleased to have you. I know you were friends with Nando. I believe he visited with you in Munich last week."

"Yes, Madame. That's why this is such a shock. I'll be flying from Munich. Is the service still at Saint-Sulpice? If so, please tell me the time."

"Yes, still there and at eleven in the morning, Herr Satie."

"*Merci*, Madame."

***

On Saturday morning, September 6, Church arrived at the pawnshop, where Jean was waiting for him.

"Monsieur, I'm pleased with the way this turned out. If you'll give me her ring and phone, I'll set it up in back and then go over everything with you." A few minutes later, Jean returned. On the counter he placed a silver-plated sun god brooch that was two inches in diameter, a ring styled similarly, Madam's smartphone, and the ring Church had brought with him.

"The brooch contains a high-resolution, wide-angle remote lens—with a Bluetooth transmitter—that is set like a center stone," Jean said. "I've already synced it to the lady's phone. Also, I installed an app that supports this lens. The brooch replaces the one on her mobile phone. If she wears it on the lapel of her suit, it will capture all the mourners in front of her as she eulogizes Nando. The ring is the shutter button. Press the stone and the camera will start taking a photograph every ten seconds. To turn it off, press and hold the stone. Her smartphone has enough memory to store at least thirty minutes at six photos a minute. It's silent and the range is thirty meters, so the lady won't have to carry it with her."

Later at eleven in Saint-Sulpice, Nando's memorial service began. Church was concealed in the organ loft taking pictures and observing from a distance. Since his dinner with Bridgette and Nando, he'd kept a low profile. And after the service and a small reception Madame had planned at La Galerie, Church intended to continue with his R & R.

There were perhaps thirty mourners besides Bridgette and Madame—friends, a small number of Bridgette's coworkers, faculty and students from the Sorbonne, and a few gallery clients. A cassock-wearing cleric from the Society of the Priests of Saint Sulpice was reverentially attending to his devotions in the rear of the large sanctuary. André Satie arrived with an elegant brunette, who was at least twenty years younger. Church learned later that Satie had introduced her as Madame Defarge, his niece, who was accompanying him on his private jet to London. Church wondered about that. It didn't seem quite right. There was too much physical contact between them, and why hadn't she just gone shopping?

Bridgette wore a dress and Madame was in a silk suit, displaying an attractive sun god brooch. When the rector concluded the service, Bridgette—standing on the steps across the transept from the mourners—spoke briefly. Then Madame eulogized Nando. Church smiled when he noticed her turning slightly—side to side—making eye contact with the mourners and holding her hands gently in front.

Church observed the reception from a small park across the street until Satie and his niece left. After that, he mingled in the gallery before taking Madame aside. He looked at the photos, which were excellent. Church texted them to Langley as well as to his own and Bridgette's phones. There were several shots of Satie and his niece.

"Madame, these are terrific, thank you. I'm particularly interested in Satie's niece."

"Niece? I'm not so sure," Madame reflected with a canny smile.

"Neither am I. I'll stop back and say goodbye before I leave Paris."

***

That afternoon at two o'clock, Satie's jet took off from Aéroport de Paris–Le Bourget for Munich; Madame Defarge was with him. They weren't going to London as Satie had said; that was a ruse to explain the presence of Defarge. In fact, she'd wanted to survey the memorial service—make certain everything looked normal. They would land in Munich, where Satie would debark before the flight continued to Rome. "Have you made up your mind?" Satie asked. "Are you satisfied?"

"I would have felt more comfortable with a body, even though his ashes were in an urn on the little table. But I'll do it subject to getting a copy of his calendar, including the classified items, when I return from Rome. Then I'll want a revised calendar every two weeks. No Wi-Fi, internet, or digital transmissions. Have hard copies sent to me automatically. Use FedEx, DHL, or the like. It makes no sense to keep going through you. I'll give you a mail drop address. The hit should probably be done in the US."

"Okay."

"Also, we need to rearrange the money."

"How so?"

"Well, the price is fine, but I want one hundred million up front and half of the expense money as well. So one hundred twenty-five million dollars."

"I don't know, but I'll find out."

"You can make it happen."

She undid her seat belt, crossed the aisle, and sat on his armrest, kissing him slowly. Then she said, "I know I haven't had much time for you lately. I promise when I come back from Rome, we can spend a week together." Impishly, Madame Defarge continued, "If you want to tell the pilot not to disturb us until ten minutes before touchdown, I can make it up to you a little bit now." As Satie picked up the cockpit phone, she was already kneeling and unzipping his pants. Several hours later, en route to Aeroporto Internazionale di Roma–Ciampino, Defarge was chuckling silently.

Christ, I drove him nuts. Perfect timing too—we finished ten minutes before touchdown. I won't need Satie any longer for the calendar, and he'll get my money any way I want! I can do without the total amount and all the expense money: one hundred million plus is plenty—more than enough to retire on. Afterward, it'll be a week with Satie, showing him the time of his life, as I promised.

That solves Satie—bye-bye, André!

"It's the least I can do!" She laughed out loud.

Now, I'll see my cousin in Rome about sneaking into the US

CHAPTER FOUR

Monday, September 8, 2014

Washington, DC

At noon the director met with the president. "Sir, we've started running the facial recognition software on Satie's visitors. We're up-to-date and had a couple of hits on low-level European arms traffickers. No one we have any particular interest in—no wants or warrants either. All were men except for an outstanding-looking blonde on Friday. She was there about twenty minutes . . . might be a lady friend."

"How's Nando doing?"

"He's digging into your calendar now. I asked him if he saw anything feasible, but he said, 'It's too early.'"

"Anything more from Jay?"

"No, but Nando has been spending time with him. Notwithstanding his rogue episode, I have confidence Medina can spot where the assassin will strike."

"That's easy for you to say. It isn't your ass," the president joked.

"Yes, sir. But do you think you should reconsider your decision to play this out? You could drastically cut back your schedule and rearrange your meetings to the White House wherever possible. Then, once we have identified the assassin, we could terminate—problem solved."

"I know you think I'm taking an unnecessary risk, but I won't let these bastards scare me into seclusion. What would the country think if they found out? No, they're not going to drive me underground. Plus, I want to nail these pricks. They'll scatter like rats deserting a sinking ship once the assassin is terminated. You know they have the means to disappear."

"Mr. President, it is a privilege to serve with you. I admire your courage."

***

Malachi "Mal" Ben-David, deputy director of the Central Institute for Intelligence and Special Operations (Mossad), was usually based in Tel Aviv but had made a special trip to Paris from Munich, where he'd been on assignment. Once he'd learned that Bridgette was law enforcement, Mal had decided they should meet. This Tuesday evening, September 9, she was having dinner in a small bistro near the Boulevard Saint-Germain with another woman. Mal had followed her onto the number 4 Metro line from police headquarters, on the Île de la Cité. Now he was sitting at the bar, nursing a glass of red wine, and watching. Mal didn't want to meet Bridgette at police headquarters or use a phone. He thought a public space might make her feel safer than if he knocked on her apartment door.

Fretting silently, Mal thought, *Shit, I've been here an hour and a half and the other woman hasn't gone to the ladies' room yet. Go figure— oh, well!* He ordered another glass of wine. Finally, the woman got up and headed toward the restrooms, and Mal walked over to their table.

"Bridgette, my name is Mal Ben-David. Please don't be alarmed. Nothing's wrong, but I need to talk to you." He was not quite six feet tall, fiftyish, and moved effortlessly with a commanding presence. Mal handed her his card. "Can we meet tomorrow for coffee, lunch, a drink, or in a public place? Wherever you feel comfortable; please, it's important. I don't want to come to your office."

Bridgette seemed startled but responded by writing the name and address of La Galerie on a napkin as well as *5 p.m.* and handing it to him. Mal thanked her and left. She hadn't said a word. Then the next afternoon, when Mal arrived at La Galerie, Bridgette introduced Madame, who suggested, "Why don't you use my office? I'll watch the shop."

Once they were settled, Ben-David began speaking. "Thank you for seeing me. Sorry for such an unusual approach, but I was having difficulty deciding on an unobtrusive one. I want our meeting to be covert. I assume Madam is completely trustworthy."

"Yes, I told her you were an old friend."

"Good. I won't waste your time. Let me fill in a bit of my CV, then we can talk. I've spent twenty-five years in the Israeli military or intelligence community, specializing in anti-terrorism. I ran the training for the Metsada and Kidon Units. In my last operational deployment, I commanded the Kidon Unit. Are you familiar with it?"

"Kidon? By reputation. The assassins, correct?"

Mal nodded. "You're well informed; most—even in the intelligence communities—haven't heard of them. I'm here because on Monday, you ran a facial recognition search through Interpol that triggered an alert. You scored a direct hit on a woman we monitor, but it was blocked from being sent to you."

"The woman with Satie at Nando's memorial service, Madame Defarge?"

"So that's what she's calling herself. That's helpful."

"I didn't see you there."

"I was the cleric in the rear of the sanctuary."

"By the way, you never offered me condolences," Bridgette remarked.

Mal paused, fighting a tiny smile. "No, let me give you the thirty-second rundown on Madame Defarge. She had been with our intelligence services for nearly eight years when she left five years ago. I trained her, and later Defarge was my top operative in the Kidon Unit. I monitor her when I can because we believe she has been freelancing in Europe since then. As far as we're concerned, Defarge has been the number-two assassin for hire in the EU."

Bridgette's suppressing a smile—message received. She's picked up that I think Nando is the number-one assassin and is still alive. Clever, Mal thought.

"Our problem is that we make these connections afterwards. But this time our intelligence suggests there's something big in process. We're determined to be ahead of it. I'm not an alarmist, but she's one of the most dangerous people in the world. Letting her roam freely is like releasing a plague—like leaving Pandora's box wide open."

"If Madame Defarge is so dangerous, why not have your Kidon Unit deal with her?"

"It's complicated."

"Why do I think everything you deal with is complicated, Mal?"

He smiled. "Perhaps we can help each other. We'll talk again."

Mal reached into his inside suitcoat pocket and handed her a number-ten envelope as he left.

***

Later that evening, after fixing a salad and changing for bed, Bridgette opened the envelope. Inside she found what was undoubtedly an internal Mossad evaluation, dated thirty days before. A quick scan showed several redactions, including where the analysis came from and who had prepared it. Bridgette read the whole thing several times. A photo was attached to the summary:

> Name: Izabella Ricci
>
> Birth Date: June 1982
>
> Sex: F
>
> Hair: strawberry blonde, frequently wears wigs
>
> Eyes: green, frequently wears colored contact lenses
>
> Height: 5′9″
>
> Weight: 125 lbs.
>
> Citizenship: Italian, naturalized Israeli
>
>> Note 1: Born in Rome to Jewish parents who immigrated to Israel in 1987 when she was five
>>
>> Note 2: Other relatives perished at Dachau
>
> Language(s): Italian and Hebrew, native proficiency; English and German, professional proficiency

Education: Tel Aviv University, B.A. in Philosophy, graduated in 2002

Employment: Mossad 2002; Kidon Unit 2004; separated 2010, reasons unclear; thereafter, believed to be a self-employed mercenary

Skills: Expert in all the following: long and handguns, bow and arrow; knives; hand-to-hand combat and martial arts. Working knowledge of poisons

> Note: Excelled in sexual training with men and LGBTQ

Performance: An exceptional undercover agent and a top performer in the Kidon Unit with **[REDACTED]** confirmed kills—showed initiative and innovation.

Threat Assessment: **[REDACTED]**

Afterward, there was a list of redacted assignments and outcomes.

Bridgette read through the file several times. *Well, about the threat assessment, Mal said, "She's one of the most dangerous people in the world." I don't think he would say that lightly.* It was eleven thirty (five thirty in Langley), and Bridgette called Nando on a burner phone.

"Hey, Bridgette—I miss you."

"I miss you too. It's hard to believe it's been barely a week. What have you been doing?"

"I have a desk with my old unit. I still know a few of the guys. I'm working with one of them, an analyst, Jay."

"Have you been in the field yet?"

"No, I've been analyzing the president's calendar. Also, I've been comparing the woman in the surveillance footage from Satie's office with the ones of Madame Defarge at my memorial service. I think they're the same woman even though the hair is different. But there's also something about her face that's dissimilar. Jay is going to run it through facial recognition software; it works off precise facial measurements, not impressions."

"I can help. Even though the facial recognition search I ran through Interpol drew a blank, I now have an unadorned photo of her from a Mossad file. I can also tell you who she is." Bridgette told him the entire story of her encounter with Mal and explained the contents of the file. She finished by saying, "I'm convinced she's who you were competing with." Then Bridgette waited for Nando to get pissed.

"Jesus Christ, are you out of your mind? Anybody can have a business card printed. Tell me you at least saw his Mossad ID."

"Nando, I went with my gut. I had to make a quick decision."

"I trust your instincts, but this is an entirely different threat level than what you're used to. Shit, you're dealing with two world-class assassins."

"Don't patronize me—I'm not a neophyte. I know exactly who they are. And you left out one of the assassins. The one I'm sleeping with."

That stopped Nando. "I'm sorry. I didn't mean to talk down to you. What you told me scares me; he is at least as dangerous as Izabella."

"I'm nervous enough to be extra careful, okay? I have a few observations, then I need to know how to send you the file. I'm thinking we should avoid a digital footprint."

"Agreed. Let's talk about it last," Nando replied.

"All right, here's what's incongruous in Mal's story. First, I don't buy that the Kidon Unit couldn't deal with her. It isn't plausible. Hell, Mal could do it himself. Remember, he was the unit's trainer. Second, why is Israel letting her run around doing what she does? I think it suits their interests. Knowingly or otherwise, is Izabella taking care of their problems? Does that sound familiar to you? Third, what's different this time? Do they know about the assassination? Obviously, assassinating your president—no matter how strained Israel's relations are with the US—is not in their best interests. But again, why not deploy the Kidon Unit? Problem solved. Shit, Izabella isn't hard to find; she isn't hiding."

"I see where you're going," Nando commented. "Also, Israel has been tied up in a ground war in the Gaza Strip since July—it's just winding down. Mal is undoubtedly a heavy hitter. Couldn't Israel deploy his talents better? Why is Izabella so important now?"

"It could be personal. Maybe he feels responsible for letting this scourge loose. Maybe Israel doesn't have a clue about the assassination attempt yet. Or maybe Mal doesn't trust his employers to do the right thing. I'm not clear about his status either. In any event, you may be his solution!" Bridgette added.

"How so?"

"Because Mal doesn't buy your death for a minute; I'm convinced, even though I can't prove it. I think you can trust him, but he's shrewd. If he knows she's after the president, Mal will help us, then let you eliminate Defarge—a clever plan."

"You make a lot of sense," Nando admitted.

"I also have thoughts on her looks and disguises. Wigs and contact lenses are obvious. But here's what I stumbled on. Izabella's gorgeous, but try to remember any of her features without a photo for reference. Close your eyes and try it. You can't, at least not after a while. It's because she doesn't have an outstanding feature. Izabella has figured this out. No matter how good-looking you think she is, Izabella blends in—she's hard to recall. The differences you're noticing are in her makeup because she's a makeup artist. Izabella can highlight her cheekbones, make her eyes look farther apart, elongate her face, and so on . . . get it?"

"I think you're right. Only a woman would've picked that up!"

"Sexist!" Bridgette said, and they both laughed. "But makeup can't outwit facial recognition."

"Now we have to figure out how to take advantage of Mal's considerable skills," Nando remarked.

"I'll let you figure that one out. I have an idea that might work for us," Bridgette said.

"What?"

"I checked online, and between United and Air Canada, there're three flights a day from DC to Montreal—all under two hours. We could meet for weekends occasionally. I can take the time, and we always have police officers moving back and forth for training or exchange programs. If anyone were watching me, it wouldn't seem out of the ordinary."

"Great, let's do it. Send Izabella's file to my hotel by DHL. We may have to figure something else out if we do this often. Let's keep Mal between us," Nando said.

"Okay, I'll start checking out Montreal. Love you!"

"I love you too!"

***

On Thursday evening, September 11, Madame called Bridgette.

"Are you doing okay?"

"Yes, I'm fine. I spoke to the US last evening, using a burner—I miss him!"

"Shish . . . be careful on the phone!" Madame whispered.

"Sorry."

"Mal stopped by to chat this afternoon. I like him—very attractive."

"I know. Sexy."

"Now, Bridgette, you're spoken for," Madame joked, and they laughed. "I think he had an ulterior motive, though."

"Why?"

"He asked me to call you. Can you meet him at my apartment on your way in to work tomorrow morning? Mal is being guarded . . . mysterious!" Madame opined.

If you only knew. "I can make it. Eight o'clock. All right?"

"Yes."

***

Friday morning, a few minutes before eight, Bridgette rang Madame's doorbell. It was the first time she'd been there. Madame was slow to answer; her hair looked tousled and she seemed unsettled. *Not her best look, but it's first thing in the morning.*

"Oh, Bridgette. You're right on time. We're having breakfast . . . through here."

We're?

Madame blushed but continued. "Mal, Bridgette's here." Bridgette was flabbergasted. He was at the kitchen table, having toast and coffee and wearing what appeared to be Madame's deceased husband's bathrobe. She dithered when she brought a cup for Bridgette, who quickly regained her equilibrium. But as Mal poured coffee from the French press, Madame continued to be flustered.

She's cute, Bridgette thought.

At last, Madame said, "Well, I'll leave you to it."

Mal was about to speak when Bridgette put up her hand, stopping him. "Mal, if you hurt her, you'll wish you were dealing with Izabella. Don't screw with Madame. I mean it!"

"Bridgette, I won't. We talked first. She knows I love my wife and kids. Madame knows I'm here temporarily. It was her choice, and I'm happy she said yes. I think Madame is wonderful. You know, Madame's a big girl."

Hearing Madame referred to as *a big girl* made Bridgette chuckle.

"That's better," he said.

"Jesus, Mal, your age difference."

He shrugged his shoulders, eyes twinkling, and said, "Think of all Madame's experience that she can impart to a young man."

"Oh, for Christ's sake, Mal!" Bridgette responded, trying to maintain a serious mien. "Why did you want to see me?"

Mal reported that he had traced Izabella to Rome after she left Nando's memorial service. Obviously, London had been a ruse. A few well-placed euros in flight operations at Aéroport de Paris–Le Bourget had obtained Satie's flight plan—Munich and then on to Rome. Mal recalled Izabella mentioning a cousin with the same last name in the import-export business there. He was apparently in organized crime as well. Mal asked Bridgette if she could run him down. "I'm heading to Rome and will be back in touch for his address through Madame. I intend to have a chat with Izabella's cousin."

On the way to work, Bridgette thought, *It shouldn't be difficult through Interpol. But why doesn't Mal simply have Israeli intelligence locate this guy? I'm convinced now that Mal is operating off-grid. But I still think he's an asset. Nando is right, though; I need to be careful. And keep an eye on Madame also.* "She's like a schoolgirl!" Bridgette chuckled.

CHAPTER FIVE

Friday, September 12, 2014

Rome

I zabella's Rome trip had gone well. She'd seen the sights again and spent time with her cousin Luca. They discussed her trip to the States. She intended to fly to Canada under a false identity but thereafter wanted to travel off-grid. The difficulty was that Izabella didn't know where she was headed. She reasoned that presidential trips east of the Mississippi River would be day trips, whereas his trips farther west might be overnight. Those western trips away from the intense security of the capital would provide better opportunities. Luca had an export-import business in Vancouver. Using an 18-wheeler that made routine trips across the border, he could arrange to smuggle her to Seattle. After that, she'd head south to either San Francisco or Los Angeles, because if she had to travel, flights from there were better than from the Pacific Northwest. They called Luca's Vancouver manager, and Izabella made tentative arrangements. Hopefully, the president would be traveling west before year end. Now she only needed the president's calendar.

Friday afternoon, traveling under another assumed identity, Izabella boarded a four o'clock Alitalia flight for Munich. There she would learn where to acquire ordnance in the US and show Satie the good time she'd promised him.

***

Nando returned to his hotel Friday evening, and Izabella's file was at reception. He reviewed it over the weekend.

When Nando entered the office Monday morning, Jay greeted him. "How was your weekend? By the way, I heard how you outflanked the director with your untimely demise—he was pissed. Apparently, the president thought it was funny as hell, and that made the director even madder!"

Nando chuckled. "He wasn't a happy camper." *Jay seems laid-back this morning. It might be a good time to see if he'll go along with keeping Izabella's file confidential.*

"Jay, I have a Mossad file that I received from a Paris source Friday evening. It has a photograph of Madame Defarge, whose real name is Izabella Ricci. Run it through facial recognition with the other two photos. I'm convinced they're all the same person."

"I'll do it while we're talking. How the hell did you acquire this?"

"I can't tell you, and I'd like to keep this just between us, at least for the time being."

Jay paused and asked, "Would that entitle me to a similar quid pro quo?"

"If possible."

"I think I know who my source is. If I'm correct, I would like you to keep it confidential for now also."

"Fair enough. Look at Ricci's file while the software is running, then I'll bring you up to speed. After that, tell me about your source."

The software and Jay's review ended at the same time. "Okay, the probability is ninety-nine percent that all three photos are of the same woman." Jay held up her file. "I wouldn't want to encounter her in a dark alley. I assume she's number one now that you're dead?"

"Yes, I'm certain, because she accompanied Satie to my funeral," Nando answered. "The only reason for that would be to confirm my death. I expect to have more shortly. I'm suspicious Izabella will be arranging to sneak into the US. I've been through the president's calendar. The time and place that makes the most sense is San Francisco. He's there before Thanksgiving; it's when and where I would do it."

"You're assuming she has access to his calendar, including classified items?"

"Yes, it's probably a safe bet. I think the conspirators have the wherewithal and clout to acquire it."

"Why San Francisco?"

"When he's traveling, security can never be as tight as in Washington, especially if he's overnighting. Before Christmas, the president isn't away from DC overnight except for a two-day San Francisco trip en route to China for the Asia-Pacific Economic Cooperation summit. It's on November tenth through twelfth. I'm certain she wouldn't try it abroad, so it's San Francisco by default. Plus, there're two venues. On Friday, November seventh, Stanford University is hosting a White House conference on global warming, cybersecurity, and other issues. That morning the president will arrive at SFO on Air Force One, then helicopter to Stanford, where around noon he'll deliver the keynote address in Memorial Auditorium. After that, the president will helicopter back to San Francisco, landing at the Presidio Golf Course before motorcading to Pacific Heights for a one-hundred-thousand-dollar-a-plate DNC fundraising dinner. It's at Holden

Ransom's mansion, where he'll spend the night. Saturday the eighth, the president will retrace his steps to the Presidio, helicopter to SFO, and then leave on his China trip."

"Ransom founded Holden Technologies, right?" Jay asked.

"Yeah, he's on the list of the world's wealthiest men. His company is in Silicon Valley and is one of the largest manufacturers of printed circuit boards in the world."

"Do you think he's involved in the conspiracy?"

"I don't know, but my gut says no."

"So what do you need from me?" Jay asked.

"First, see if you can electronically retrieve building plans from Santa Clara County for Memorial Auditorium and from the City of San Francisco for Ransom's mansion. Don't leave a trace. If you can't do that, we'll have to do it the old-fashioned way—in person. Next, see if you can electronically surveil any other requests for those plans."

"If the files have been digitized, it shouldn't be a problem," Jay responded.

"Also, we should go to San Francisco before we start in-depth planning and check out the two sites. Now tell me about your source."

"Around the middle of July, I started receiving occasional anonymous calls here in the office. The person uses a voice changer to disguise who they are, but I think it's a woman. Here's what I learned. She's apparently an assistant to a high-ranking officer at a major tech firm. He travels frequently on a private jet, and she usually accompanies him. For the last four months, there've been peculiar trips to different domestic locations. On these trips, the boss takes a large suite with a separate living room. There's a meeting, and my source is relegated to the adjoining bedroom or shopping. It's unusual, because on other trips she attends all his meetings, taking notes, distributing handouts, and providing support. Notwithstanding that precaution, she once saw one of the other participants—an Asian man. Also, she has gleaned from overhearing several—animated, raised-voice—conversations that there's a conspiracy underway between six or seven men. At first, my source thought it might be price fixing, but she now thinks it's something else. Specifically, she has heard snippets mentioned such as one hundred-fifty million dollars plus expenses, the name Satie, a pipeline, a crackdown on intellectual property transfers, child labor, and new financial regulations."

"It's quite a shopping list," Nando said. "I think your source is correct about it not being price fixing because of Satie and the fee. Plus it fits the assassination theory and may give us an idea why. It seems like this group is pooling their resources to solve a common problem, even though their reasons may be different. What is it you want me to keep confidential? The director seems to have inferred all this."

"There's more. I think it's my cousin Anna, who lives in the Bay Area and works for a big tech firm in Silicon Valley. I don't know what she does. I'm sure I recognized her speech pattern, and once, she let slip something about the Bay Area. Plus she calls on my direct CIA number. That's not easy to obtain; I've just given it to a few family members. If it's Anna, I need to protect her."

"Agreed. She might be in way over her head. But do you think Anna would still be willing to help if we approached her and guaranteed protection?"

"I don't know what her motivation is. She hasn't asked for anything yet."

Nando thought for a moment. "How about the next time she calls, before you hang up, say something like, 'We need to talk.' Then take it from there."

"Okay, and perhaps we can see her when we go to San Francisco. I don't want to discuss this further by phone or email," Jay said.

"All right, let's see what happens when she calls. We'll keep both Mal and Anna to ourselves."

***

Bridgette had reached out to her Interpol contact on Friday. On Tuesday the sixteenth, she received a call back. Apparently, Izabella's cousin Luca Ricci was well known to Rome's police. He had ample underworld contacts and was believed to be involved in smuggling in Italy, the US, and Canada. Bridgette obtained his address and phone numbers before calling Madame.

"Bridgette. Nice to hear from you."

"I have the information Mal asked for."

"Oh, good. I'll be seeing him tonight. I'm sure he'll be pleased."

Bridgette gave Madame the information, after which an awkward silence developed. Finally, Madame said, "Don't judge me harshly. I know this is going nowhere. Mal has been honest. Well, at least about his family and how he feels about them. Mal is a lovely man . . . to me."

"Madame—"

"I understand you know more about him than I do. I don't want to hear the rest."

"Okay . . . it's difficult once you do. I'm struggling with knowing *the rest* about Nando."

"Oh dear. I was always suspicious. But I judge Monsieur as he is now."

"I focus on that too. But I don't want you to be hurt."

"Bridgette, it has been so long. I forgot how wonderful it felt. How lovely it is to be wanted. I hope Nando will always make you feel special. My husband did. But this may be my last opportunity. Isn't it worth a bit of pain?"

After they hung up, Bridgette thought, *Mal was right, Madame is a big girl.*

***

Arriving in Rome on Thursday afternoon the eighteenth, Mal rented a car, checked into a hotel, and began staking out Luca Ricci's office. Around seven o'clock that evening, Luca went home. Early the next morning, Mal returned and parked down the street from the office. He observed Ricci arrive. Luca didn't leave the office until six o'clock, when he drove to a small, detached, two-story house in a suburb. Luca honked, and an attractive, much younger woman came out, got into his car, and kissed him. Mal followed them to dinner and several hours later back to the house.

Mal waited, checking his courier bag: gloves, lockpicks, silenced .22 LR semiauto, zip ties, syringes, and so on. After an hour, the downstairs lights went off, followed by the upstairs ones coming on. He waited twenty minutes after those lights were turned off before putting on his gloves and slipping the pistol in his waistband. Then grabbing his bag, he crossed the street, picked the front door lock, and entered. Mal could hear them; it sounded like they were having a whale of a time. That's what he'd been counting on—a lover.

Mal waited for his eyes to adjust before surveying the rooms. The dining area, which was open to the living room, looked fine for his purposes. He drew the downstairs curtains, after which no one could see inside. Mal rearranged two chairs in front of the dining table, facing them toward the living room. Then he moved a third chair in front of the others; now Mal could sit and watch. Last, he took the zip ties and syringes out of his bag and put them on the table before starting upstairs.

The bedroom door was open, and with the ambient light coming through the window, he could see her on top, her back to Mal. He flipped on the light. After their spasmodic decoupling and stereo exclamations of "What the fuck," he marched them downstairs at gunpoint and into the dining area. As soon as they were seated, he stood behind them and quickly injected each in the neck. They were unconscious almost immediately. Mal zip-tied their wrists and ankles to the arms and legs of the chairs. Afterward, he sat watching the naked couple. *They ought to be coming around in about ten minutes. It won't take long after that.*

***

Izabella had stayed at Satie's for a week. During that time, her Zurich private bank confirmed that her account had been credited with $115,000,000 from André—her full payment less his ten-million-dollar commission. She transferred the funds to the Banque des Antilles Francaises in Grand Case, Saint Martin, where she had an upscale condo. Later, her mail drop in Berlin confirmed receipt of a FedEx envelope from the US—the president's schedule. And finally, Satie gave her a contact in San Francisco, José, who could provide ordnance. And as promised, Izabella showed Satie a grand time. They were together a great deal, although he still went to the office. Satie gave Izabella the keys to the Mercedes wagon so she wouldn't be housebound.

Friday morning the nineteenth, Satie was awake and out of bed quickly. Izabella was suspicious he was avoiding any further amorous overtures from her. She chuckled silently. *I've truly worn him out! But he should be recharged by tonight because he knows I'm leaving early tomorrow. And André won't waste a last opportunity to have me!*

Today, Izabella intended to visit the Nazis' first concentration camp at Dachau. It was scarcely twelve miles from Munich. Her family, who were Italian Jews, had suffered during the Holocaust, especially after 1944, when Hitler pressured Mussolini into dealing with the "Final Solution." Some of her relatives had ended up in Dachau, where they were worked to death. For years a compulsion to visit the camp had plagued her, yet she'd never understood why. After all, death was her profession. But Dachau seemed different. Maybe because it was an assault on humanity. Seeing where and what her family had endured might provide her with relief—*but from what? I don't know. It's confusing . . .*

After André left, Izabella had breakfast, packed her duffel, took it to the Mercedes, and left for Dachau. She stopped at an OBI big-box store and bought three jerry cans. At the work camp, she took a tour and walked around. *Hardly a pleasant afternoon.* While returning to Satie's, Izabella filled the jerry cans with petrol and covered them with a blanket. Next, she picked up things for supper. When Izabella arrived at the house, she left her bag and the gas cans in the Mercedes. Then, sipping wine as André walked in, she said, "I thought I'd fix a light supper tonight. Is that okay?"

"Excellent. We don't want to overeat and fall asleep too early," André joked.

"Yes, my thoughts exactly. We should probably go up early because I need to be up first thing tomorrow."

They were in bed by eight o'clock. Izabella took her time with him, doing everything he liked but not exhausting him, wanting him to have something left for his last time. After a while, it was time to start her endgame: there was plenty to do after she had finished with him. Izabella began making love once more, taking the top, facing him. Hardly moving, she started rhythmically nudging him forward, then pulling him back, holding him near the edge. Eventually—when he was pleading for his release—she leaned closer and began moving her hips. Izabella put her hands around his neck, gently constricting his airway. Soon Satie began climaxing, clutching and tugging at her. He hadn't noticed Izabella unobtrusively but firmly squeezing his carotid arteries closed. He blacked out, and she began moving rapidly. *No point in squandering his erection!* After making it, Izabella kept compressing his arteries for several minutes. *Bye-bye, André!*

She wasn't flying from Munich tomorrow as she had told him. Instead, she was driving to Frankfurt, about four and a half hours away. She needed to leave by midnight to arrive at the airport in time to check in for her Berlin flight. Izabella showered, dressed, and policed the entire house to be certain she hadn't left anything behind. She went to the Mercedes, making two trips for the jerry cans. Izabella drained one can over both André and the bed, making sure his pyre was well soaked. The other two cans she poured down one side of the carpeted stairs and then below over cloth furniture, carpets, and draperies. Avoiding the gasoline-soaked areas, Izabella rechecked downstairs and returned to the bedroom. After another quick look around, she lit a match and threw it onto the dead man. She hurried downstairs, dropping lit matches along the way. Then Izabella was out the front door and into the Mercedes. There'd be no forensic evidence to link her to Satie or his house.

Izabella drove carefully to the Frankfurt am Main Airport but not so slowly as to be noticed. She paid for two weeks' long-term parking, thoroughly wiped down the car, and took the shuttle bus. Then, using another false identity, Izabella was on the nine-fifteen flight to Berlin.

CHAPTER SIX

Saturday, September 20, 2014
Berlin

The airport cab dropped Izabella at Elsa's apartment in the chic Mitte neighborhood. For nearly eighteen months now, Izabella had been living under the pseudonym of Katja Schmidt with her lover, Elsa, a young freelance fashion designer.

"Is that you, Katja?" Elsa called from her work space in a spare bedroom. "I missed you. Glad you're home."

"Yes, I finished ahead of schedule."

Izabella reminisced wistfully about their first meeting at a new nightclub that had been all the rage. Izabella was passing through Berlin and thought she could get lucky at the club. She hadn't been there long when Elsa sat at the bar next to her. She was cute as hell: blonde, five foot nine, nice figure, and she looked hardly old enough to drink legally. They talked, hit it off, and there was no question Elsa was picking her up. Izabella was puzzled because, while she'd had many lesbian lovers on the job, she had never been with a woman on her own time. She considered herself straight and was positive she didn't give off an encouraging vibe. *Go figure.* It wasn't long before Izabella was surprisingly aroused. After two drinks, Elsa slid off her stool, took Izabella by the hand, and said, "Let's go to my place." Shortly after that they were in bed sixty-nining, Izabella on the bottom, playfully teasing Elsa—arousing her until she couldn't attend to Izabella any longer. All Elsa could do was mewl for release.

Ever since then, Izabella had lived there. And if she shone in bed, Elsa didn't give a damn what she did for a living. *I like being here. Elsa makes me happy, and it's fun*, she thought. *An excellent deal as well, because her father pays the bills.* Izabella decided to wait until after Elsa made love to her before disclosing she was heading to Canada soon.

On Monday morning, Izabella shopped along Unter den Linden. Elsa met her for lunch, and afterward, they returned to the apartment. They hadn't been back long when Izabella's phone rang. Luca's wife, Nina, was calling to tell her that Luca and his mistress had been murdered. It had occurred at his lover's place, and she'd been tortured before being killed. Nina was nearly hysterical trying to take it all in: torture, murder, and a girlfriend too!

"What's the matter, *Liebchen*?" Elsa asked. After Izabella told her, Elsa held her for a long time.

I gotta pull it together, Izabella thought, and finally went to the kitchen for a glass of water. *This is all screwed up now. I can't use Luca's contact in Vancouver anymore. Obviously, there's a new player who knows something about what I'm up to. That's why he went after Luca. And now he must know where I'm heading. Shit, I need to get to the US, but not through Vancouver.*

Izabella called her emergency contact. When he answered, he asked, "Are you using a burner?"

"Yes."

"You haven't called before. Is this an emergency?"

"Yes, my route into the US is blown. I need help."

Brandenburg Gate & Unter den Linden

"What about Satie?"

"Dead."

"All right . . . go to Montreal ASAP—stay at the Gault—I'll call you Thursday afternoon before six o'clock. You'll deal with me directly from now on. Here's a new burner number."

Izabella checked Montreal flights and went to the living room, thinking, *Elsa won't be happy.*

***

At nine o'clock Monday morning, Jay's source called. She was calling from home before going to work, saying she'd been on one of her boss's unusual trips on Thursday the eighteenth and hadn't returned home until late Friday evening. They'd been at the Camelback Inn in Scottsdale. She told Jay about the meeting—no new information. After she finished, Jay spoke up; he had decided to bring the question of her identity to a head.

"Anna, is that you? Please don't hang up!"

"Who's Anna? Why would you think I was Anna?"

"I'm an analyst—a spy. I figure stuff out."

"If I were . . .?"

"I would tell you that my partner Nando and I can protect you, whatever it takes. You've already surmised this is more serious than price fixing, but if Nando and I are correct, you've no idea the gravity of the situation."

"Perhaps I do. Why do you think I keep doing this? It's not without risk."

"If you're Anna, we would like to meet in San Francisco. We'll be there in the next couple of weeks. If we're on the same page, you don't have to say anything." The line was silent. "All right, buy a few burner phones. Then call me back so we can make plans . . . and thanks."

***

Madame called Bridgette early that afternoon. "Bridgette. I heard from Mal. He's back from Rome. I didn't even know he'd gone. Mal has information for you on where Madame Defarge might be headed next. I guess he visited with her cousin."

"I didn't know Mal had gone either. Are you seeing him?"

"Yes."

"Should I stop over before work tomorrow?"

"I'm certain it will be fine, but if not, I'll call you."

Bridgette was about to start home at six o'clock when her phone rang. She vacillated, not wanting to answer because it had been a tiring day. Ultimately, Bridgette did, and it was her Interpol contact, the one she had called to locate Izabella's cousin for Mal.

"I just heard from the Rome police. They called as a courtesy because of my inquiry about Luca Ricci. Sunday morning, they found him and his mistress murdered in her home."

Silently sighing, Bridgette responded, "Oh no. What happened?"

"It's not clear why or who. The couple was found naked and zip-tied to chairs in the dining room. They were both shot with a small-caliber gun. Luca was shot once in the forehead, but the woman was shot multiple times on her left side: ankle, knee, hip, wrist, elbow, and finally in her forehead. Our medical examiner opines that she was tortured—crippled slowly, shot by shot—until Luca told the killer what he wanted to know. After that, they were executed."

"Jesus, that's cruel."

"Be careful, Bridgette. Whoever this fucker is, stay clear of him. I'll let you know if I find out anything else."

Bridgette didn't have a calm night. *Nando is right. This is an entirely different threat level than I'm accustomed to.* She was still upset on Tuesday morning when she arrived at Madame's apartment. Madame answered the door but didn't seem to be flustered this time. She simply looked happy. It was like last time: Madame brought a cup, and Mal poured coffee. But this morning he was wearing what looked like a new bathrobe. When Madame left them, Bridgette tried to act normal. "You have a new robe. It's attractive."

"Yes, it's silk. Madame bought it for me. It's silly, but I felt uncomfortable in her husband's robe. But more important, I have information for you. I visited with Izabella's cousin in Rome." Mal handed her a note with the details. Bridgette struggled with her composure. Mal quickly noticed and asked, "Are you okay, Bridgette?"

"You don't feel comfortable in her husband's robe—bullshit!" Bridgette snapped, then stifled a sniffle.

"What's happened?"

"So I'm supposed to believe you're so sensitive—you're a son of a bitch! Interpol called me yesterday about Luca Ricci."

Mal paused. "I'm sorry they did that."

"That's all you have to say? I suppose you think I'm blowing this out of proportion?"

"No, you're not. It was a shock, an unexpected look into my world." Mal reached out and took her hand. "Please don't upset Madame. I hope we can still work together."

On the way to Île de la Cité, Bridgette was disconcerted. She had let him hold her hand—why? Bridgette didn't want him to touch her again and couldn't stand the thought of him making love to Madame—not cute anymore. Bridgette wasn't naive, so why was this so upsetting? But she knew why. She was trying to avoid the truth. Mal hadn't needed to point it out. It had been an unexpected look into Nando's world too, or at least what Nando's world had been.

***

When Bridgette called Nando that evening, she tried not to act upset. But after she had given him the details of Izabella's plan to be smuggled into the US through Vancouver, he asked, "What's the matter?"

"Nothing. A bad day. I'm okay."

"Bridgette?"

She paused for a while, then told him about what Mal had done and waited silently.

"I'm sorry you found out."

"You weren't like that, Nando. Were you?"

"I wasn't trained as an interrogator."

"You didn't answer my question."

"I know," he admitted.

"Well?"

"I'm happy with my life now. Especially the last few years, after I met you and the CIA and Satie started leaving me alone. I want this job over with ASAP so I can return to normal."

"You're still avoiding my question."

"I know. Just love me the way I am."

"I do love you—no matter what."

"And it means the world to me," Nando said. "I've never been happier. You know about CIA black sites and renditions. It has been all over the news. Can't you infer from those stories and what you just learned? If you must know, I'll tell you, but not on the phone—in person. Are the details that important?"

"No, I guess not. But I'm still unhappy."

"I'm not happy either. It upsets me that you had to deal with what's been my world. I never wanted you to see it. Look, I was rarely involved with that shit. It wasn't my job. If I did, I stuck to the manual that was authorized at the time. What Mal did was well outside our rules. Does that help?"

"A little."

"Bridgette, you'll work your way through this. So let's plan on meeting in Montreal as soon as we can—we need to be together. Jay and I are headed to San Francisco on the thirtieth for three or four days, so after that."

"All right, I'll call you with dates." They found it hard to hang up and were quiet. At last, Bridgette said, "Love you."

"Love you too."

***

In the late morning on Wednesday, September 24, Mal reached out by burner phone to Zerubbabel Levie. Levie was known as Zeb, a nickname resulting from his childhood inability to pronounce his polysyllabic first name. He was a senior analyst in the Kidon Unit and perhaps the best one in all Israeli intelligence. Because they had worked together frequently during their careers, Mal had contacted Zeb when he'd begun this investigation. He recalled their conversation.

"Long time no speak. How are you? How's the family."

"All is well, and with you?"

"The same. I was wondering if you'd be able to help me out."

"Sure. What's up?"

"I'm working on a project. You'll be the only person I'm going to read in—for your eyes and ears alone."

Zeb paused, focusing on Mal's unusual approach. "So you're back in the field?"

"Sort of—for a short time."

"Mal, is this off book?"

"Can I count on you, Zeb? It'll be limited."

"What do you need?"

Mal had made two requests then, both regarding the surveillance of Satie's office. First, he sent Zeb the photos of Church Gagne and Nando Medina. Zeb's searches turned up nothing on Gagne yet easily identified Medina, disclosing his full CIA history. Zeb opined that Medina had been the go-to guy for assassinations before he went dark. Someone called Defarge was rumored to be replacing Medina. The second request had come after Mal observed a CIA communications team installing wireless surveillance cameras covering Satie's office. He had asked Zeb to hack into their feed, then stream it to Kidon headquarters.

This morning, Zeb reported. "The photos from Satie's office have continued to come through fine, but there has been no activity since last Friday the nineteenth."

"I wonder why? Let's keep watching," Mal suggested. "I have several bits of information for our file on Ricci. I located her cousin's address in Rome through a French inspecteur I know. I visited him and can report the following: her home address is in Berlin, and I'll give it to you before we hang up. She's living there with her lesbian lover, but I don't know what name Izabella is using. Also, I learned Izabella is going to sneak into the US using a false identity. She'll fly from Europe and then make her way to Vancouver, where her cousin's associates will smuggle her across the border."

"That ties in to what I discovered," Zeb continued. "Monday evening the twenty-second, we had a high-probability hit—eighty-five percent—on our facial recognition software we're running on flights from Berlin. Izabella headed for Montreal; I don't know what identity she is using either."

"See if you can hack Montreal airport's CCTV where Izabella would grab a cab and trace her. It looks like I'm heading to Montreal."

***

Before lunch on Wednesday the twenty-fourth, the Republic of South Korea's ambassador was ushered into the Oval Office. The president was meeting with him alone and had instructed his secretary not to show the appointment in his classified calendar or the White House visitors log. It was a short meeting.

"Mr. Ambassador, I have an unusual request. I'm asking you because I trust your discretion completely."

"Certainly, Mr. President. What can I do?"

"I need to borrow your consulate in San Francisco for a top secret meeting on Saturday morning, November eighth. I'll need it for about two hours. I assume your consulate is closed on Saturday?"

"Yes."

"Fine. I'll have one guest, and we'll each have a translator. There will be minimum security. I would expect your consul general to be there to greet us but not attend the meeting. Plan on just two staffers to provide refreshments and so forth. We'll work out the specifics later. Is it doable?"

"Of course."

"I'm not going to disclose anything else now. You can tell your consul general about a meeting, but that's all. This is a matter of the greatest national security."

"Mr. President, I'm honored you value our alliance and are willing to entrust your national security to us. We won't let you down."

The two men shook hands. As the ambassador left, the president chuckled. *He looked bewildered. Better to keep it that way until the last.*

***

In the early evening on Wednesday, the director met with the president in the Oval Office. "We have additional information from both sources. We've identified who Defarge is. She is Izabella Ricci, a former Mossad agent who freelances much as Medina did."

"Do you think she's deep-cover Mossad?"

"No, I think she's rogue. Izabella was a member of the Kidon Unit and is characterized as one of the most dangerous people in the world. We believe she has already made her way to Canada."

"What's your plan?"

"Well, obviously, find her. But it might be difficult. Also, Satie's house burned down early Saturday morning. We believe he was killed in the blaze."

"Ricci?" the president asked.

"Perhaps. I have a question for you. Do you want us to terminate her as soon as we locate her, or do you want to play this out? If we play it out, we may be able to unearth the conspirators."

The president continued without answering. "What else? What do you have from your other source—the US one?"

"Nando and Jay have concluded that San Francisco is the likely spot. They're going there on the thirtieth, and their source will meet with them then."

"That's a break. Maybe their source will flip on a conspirator. Then we could nab the bastards without playing out the Ricci scenario."

"Yes, but it assumes Ricci doesn't act before that."

"So you're recommending termination," the president observed.

"I didn't say that. It's your call. You know the risks you'll be taking the longer she's operational."

"I do, but it makes sense to keep both options open. Don't you agree?"

"If it's what you would like, I'll support it."

"Fine. How about getting the other services involved now?" the president asked.

"Mr. President, I haven't changed my mind on that. No, let me keep it in-house with the CIA. I'm too anxious about leaks."

"Speaking of leaks, we must keep my meeting at the South Korean consulate in San Francisco the morning after the fundraiser absolutely secret. You know how important it is."

"I do. It's not even in your classified calendar. I think there'll be less than five people besides you and me who know."

"Fine, then don't terminate her yet," the president said. "But for Christ's sake, find her."

***

Later that evening, a man in Silicon Valley received his first text from the emergency contact Satie had provided: THURS.—SEPT. 25, 4 P.M.—YOU'RE ALIAS JACK, SEE MATT—NOTRE-DAME BASILICA OF MONTREAL.

Shit, he thought. *This must be serious. And everything was going well.*

***

Father Matt had been at the Notre-Dame Basilica of Montreal since 2009, having been called there after the monsignor passed away. The old man and his beloved chocolate Lab, Jacques, had been there longer than anyone could remember. Father Matt had met him a few years before he passed at the prompting of their bishop, who had suggested that Father Matt discuss a personal crisis with the old priest.

"Let's walk to the Promenade, Matt," the monsignor had said. "You can talk to me; I'm an excellent listener."

Father Matt recalled studying the old man's face. His eyes were gentle, coaxing, yet insistent. Father Matt was convinced the old monsignor already knew everything. As they walked and talked, Father Matt had begun to see, to calm down, to understand, and he felt better about his problem. Now he was constantly reminded of their meeting because the monsignor's well-worn red parka still hung in the coat closet. The old priest had worn it that day, and Father Matt couldn't get rid of it. And of course, there was Jacques, who was still at the basilica, having accepted Father Matt without hesitation.

This Thursday morning, Father Matt was restless. It was three o'clock. Today he was having *those* visitors again. Even though the visitations had happened only five or six times since he had been there, sometimes Father Matt—now the monsignor—questioned his judgment. Would the old priest have approved of the visitors? Father Matt wasn't so sure he would've. It had started after a childhood friend and his roommate at the University of Toronto requested a favor. The friend, now a senior officer in the Canadian Security Intelligence Service, asked if the service could use the basilica for hush-hush meetings. Meetings that were a matter of national security. The drill was that Father Matt, when requested, would close the confessionals for several hours. Then a host would arrive and wait in the sacristy. After the other party showed up, the visitors would meet in a confessional. A couple of times, the hosts had been Americans. The priest had recognized one of them because that man served high up in both the current and previous administrations. Other than that, he had no idea who the visitors were—spies, double agents, defectors, confidential informants. Father Matt continued to ponder whether he was doing the right thing; secrets never boded well. He just didn't know. And adding to his quandary was that after each meeting, the priest would find an envelope on his desk addressed to RECTOR'S DISCRETIONARY FUND, containing five hundred Canadian dollars. The monsignor made sure the money went to worthy causes.

CHAPTER SEVEN

Thursday, September 25, 2014
Montreal

Thursday afternoon at three forty-five at the Notre-Dame Basilica, the man from Silicon Valley arrived and sat in the front pew. Soon a priest entered from the sacristy and approached him. They shook hands. "I'm Jack," the man said.

"Yes, and I'm Matt. This way, please." Their simple recognition code had been correct, so the priest led Jack to a confessional. After he was inside, Father Matt retraced his steps. The priest came back straightaway with another man from the sacristy, whom he led to the unoccupied side of the confessional. Then Father Matt returned to his office.

The sacristy man said, "Satie is dead."

"Jesus. I just spoke with him last week."

"About what?"

"Satie said he arranged for a different contractor because the one he was hiring had been killed in a hit-and-run accident in Paris."

"Did he say who the replacement was?"

"Someone called Defarge," Jack answered.

"That confirms my understanding."

"Also, Satie gave me an address in Berlin. Apparently, the contractor lives there with a girlfriend," Jack continued. "I have an emergency contact number for Defarge. But I couldn't call you because I don't have yours. I'll give you this information before we leave."

"Did you make the payment?"

"Yes, on the seventeenth, so the scenario ought to play out by itself. Will you be control now and deal directly with the contractor?"

"Yes. Here's how you can reach me, but only in an emergency— it's a burner. Get yourself several; we'll communicate that way from now on."

The men continued to talk for a while before Jack left by the center aisle. The sacristy man departed shortly thereafter and walked toward the Old Port.

***

Cole sat in his car and waited on Saint-Sulpice Street. If Cole had ever needed to prepare a job description, it would've been difficult. *I guess a smuggler might cover it*, he mused as he waited, *but not really. I'm not a coyote, drug smuggler, sex trafficker, or anything like that—not involved with that shit.* Cole worked the northern and southern borders of the US— in either direction—bringing people across. He handled those who needed to disappear or cross off-grid. And whatever it took, Cole brought them across: on foot trudging over unmarked trails in the middle of the night, in the backs of trucks or trunks of cars, by boat—even flying under the radar. He was comfortable at sea as well as in mountainous or jungle terrains. Mostly he worked for the alphabet spy agencies, providing logistics or running extractions, defections, or escapes. But now and then, his clients were organized crime figures or wealthy white-collar criminals. All of them disregarded the fact that Cole worked both sides of the aisle.

Cole had been well trained via a ten-year stint as an Army ranger and, afterward, bush piloting for an outfit Cole suspected was a front for the CIA. That's how he had met today's client. Cole checked his watch—four thirty. *Still plenty of time to take him to the airport for his six o'clock flight.* When he looked up, his client—the sacristy man—was walking toward the Old Port on the other side of the street. Cole tooted a couple of times; the man crossed over and walked behind the red Dodge Hellcat, looking it over before getting in.

"Nice car. New? Glad you're not trying to be inconspicuous."

"Yeah," Cole joked. "It gets me where I'm going."

"Thanks for picking me up. It's easier than trying to meet somewhere surreptitiously."

"Not to mention a free ride to the airport," Cole said.

"That too."

"So what's up?"

"Drive to Sioux Lookout by noon on Monday. At the Sunset Inn Motel, you'll find an untraceable Ford 150 pickup parked. It's outfitted with an oversized toolbox behind the cab. Then pick up a woman at the train station, head for the bridge at International Falls, and hide her in the toolbox before crossing the border. After that, take her to Falls International Airport."

"Sioux Lookout's a haul. I think it's about twelve hundred miles. I'll take two days and be there sometime on Sunday."

"You'll leave your car there?"

"Yeah, I'll check in for a week, drop her at the airport, ditch the truck, then probably make my way back there by bus. No one will ever think to look for me traveling that way."

"I gotta give you a heads-up on this broad: she's lethal. I'm not shitting you—one of the most dangerous people I've come across."

"I'm not worried. You know my background."

"I know, but don't underestimate her. If she gives you any trouble, you know what to do."

They arrived at the airport in plenty of time for the sacristy man to catch his flight.

***

Mal took an Air France afternoon flight; it arrived about five fifteen local time. When he landed, he called Zeb, who said, "I have information for you. I was able to track Izabella. She is staying at the Gault on Sainte Hélène Street in the Old Port. I've been able to hack into the CCTV of their lobby and corridors, so I can help you with surveillance. Also, after we talked, I was curious about why Satie wasn't showing up at his office. I don't know how the hell we missed it right away, but his house burned down early Saturday morning—a total loss. They found remains in his bedroom."

"Satie?"

"I assume so. The Munich authorities are waiting for DNA results."

"Shit. Izabella's covering her tracks."

"Apparently. Anything else you need?" Zeb asked.

"I'm going to need a sidearm."

"Do you remember Ezra Grossman?"

"Ezzie? Sure."

"He's now our cultural attaché at our Montreal consulate."

"You mean chief of station?"

"Yeah." Zeb chuckled. "I'll give him a call and ring you back. What do you want?"

"A .45 ACP semiauto—short barrel."

***

After six Thursday evening, Izabella received a call from control. The conversation was brief, telling her how to travel to Sioux Lookout for a pickup at noon on Monday. Izabella also learned that Nando Medina was alive and in Langley, investigating the assassination conspiracy. She and control agreed that they would switch to new burners after their call ended.

***

Mal was concealed across the street from the Gault, ready to tail Izabella. Thursday evening she had dinner at a bistro and returned to the hotel.

Later that evening, Zeb called, sending Mal to a gentlemen's club called Chez Camasutra. When he arrived, Mal asked for Ginger, a cute American stripper. After giving the recognition phrase "Ezzie sent me," Ginger took him to the VIP room and handed him a bag containing a Kimber with a three-inch barrel, two magazines, and a box of fifty rounds.

"How much?"

"It's paid for. So is my time—but we need to stay at least twenty minutes to make it look legit," Ginger said as she took off what little clothing she still had on and came over to him.

Afterward, in a cab to a small second-class hotel near the Gault, Mal thought, *Jesus, "Ezzie sent me" . . . really!*

***

Friday morning, September 26, Izabella checked out, and Mal followed her by cab to Montreal's Central Station. Once inside, he saw her buy a ticket. A few dollars to the ticket agent disclosed that Izabella was traveling to Toronto's Union Station on the eight fifty. Mal stayed out of sight and boarded a separate car. The train arrived in Toronto at two fifteen p.m. Then Izabella made two stops within the station. The first was to the Via Rail ticket booth. Another few dollars revealed that she had purchased a one-way ticket to Sioux Lookout on Sunday morning's nine forty-five departure of the *Canadian*. It arrived the following day at noon. *What the hell is Izabella doing in Sioux Lookout?* Mal purchased a similar ticket and picked up a brochure about the train. Izabella was at the hotel desk now. Mal decided not to follow her because he knew where she would be on Sunday morning. He sat in the waiting room and perused the brochure's map of the train's route. Sioux Lookout appeared to be one of the closest stops to the US border. Driving from there on Ontario's Route 502 south, International Falls, Minnesota, would be less than two hundred miles away. A quick search of the internet revealed that Falls International Airport had service to the Twin Cities.

Mal waited until Izabella left the station and called Zeb at home, explaining what was going on.

"What's next?" Zeb asked.

"It's likely Izabella's heading to San Francisco, because Bridgette said that's where Nando thought she would go. So I'll follow her to Sioux Lookout and see what she does. If Izabella heads for International Falls, that would confirm what I'm thinking."

"Let's do this," Zeb said. "I'll get teed up over the weekend to hack CCTV at International Bridge, Falls International Airport departure gates, and arrival gates at SFO. If you can send me a plate number and description of the car she'll be in, it would be helpful. Anything else you need?"

"No. Talk to you later."

***

Friday evening, Nando asked Jay if they could talk somewhere inconspicuously. Without hesitation, Jay agreed, suggesting dinner at his house on Saturday evening. Jay quietly joked, "Less chance of eavesdropping."

He's on the same page as I am, Nando thought.

So on Saturday evening at seven o'clock, Nando rang Jay's doorbell. Jay and his wife, Joan, lived in a suburb near Arlington. They all went to the deck, where they chatted over wine and cheese while potatoes baked on the grill. When Joan left to make a salad, Jay said, "Regarding tonight, I'm glad you spoke up. I'm mixed up about our investigation. After dinner we can talk safely here; I sweep the house for bugs every week."

Jay grilled steaks, and when dinner was over, Joan left them in the dining room to talk. Nando began, "Before we start with what's concerning us, can you fill me in on some of the background? I believe an assassination attempt is underway. There's too much circumstantial evidence to deny it. But I've been out of the States a long time and don't understand why; I'm curious."

"It's complicated," Jay said,

"The president was elected as a transformational leader. When he took office in 2009, his approval rating was sixty-seven percent. But as of this September, he is upside down, with an approval rating of barely forty percent. Key issues aren't any better, with approval ratings for the economy and foreign affairs at about forty percent each. Government isn't functioning well either, with Congress' approval rating near an all-time low at fifteen percent."

"That doesn't bode well for the upcoming midterm elections," Nando said.

"No, and the emergence of the Tea Party is portending a meaningful shift to the right. So the smart money is that the Republicans will control both houses of Congress, which will tie the administration's hands. Thus, since January this year, to avoid a congressional gridlock, the president has been threatening to double down with executive orders. Orders that are deleterious to the conspirators."

"Can the president create that much havoc using those?"

"Apparently they think so. And they can't count on the Republicans. They aren't litigious like the Democrats. The RNC doesn't run to court or have the equivalent of the ACLU or other watchdog groups to file injunctions and so forth. So the executive orders may well go unchallenged and be effective."

"Assassination is a drastic solution for a two-year problem," Nando observed.

"Maybe, but even if the president is ineffectual, it doesn't solve the longer-term problem. The assassination is a preemptive strike. The vice president isn't merely a stopgap until the 2016 elections. He is viewed as more moderate and has worked across the aisle in the Senate for nearly fifty years—a deal maker and negotiator. The group behind this thinks he is malleable and controllable. Also, it's still a bit fuzzy, but the vice president is believed to be sympathetic to China because of indirect business interests he has there. So they want to put him in the Oval Office as soon as possible and afterwards elect him president. The Republicans look like they will field at least a dozen primary candidates for the presidential. There's no guaranty their presumptive nominee will prevail. And if he does, he lacks charisma and is carrying around the baggage of a dynasty. I think the Republicans will be in poor shape to compete in 2016. But it's not necessarily great news for the Democrats either, because their presumptive nominee has low likability numbers in all the polls. Not to mention other problems, such as the 2012 attack in Libya and increased scrutiny of a family charitable foundation. So, if the vice president is installed in the White House shortly and is properly handled, he'll stand a likely chance of winning both the Democrat nomination and presidency."

"So," Nando said, "we have a consortium of construction, banking and finance, industry, energy, big tech, and a foreign actor behind the assassination plot?"

"Yes, and it's all about money. They all have individual or joint issues that affect their bottom lines. China is probably the international actor because of what Anna reported. So let's deal with them first. I don't think it's state sponsored. Even though China's current administration has been shifting policy back towards governmental ownership, the private sector still accounts for much of the country's economic output."

"So you think it's the private sector?"

"Most likely. They are concerned about issues such as currency manipulation and human rights, including both child and slave labor. Those policies keep their export prices low, and any interference would adversely affect their profits. Our administration is openly critical. A related problem is our imbalance of payments—trade—with China; we are on the short end of the stick.

"But China overlaps with domestic issues as well. Silicon Valley isn't happy with any potential disruption in trade with them because they import components for smartphones and other electronics manufactured domestically. It becomes complicated for the US manufacturers that operate in China too. They aren't supposed to use child labor and so on, but it's questionable if they're complying—who knows. More important, in order to gain permission to operate there, these companies along with big tech must share their technology. It's tantamount to a theft of intellectual property. The president is threatening to crack down on all of this.

"But there are domestic matters that don't involve China. Big tech has issues because there are grumblings from the administration about breaking up their oligopoly and a repeal of Section 230 of the Communications Decency Act. Oil and construction share common interests such as the Keystone XL Pipeline. Its approval continues to be tied up in a Nebraska court and the Department of State. Then there're upcoming new regulations with mixed messages on oil and gas fracking as well as greenhouse gases. These are hot buttons with environmentalists, and the administration is supportive of stricter policies. Also, there's the issue of government overregulation. It affects everyone in this group and business in general.

"The current president is seen as liberal—far left wing—with progressive policies harmful to all of them. They're gambling on being better off without him, thus preferring the vice president. Think about it—

an administration in place for ten years that's preferential to their wants," Jay concluded.

"Jesus, Jay, you've thought a lot about this."

"It's what I do." He chuckled. "When I started with the company, I used to work on *The World Factbook*."

"It's exhausting, and we haven't even talked about what's bothering us," Nando kidded.

"I know. Why don't you go now? I've been doing all the talking."

"Okay," Nando said, "something isn't right with how this is unfolding. Think about it. It's a problem with a simple solution. First, why doesn't the president change his schedule and stay close to the White House. Or why not give the order to terminate Ricci? The CIA found her once already in Munich, and we're sure she's headed to San Francisco. We even have an idea where Izabella will attempt it. For some reason, the president wants to play this out. Is he being manipulated? And if so, by whom? Also, is there someone close to the president who's providing information to the assassin, and if so, is it the same person as the manipulator?"

Then Nando shared what he knew about Mossad and Mal's involvement. "He's well informed. But how did Mal suss out my fake death so fast? Is he on our side? I think so, but I don't think we know what his motivation is. Is he on assignment from Tel Aviv? If so, why not liaise directly with the US? Why Bridgette? Mal identified her quickly. Sometimes he is using her instead of Israel's intelligence services, but Mal has more information than Bridgette can provide. It's confusing, and I'm concerned he's rogue. In any event, Mal isn't our unknown actor; it isn't possible he could influence the president."

"What's your conclusion?" Jay asked.

"I don't have one yet. What do you think?"

"I've thought about all you've said, and they are my concerns as well. Two quick observations: First, we must keep Mal's identity to ourselves. No one else but Bridgette knows. The same for Anna—she'll be in jeopardy if she's identified," Jay replied.

"Agreed. And I also think that since her cousin's murder, Izabella will change her plans to use Vancouver to enter the States. Izabella will be harder to find now."

"Yes," Jay said. "Also, Satie was controlling the process, even though he probably only knew one of the conspirators. There's no evidence he knew about the consortium Anna's been describing. Satie's death was unexpected. So I think our unknown actor may become directly involved now. Perhaps he'll make a mistake."

"So what's next?" Nando asked.

"I have two further concerns. I anticipate my hacking will be needed. The only way around that is through warrants or the FISA court. I'm not sure they're feasible because of time and potential leaks."

"I hadn't thought about that."

"Next, let's think carefully about what intelligence we pass along. It must be strictly on a need-to-know basis. But, while I'm convinced there's someone close to the president behind this, we can't shirk our duties on a hunch either. It's a dilemma," Jay concluded.

"And?" Nando probed.

"Like you, I'm not willing to say. Not yet."

***

After noon on Monday the twenty-ninth, Mal remained out of sight in the Sioux Lookout station. It was a bit of a challenge because the station was small. Shortly after Izabella detrained, she was picked up by a man in a blue recent-model Ford 150 pickup truck with tinted windows. She threw her duffel in the truck's bed before climbing into the cab. As the truck pulled away, Mal noted the number of the Minnesota license plate and called Zeb, relaying the information.

"I'm all teed up to pick up the truck at the International Bridge. If they drive through with only one pit stop, it'll be about four hours. I'll call you when I pick them up. In the meantime, I'll run the plate. What are you doing?" Zeb asked.

"I'll hang out here and probably spend the night. I want to be sure Izabella is in San Francisco and know where she's staying before I head west."

Zeb called back in less than an hour. "The truck is untraceable. It's owned by a corporation that's a subsidiary of a subsidiary and so forth. That probably tells you what you want to know. I put the search on hold for the time being; I can use my time better. Talk to you later."

Mal sat in a coffee shop having an early dinner. He kept thinking about Izabella's actions. *She adjusted rapidly. Izabella planned on her cousin's associates getting her into the US, so she didn't have her own network in place. But despite that, shortly after learning her plans had been compromised, Izabella was on a flight to Montreal. And as soon as she landed, an atypical alternate route with ground support was in place. Izabella is good, but is she that good? Perhaps there's someone else involved behind the scenes—someone with resources.*

Zeb called early Tuesday morning, the thirtieth, and confirmed that Izabella had made it to San Francisco the previous evening. She stayed at an airport hotel. Because it didn't make sense for her to use that location, Mal surmised that Izabella would probably find another hotel in the city. "I'll let you know as soon as I have additional information," Zeb told him. "Are you going to SF?"

"Yes, but I want to check in with Bridgette Dubois first. Talk to you later."

"Okay, but before you go, Mal, there was one curious thing. I enlarged a shot of the truck entering the US. I wanted to see if I could ID who picked her up. There was one person in the cab, a man, but I couldn't make a clear blowup. I assumed Izabella was in the big toolbox in the truck's bed. So I went to the shot of the truck entering the airport. Odd. By the time the truck reached the airport, there was still only one person in the cab, but now it was Izabella. She parked and took a shuttle to the departure gate. Maybe Izabella's covering her tracks again."

"I wouldn't be surprised," Mal replied, and rang off.

After Zeb called, Mal caught up with Bridgette in Paris.

"Hi, Mal. Where are you? Madame is wondering."

"This all came up suddenly. I'm in Sioux Lookout, Canada, now. I've been tracking Izabella. She has made it to San Francisco, and I'm heading there next. Would you ring Madame and tell her I'll call when I'm settled?"

"All right." Bridgette knew Mal was a valuable resource, so she'd reluctantly pushed aside her upset over his ruthless methods. She volunteered more information. "Nando and his analyst flew to San Francisco this morning to meet with an asset. They're pursuing a second line of investigation besides Satie. Then they'll look over the two likely sites. I think Nando will be back by this weekend, because we're taking a few days in Montreal beginning Friday, October third."

"Do you have a place to stay yet?"

"I'm working on it now."

"Izabella stayed at the Gault in Old Montreal. It looked fine, but it's pricey."

"Did you stay there?"

"No, too expensive for a mere government functionary."

"Oh, please," Bridgette laughed "But I'll check it out anyway."

"Anything else going on?"

"No, all is quiet."

"I look forward to seeing you soon," Mal responded. As they rang off, he thought, *I think a quick trip to Montreal this weekend is in order. Hopefully, Bridgette will take my hotel recommendation, and they'll be easy to find. It's time Nando and I met—apparently he is on a different tack.*

CHAPTER EIGHT

Tuesday, September 30, 2014
San Francisco

Anna had taken a vacation day so she could pick Jay and Nando up at the airport. They had taken an eleven o'clock nonstop that arrived in midafternoon. On the way to the Sir Francis Drake, where they were staying, Anna said, "I thought we could talk in your room after an early dinner. Then I can head home at a reasonable hour." Anna left her car with the valet, and after they registered, she said, "I'll walk over to Sears and make a reservation—give you guys a chance to freshen up."

After dinner, when they were back in the room, Anna began the conversation, despite being uneasy. "What do you want to know? I hardly know where to start."

Jay said, "Why don't you tell us why you're doing this? It's a big risk."

"This isn't easy for me. I'm embarrassed, but you need to know how serious I am. It's time for payback; that's how it started, anyway. But it has become more important to me now that I have a clue about what's going on."

"You don't have to tell us anything embarrassing." Jay responded.

***

Anna hadn't told anyone about her situation, but now she was ready to talk. After high school, she'd worked as a secretary. Not long after, she got married and had a child, and she stayed home with the baby. The family seemed to be doing fine, but her husband wasn't crazy about marriage and took off. Anna moved back in with her parents and never heard from her husband again. Later, her father died, and they lost his pension. So she went to work as a clerk in the company she was still with today. In time, her boss noticed her, and Anna was transferred to his office. She did well and was promoted to administrative assistant, working closely with him. Eventually, her boss was promoted to CEO, and Anna moved with him to his new job.

Anna's recent problems had started when her boss boxed her into a tough spot. Four years ago, he'd called her into his office and said a staff realignment was underway and there wouldn't be a place for her. Anna was dumbfounded and started crying, but her boss was unsympathetic and finally said, "If you don't leave, I'll call security. You'll hear from personnel about your last day."

Later, Anna received a week's notice with two weeks' severance pay. Then, on the day before she was supposed to leave, her boss called. "Let's go to the Hilton Garden Inn. I have an idea, but I don't want to talk in the office."

So Anna went. He sat on the edge of the bed just staring at her. In the end, Anna asked, "Why are we here? What's going on?"

"I'm deciding if I've made a mistake about giving you another chance."

"I don't understand."

"Let me help you out, then: take off your clothes."

"Huh! So that's it. You want to screw me . . . right?"

"Well, duh. But this isn't going to be a one-off. Get undressed and stop messing about."

Anna convinced herself she was merely doing what was necessary and did as she was told. But it took all her resolve to stand there naked while he looked her over. He continued watching as she teared up. Finally, he called her to where he was sitting and said, "Kneel down . . . and for Christ's sake, stop sniveling. You won't be able to breathe."

Since then, their relationship had developed into a complicated and confusing one. Anna's boss told her he loved her, and she believed he did—in his own way. He had never acted like that again, but Anna understood the message: her tenure was only as secure as her last performance was up to snuff. Nevertheless, her boss treated her well and continued to increase her pay. Anna made good money now.

***

Their meeting continued and Nando said, "Don't be embarrassed. You were simply taking care of your family. Your boss bullied and abused you, making you into both his sex and wage slave."

"I never looked at it that way—I mean about the wages—but you're probably correct. I'm not qualified for a job at my present salary level."

"What about the MeToo movement and whistleblower protections? It doesn't seem like you're out there all alone," Jay said.

"I've thought about it, but it would only end badly. I can't risk it because I'm the breadwinner. Besides, my boss needs to pay for what he did to me, and this conspiracy is giving me an opportunity."

"All right," Jay said. "What else is going on?"

"I told you we had a meeting in Scottsdale on September eighteenth. There was nothing unusual, and I didn't learn anything new. But here's something odd. My boss took an unscheduled trip to Montreal on Thursday, September twenty-fifth. He didn't come in to the office but called me from the airport while waiting for his jet to be fueled. He must have had to scramble to put the flight crew together. He sounded . . . it's hard to describe . . . maybe anxious. I don't know what it was all about, but he was back in the office as usual the next morning."

"He didn't say anything about it?" Nando inquired.

"No, I asked him, but he told me it turned out to be nothing—a family matter. I didn't push."

"Do you have any more of those unusual trips scheduled?" Jay asked.

"Yes. We're going to New Orleans on Thursday, October sixteenth. I'm making the arrangements at the Ritz-Carlton—we're taking the Ritz-Carlton Suite."

"How do you feel about proactively wheedling information out of him?" Jay continued.

"I think I can . . . especially in bed. He seems more open then. But you're asking a lot. You need to cover my butt—I mean it. I need guarantees.

"The way I see it, I didn't have to do any of this. Life would've gone on as usual and their plan would've succeeded or not—no skin off my nose either way. But now that I've put two and two together, figured out what is happening, I can't ignore it either. Not with a spy in the family," Anna joked.

Nando was watching her carefully. "And a perfect opportunity to get even with your boss."

Jay shot Nando a glance, but Anna didn't pause before saying, "Yes."

"What's your solution?" Nando asked. "What do you want?"

"Security and safety for my family. If I provide you with sufficient information to arrest him, I'll have to testify. It's all going to come out. My boss may go to jail, but I'll be utterly unemployable despite the whistleblower protections you mentioned. I'm also guessing there's a more powerful person behind this than my boss. Look at how he scurried off to Montreal. My life will be worthless—revenge is a bitch. That leaves witness protection. Are you going to be able to place me in a position equal to or better than my current one? I'm skeptical about that.

"So the best thing for me would be if my boss offed himself or had a fatal mishap."

Jay appeared to be alarmed.

But Nando said, "I understand."

Anna continued, "If that were to happen, I'm certain I could weasel my way onto the staff of another man in the executive suite. One of them ought to jump at the opportunity, because I have no illusions that my boss has been discreet. But that is not to say we have an understanding yet."

They were quiet. Finally, Anna continued, "All right . . . I'll go with my instincts. I'll cooperate, but don't hang me out to dry. I work for Orwell MegaData in Palo Alto. My boss is Bruce Campbell."

Anna left shortly thereafter, and Jay said, "Jesus, I never saw that coming. Scary."

***

Wednesday, Mal flew to San Francisco. He found a small hotel near Union Square. After he was settled, he called Zeb.

"I tracked Izabella from her airport hotel by cab," Zeb said. "She's staying at a small hotel on Bush Street near Powell. Where's your hotel?"

"I'm on Geary Boulevard a few blocks from Powell also." Mal could hear Zeb typing.

"You're a three-minute walk away—just three streets south of her."

"I'll have to be careful not to encounter her." Mal chuckled. "Anything else new?"

"No, but I keep going through all the surveillance footage of Izabella's trip to International Falls. The man who took her across the bridge disappeared between there and the airport. It's only about three miles on Route 53. I'm checking news feeds to see if there're any reports that shed light on it."

"Okay, keep it up. I think I'm going to Montreal on Saturday. Nando and Bridgette are having a long weekend together. I suggested to Bridgette that they stay at the Gault. I think it's time we shared what we have."

"Do they know you're coming?"

"No, I think I'll surprise them." Mal chuckled as he rang off.

CHAPTER NINE

Thursday, October 2, 2014
San Francisco

Nando and Jay rented a car and set out on the forty-minute drive to Palo Alto. Their plan for the day was twofold: first, perform a site assessment at Stanford University, where the global warming conference would be held, and second, return to the city and reconnoiter Holden Ransom's. During the drive, Nando asked, "Have you been able to find out if anybody has been requesting plans for either location?"

"No, nothing yet, but I'm following up regularly. I printed copies of the auditorium's floor plan from the internet. We should be able to look around inside if it's open."

"Are you still concerned about warrants?"

"Yes."

"I'll discuss it this weekend with Bridgette. Maybe she has an idea."

"Cool."

Jay had brought along a map of the campus, which he'd also printed from the net. When they arrived at Stanford, they parked and headed for Memorial Auditorium. Nando intended to work out a feasibility assessment: could it be done, how, how difficult would it be, and what would be the likelihood of success and escape. They were able to access the public areas of the auditorium. After that, they scouted the campus for likely spots a sniper might set up. Nando paid particular attention to sight lines and distances.

By noon, they were on their way back to San Francisco. In the car, Jay asked, "So what do you think? It looks like there're plenty of possible sites to set up—not too far away, either."

"I don't like it, although you're right about outside. There're excellent sight lines and reasonable distances. That's not much of a concern if Izabella's as skilled as I think she is. But here's what you don't see. Snipers set up ahead of time. Their window of opportunity is small; it's hard to adjust to a different location on the fly. There are too many possible scenarios here—all with no better than fifty-fifty odds. First, there's more than one landing location. Sometimes a second chopper is deployed like a decoy and doesn't land near the first one. So if the attempt is made when he'll be moving from Marine One to his car, which chopper is it? What if they use two cars—which do you set up on? When the president enters the building is the best scenario, but there's a garage in the rear. They can pull his car in there and close the door; that would fuck up any shot. No, the only workable scenario is at the front entrance—then bang, he's dead. Nothing else works."

"I never thought of all that," Jay said.

"There's no reason why you should have—you weren't trained for it. If we didn't know who the sniper was, I might consider it a possibility, because to a novice it has a simple, straightforward appeal. There's no doubt that the mansion is complex, with a lot of moving parts, yet I'm betting it's doable. We'll see," Nando concluded.

After lunch they drove to Pacific Heights. It was quite a home, with multiple entrances and three floors below a full attic. The first floor had large, open rooms for entertaining along with a commercial kitchen. On the second floor was a huge master bedroom suite, a guest suite, and nursery. The third floor had other bedrooms and showers. The attic was about thirty percent finished, with smaller staff accommodations. There was even an underground four-car garage. This was all easy to divine, as Jay had electronically retrieved recent renovation plans from San Francisco's Building Department, and everything was clearly marked.

There wasn't much to do but review the plans, find all the entrances, see which streets were best escape routes, and so on. On the way back to the hotel, Nando said, "Izabella will do it there. It's what I would do."

"How?" Jay asked.

"That's the tricky part. Yet if it's done properly, there's a likely chance of success and escape. It's also not for the squeamish—it'll be up close, no eight-hundred-yard shot. But we need additional information."

"Such as?"

"Well, who's going to cater it. Who's supplying the booze and bartenders. How much additional staff they're going to put on. Who's providing them. What security will be in place besides the Secret Service. Which bedroom will the president use, and so forth. I think, as we acquire this information, a plan will begin to emerge; it always has in the past."

Then Nando paused. "But there's a different topic we need to talk about. I don't want to disclose Anna's upcoming meetings or who her boss is yet. We both know about him, so it gives us some cover if this blows up. The less we pass on, the better, until we know what's what. I don't even want to use our internal sources to develop the information we need to proceed in analyzing the assassination plot."

"So what do we do then?"

"I have an idea. I'll talk it over with Bridgette this weekend—it involves her."

***

On Tuesday the thirtieth, after leaving the airport hotel, Izabella checked in at the White Swan Inn on Bush Street. It was a fifty-room English-style B and B located in the Nob Hill neighborhood near Union Square. While not off the beaten path, it mostly went unnoticed by tourists—just what she was looking for.

On Wednesday, Izabella slept late, because she needed to recharge from her travels. In the afternoon, she intended to visit José, Satie's contact for ordnance. José was in the heart of the Tenderloin District, and Satie had told her it was one of the highest-crime areas in San Francisco. She'd be on guard because she didn't have a firearm yet. While Izabella had no reservations about taking care of herself in hand-to-hand combat, she wasn't foolhardy either. So Izabella slipped a stiletto into her bootie and called for a taxi. The cabbie was reluctant to take her, but her charm and a $50 tip persuaded him. As she left the car, the driver said, "Lady, I can't wait for you—it's too fuckin' dangerous. I hope you know what you're doin'."

That sure as shit doesn't make me feel comfortable, Izabella thought as she started walking to a dilapidated tavern on the next corner, where five or six thugs were loitering. Izabella checked Satie's note as she approached; this was it—José's address. Izabella was used to being checked out, but these guys weren't even trying to hide it. As she came closer, one guy started flicking his tongue lewdly, while another—a big son of a bitch—began calling out, "Chica. Chica, you come to see Papi. Papi ready for you, chica." He grabbed his balls and squeezed them while keeping up his mantra.

Breathe slowly. Shit . . . can't remember the last time I was this nervous. Okay, don't hesitate. Look that big son of a bitch right in the eye. You can do it. Act like this is par for the course.

"Hey, guys, what's up?"

"What the fuck you want, chica?" the big SOB asked aggressively.

"I'm here to see José. Satie sent me."

"Who the fuck's Satie?" the big thug continued, but another loiterer whispered something to him before entering the tavern.

"Get your skinny ass over here," the SOB ordered. "I'm gonna pat you down. Up against the wall; spread 'em." He took his time, touching her everywhere—fondling her, toying with her nipples, and rubbing between her legs—it seemed to go on forever.

"Oh, yeah! Papi making you feel good. You like it like that, don't you? Papi can tell."

Stay calm . . . under control. What an asshole. Stupid too—missed the knife. Izabella had no doubt she could take this prick out hand-to-hand before he knew it. But she couldn't handle the others at the same time—not even with her knife. *Later, dude.*

He finally stopped when the other thug returned. "This way," the second thug said, holding the door open and pointing to José, who was seated in a rear corner at a round table with a .45 semiautomatic on the table beside his right hand.

José sized her up. "What should I call you?"

"Chica will do."

"Yeah, about that. I'm sorry . . . Pedro was rough. I'll speak to him—it's bad for business when he acts up."

"No harm, no foul," Izabella said.

Why the hell don't I believe you? José thought, but instead he said, "Okay, what do you want?"

"Satie said you can provide any armaments I need."

"What exactly?"

"I need a handgun, either a ten-millimeter or .45 ACP semiauto—full size. Also a Steyr SSG 69, a scope, silencer, and ammo for both."

"That's an impressive sniper's rifle, light, with a five-round magazine. It'll take a week. I need to call for a price. If you want a 1911, I have either a Springfield Armory ten-millimeter or a Sig Sauer .45 ACP in back."

"I'll take the Springfield, with two magazines and one hundred rounds. I'll need to do a function check, clean, and lube it before I leave. How much?"

"Five thousand dollars. I'll bring it out along with the cleaning supplies. You can do that while I make the call on the Steyr."

Izabella attended to the semiauto while José was on his mobile. *She's quick—knows what she's doing*, he thought. *Shit, chica already has it loaded and racked, with the safety on.*

"All right, it's ten thousand dollars for the rifle, scope, silencer, and all the ammo—fifteen in total. Give me ten thousand now. It covers today and fifty percent of the rest—then five thousand at pickup."

Izabella slipped the handgun into her waistband at the small of her back. Then she put the second magazine and ammo into her bag and took out an envelope containing $10,000, handing it to José.

"Give me your phone," he said, and called his own number. "I'll call when the rifle is here."

"Okay, phone me a taxi. My driver wouldn't wait."

Not surprised, José thought as he called.

***

Friday afternoon in Paris, Bridgette was on a three o'clock flight to Montreal. It arrived about four—plenty of time to make it to the Gault and check in ahead of Nando.

Meanwhile, in San Francisco, Jay took Nando to the airport. He was on a 7:00 a.m. nonstop to Montreal. It would arrive around five o'clock that afternoon, and by then Bridgette would already be there.

"I'll be heading back to DC as early as I can on Tuesday," Nando said as they pulled into the airport. "Was your mother able to put together Sunday dinner with Anna's family?"

"I'm still waiting to hear. I don't come west often, so it's a big deal for Mom. In any event, I'll probably leave on Monday."

"I hope her dinner works out. See you Tuesday," Nando said as he got out at the DEPARTING FLIGHTS sign.

***

Friday evening, Izabella drove to the Tenderloin District and parked one street over from where Pedro lived.

On Wednesday evening after leaving José's, Izabella had rented a car and later returned to stake out the dilapidated bar. The thugs were still hanging out, so she parked down the street and waited. About seven thirty, when the sun was down and it was growing darker, they broke up, and Pedro left. Izabella followed him for four or five blocks until he parked across from an apartment building and entered. She waited a few minutes, then drove by slowly. Izabella spotted an alley on the right side of the building. She drove around to the street behind, parked, and explored the alley. As Izabella had hoped, it went through to Pedro's street. And even when she stood deep in the alley—back in the shadows—she had a clear view of Pedro's car.

This evening, waiting in her car on the street behind, she checked her watch—seven fifteen. Time to go. Izabella, dressed all in black, wore running shoes, jeans, and a hoodie, and her handgun was tucked into her waistband. She headed for the alley and stood in the shadows at its entranceway. Izabella pulled on black gloves and waited. Seven thirty came and went. Finally, at seven fifty, Pedro's car pulled into a spot across from his building. It was much darker than the previous night—*better*. Izabella went straight up to Pedro as he stepped up onto the sidewalk.

"A little OT tonight, Pedro?"

Not recognizing her at first, Pedro looked confused. Then he smiled and said, "Chica, you come to see Pap—"

But Pedro couldn't finish his question. His voice box exploded with a crackle and pop, and his head snapped back. He tried to recover from Izabella's vicious closed-fist throat punch before he collapsed. Pedro made an awful racket trying to breathe. Prostrate on the sidewalk, he continued to struggle while Izabella stood over him, rubbed her fist, and calmly said, "Oh, Pedro, shut up. Take it like a man . . . you're such a fuckin' pussy."

Izabella looked about—no need to run. Nobody was around. *I guess this is the kind of neighborhood where people stay inside, see nothing, hear nothing—cool.* She squatted on her haunches, out of Pedro's thrashing range, watching him die. Afterward, Izabella smiled and returned to her car.

CHAPTER TEN

Saturday, October 4, 2014
Montreal

It was nearly noon. Bridgette was still in bed—dozing, stretching, smiling, and feeling terrific—while Nando showered. Yesterday afternoon had worked out perfectly. She'd arrived on time at four o'clock and been at the Hotel Gault before Nando's flight landed. Originally, Bridgette had thought of waiting for him at the airport, but then she'd reconsidered. In the end, she'd come ahead and checked in for them, then taken both key cards and texted Nando their room number. As soon as she was in their room, Bridgette showered and put on a courtesy terry robe. In less than an hour, Nando tapped on the door. When Bridgette opened it, she pulled him inside and began kissing him.

"You smell wonderful," Nando said, after they stopped kissing.

Bridgette smiled and led him to the bed.

"Should I take a shower too?"

"Not on your life, Monsieur. I intend to have my way with you right now—no excuses."

They stayed in bed and later ordered room service. When they were both tired out, Nando took a shower. *I don't remember him coming to bed. The last thing I recall was the sound of running water. I must've fallen asleep right away*, Bridgette mused.

So today they were going to relax, walk around Old Montreal, boutique shop, and work their way to the Old Port.

It was one o'clock before they left the hotel. Since they hadn't had breakfast, they found a bistro and ordered fresh-squeezed blood orange juice, strong coffee in small mugs, and croque madame and monsieur sandwiches. After they ate, they strolled along Notre-Dame Street West and went into the basilica. They spent an hour there, sitting in the quiet or walking around, enjoying the basilica's beauty. When they left, they shopped and slowly made their way to the Promenade du Vieux-Port, watching the traffic on the Saint Lawrence River for quite a while. The weather was warmer than usual—in the high seventies—so they were in no hurry to leave. Bridgette and Nando finally arrived back at the hotel around five thirty, took a short nap, and got ready for dinner.

"While you were in the shower, I called down to the concierge for the name of a small bistro the locals like, with authentic French country food," Bridgette said as they rode the elevator. When they left the hotel, Bridgette hadn't noticed Mal, who'd been sitting with a newspaper in one of the lobby's nooks.

It was a short walk to the bistro. It was still early, so the restaurant wasn't crowded. They sat at a small table in the rear corner. Bridgette instinctively took the seat with the best view of the entrance. She noticed Nando smiling. *He's laughing at me about my cop thing. I'll bet Nando did it also when he was on the job*, Bridgette thought. They both ordered traditional dishes—Bridgette ratatouille and Nando cassoulet with duck and garlic sausage—along with a bottle of Côtes du Rhône. They'd scarcely raised their glasses to toast when Bridgette's smile disappeared; she was looking at the entrance. Nando turned and saw a man walking in: well built, about six feet tall, fiftyish, with a self-assured bearing. Nando had no doubt who he was, even though he had never met the man before.

"Mal?" Nando said as he turned back to Bridgette.

"Shit, what does he want? Mal recommended the Gault, but I had no idea. Dammit—he set me up." Mal walked over to the table and sat down as if he were expected. Looking at Nando and extending his hand, he introduced himself.

"I hope you don't mind if I join you. I know you're on R & R, but we need to talk—not now, after dinner. And I think we should let the Central Institute for Intelligence and Special Operations pay," he said, and waved their waiter over. Mal ordered coq au vin and another bottle of Côtes du Rhône.

Bridgette noticed Nando smiling. *He's picked it up as well. Mal's telling us he is legit—on the job.*

This was Bridgette's first experience with Mal when he wasn't talking business. He was an excellent conversationalist, humorous and engaging. *I get it now,* she thought. *Mal's hard to resist. He makes you feel important and relaxed. That's how he got Madame in to bed so quickly—a perfect friggin' spy.*

When they had finished dinner, Mal began. "I do apologize. I'm pleased you picked up on my suggestion about the Gault. If you'd stayed elsewhere, I'm not confident I could have located you."

"You could have simply asked," Bridgette observed.

"I know, but I was afraid you'd put me off. We need to talk, and I have to clear the air." Nando and Bridgette looked at each other. "I know you've been confused about my status; it's complicated."

"Why is everything so complicated with you, Mal?" Bridgette asked, a bit pissy.

"It always is. I don't try to make it that way. I live in a more shadowy world than you might expect; that's all I can say."

Bridgette pushed. "Well, obviously you have an expense account," she said, indicating the table with a hand gesture. "So you're not rogue."

"No, not totally."

"Oh ... for Christ's sake, Mal. Just fuckin' tell us!" Bridgette snapped.

Mal looked genuinely startled, and Nando tried not to break out laughing.

"I didn't mean to upset you." Mal paused, apparently hoping this would reduce the tension. When Bridgette didn't say anything, he continued, "You have my business card. That's my real job, and my CV I told you about is accurate. When I'm not in the field, I'm an administrator. But I have talents that senior ministers in our government like to take advantage of at times like this. Issues they think are so sensitive they don't even want them run through our intelligence services. These are approved missions; please take my word for it. But I'm supposed to handle these problems on my own. Unknown to my superiors, I use one analyst sparingly. He's the best we have. Bridgette, you must've picked up on the incongruity that I can develop information you can't, yet at the same time, I need your help."

Bridgette remained silent.

"You're not making this easy, Bridgette. All right, my assignment that came from the highest level was to deal with Izabella. She's a total embarrassment to our government. I didn't need to be told what to do. So I was working the Satie angle to track her down. That's when I spotted Nando and Gagne. We ran you both through facial recognition. You were easy, Nando—we still had a file, even though you'd been inactive. We didn't know Gagne.

"It becomes confusing now. Is that a better word for you?" Mal asked with a chuckle. When Bridgette didn't respond, he continued. "I'm not even positive I have this in the correct order anymore. I was waiting in Munich for Izabella to eventually show up at Satie's. Meanwhile, my analyst discovered something big was afoot with the US and that it involved one hundred and fifty million dollars. Gagne showed up. Then after you arrived, Nando, I started to form an inkling about what might be happening. I kept watching, and both of you returned to Paris. After you were run over. I took it at face value when I heard about it. Later, Izabella appeared at Satie's. I didn't have a clean opportunity to deal with her then. If I had, we wouldn't be here now.

"On a hunch, I decided to come to Paris and went to your memorial service. I was the cleric in the rear. I kept waiting and watching. After that, it started to fall into place. Gagne hiding in the organ loft; I assumed he was taking pictures. Madame's eulogy, with the way she kept moving side to side; Madame was taking pictures as well. And then the service with no body and absolutely no proof that you were dead, Nando—it was effectively staged, but I was positive you were still alive.

"I'd guessed correctly that Satie and Izabella might show up. But why had Satie come? The two of you weren't that close. And why Izabella? Were they verifying your death? Then I toyed with the idea of doing her there. But I was fearful there wouldn't be enough chaos for me to escape. So I reconsidered and opted to check back with HQ before I proceeded. They decided I should work with the US government— unofficially, if possible. Eliminating Izabella was temporarily off the table.

"So afterward, I tracked Izabella's flight to Rome. Then, on the Monday after the service, Bridgette ran facial recognition on Izabella through Interpol. I was notified immediately. I knew Bridgette's name from the funeral but didn't realize she was law enforcement until then. I wasn't certain if you two were working together yet. Before I sought

Bridgette out, I learned from my analyst that he was convinced Izabella planned to assassinate your president. But he didn't know why, how, or who was behind it. When I met Bridgette, I brought Izabella's file to gain her trust. Bridgette never said anything directly, yet I inferred that the CIA had reactivated you and you were probably in Washington. It made absolute sense. Who better to capture the number-two assassin than the number one? I've been operating on that premise since then."

"You forgot to mention your quick trip to Rome," Bridgette said coldly.

"Yes, that too. I realized, Nando, that you were working a different angle than the Satie-Izabella one. I don't know anything about it. We ought to work together. After I talked to Bridgette last week, I decided to try to meet you this weekend. I want you to trust me, so I'll share what I've learned. I tracked Izabella to Montreal and then to Sioux Lookout. I determined she was heading to the airport at International Falls. My analyst tracked Izabella to San Francisco, where she has been staying since the thirtieth at the White Swan Inn on Bush Street. I'm suspicious an unknown highly placed US player is calling the shots. There's no way Izabella could've put all that together on the fly. So on Wednesday morning, I flew to SF and arrived in time to tail her that afternoon to a run-down bar in the Tenderloin District, but I lost her cab when she left. I flew here this morning and picked you up at the Gault."

"How did you know we were at the Gault?" Nando asked.

"My analyst hacked their lobby's security camera on Friday afternoon and evening."

Then Bridgette and Nando shared the information they had about the conspiracy without revealing Anna's or her boss's name. Finally, Nando said, "Obviously, I need boots on the ground to investigate the Ransom mansion scenario and track Izabella's movements. And we all share the concern that there's a highly placed insider in Washington who might be leaking information to Izabella. Bridgette and I talked about a possible solution while we were walking around today. Bridgette, why don't you fill Mal in on what we're thinking."

"It's a simple solution. But it might be tricky to implement because we don't want to go through official channels. If we can pull it off, it'll be completely off the record, but we're going to need to divulge information we normally wouldn't. And God help us if it blows up," Bridgette concluded.

Mal smiled and joked, "Haven't you been listening? I'm completely comfortable in such an environment. Let's explore it."

Then Bridgette filled Mal in on Dr. Sandler, Captain Joe Cancio, and Lieutenant Gabi Müller. Her relationship with them. How she had assisted with their investigation in the Warehouse Murders in 2011. They continued talking for a while until Mal said, "If you trust them, I'm in. It sounds like a fine idea."

"I'll run point on this, at least in the beginning," Bridgette offered. "I'll talk to Dr. Sandler first."

"Bridgette, it's going to be a real pain in the ass for you, running it from Paris. Especially since you can't tell your bosses what you're up to," Mal commented.

"It shouldn't be difficult. They don't bother me if I do my job."

"Before we wrap up, there's one more thing Bridgette and I discussed that we don't have a solution for," Nando interjected. "My analyst and I are concerned about the hacking we'll obviously have to do."

"Your FISA court and so forth?" Mal asked.

"Yes."

"If my guy Zeb does it and we funnel it to Bridgette, who passes it along to you anonymously, are you covered?"

"I think so; I'll check with Jay."

"Okay, we'll do that if he's on board. Also, let's exchange mobile numbers."

***

On Monday, October 6, when Detective Captain Joe Cancio, commander of San Francisco's Serious Crimes Unit, entered the office, his number two, Detective Lieutenant Gabi Müller, was already at her desk. She was a team leader of one of the two groups under Cancio's command.

"'Morning, Gabi. You're in early today."

"'Morning. How was your weekend?" Gabi asked, getting up from her desk and following Joe into his office.

"All right, and yours?"

"Fine, until last night. Danny called me. There was a brutal killing in the Tenderloin on Friday night. They've identified the victim as Pedro Mahia, part of José's crew."

"So that's why they called Danny," Joe said.

Lieutenant Danny Wong was the team leader of Joe's second group. He had served many years in the Tenderloin District before Joe promoted him to the Serious Crimes Unit. José was Danny's CI and had acceded to the top of his crew in May 2011 when its former boss, Tyree, was gunned down in a drive-by shooting. Danny had always suspected that José was behind Tyree's murder, although there was no prosecutable evidence.

"Yeah, their commander is concerned about a gang war. Because of Danny's relationship, he called him before kicking it up to the Gang Unit. Danny is there now and asked me to come over—he wants a second opinion."

"Do we have anything from the medical examiner yet?"

"A preliminary—she said it doesn't look complicated, just peculiar. I'm going to stop down and see her before I head out."

"Curious. Okay, help Danny, but see me later today. If we want the case after you fill me in, I'll straighten out the jurisdiction."

***

Gabi looked at Pedro's body on the slab. *Big bastard*, she thought. The ME came over and reported what she had already concluded.

"This is a bit unusual, so I'll do a full autopsy to make certain I'm not missing anything. He appears to have been killed by a single powerful punch to the throat that crushed his windpipe. His voice box would have literally exploded. The victim probably suffocated; look at his bloodshot eyes. But I'll confirm that during the autopsy by checking for foam in the airways and higher carbon dioxide in the blood. If he'd had medical attention—a tracheostomy—he would have survived."

"What's peculiar?"

"The blow was extremely powerful and precise; I would say by an expert in martial arts. Also, look at the marks on the neck. The scratches are self-inflicted from struggling. But this circular bruise right at the larynx is the cause of death. Probably from a closed fist. It's smaller than what you'd expect from a man. I think the killer is a woman. Plus, look at the scars on his body. He was no stranger to violence, yet his killer got in close—closer than an arm's length. And there're no defensive wounds. The victim knew his killer."

"Well, being a woman might explain it—he didn't feel threatened. He might've messed with the wrong lady," Gabi said.

"I know I'm straying into your territory now, but this isn't a typical gang killing. I would expect a bullet wound, stabbing, beating with a bat or chain, or so on. And I can't stress the violence of the punch; most trained men couldn't pull it off with a single blow. Because it happened outside his apartment, it wasn't random either: the woman was waiting for him. This was personal."

As Gabi got in her car, heading for the Tenderloin, she thought, *How the hell did Pedro run afoul of a trained killer? They hardly would've moved in the same circles.*

CHAPTER ELEVEN

Tuesday, October 7, 2014
CIA Headquarters, McLean, Virginia

J ay had flown in from San Francisco on Monday and was at his desk first thing Tuesday morning. His mother had been able to put together her dinner with Anna's family. They'd had a pleasant time catching up, even though Jay was still perturbed over Anna's coldhearted solution to the situation with her boss. Nonetheless, Jay felt Anna would continue to provide useful information. Nando arrived in the office a little after noon. "How was your weekend?" he asked.

"Fine. Mom's dinner came off; we had a good time. Anna and I didn't have much of an opportunity to talk about our plans, though. Did you and Bridgette have a good weekend as well?"

"Sort of. A mixed bag. We had a wonderful time, but friggin' Mal showed up unexpectedly at dinner on Saturday."

"What'd he want?"

"To meet me, among other things. Bridgette was pissed and ripped him a new one." Nando laughed. "Mal was more candid than he has been before, so we now know what he's up to. I think we're going to take a different tack. We need to talk, so let's get together this afternoon—off campus—and I'll update you."

Later, they met at a coffee shop in Falls Church that was convenient to Langley, Jay's home, and Nando's hotel.

When they were settled, Jay said, "So tell me."

"I'll give you the concise version. Mal is legit; he is who he says he is. His mission is authorized, and he reports to the 'highest authority'; I'm suspicious it's the prime minister. His assignment was simple at first: terminate Izabella. Then, after Israeli intelligence discovered the likely assassination plot, Mal was redirected to help the US prevent that before continuing with the Izabella mission. To keep Israeli hands clean, he wasn't supposed to use their intelligence services unless necessary and then only on a need-to-know basis. Nevertheless, Mal judiciously uses an analyst in the Kidon Unit, who is a longtime friend and the best, according to Mal. But to avoid getting his analyst in trouble, he uses Bridgette whenever feasible. As things unfolded, he decided it was best to make contact at my level."

"So what's your take on him?"

"Undoubtedly lethal, but he'll be an excellent asset. I think Mal's honest and trustworthy if our interests don't conflict with Israel's. But I gotta tell you, he's a clever bastard. Mal figured out my death was a ruse and that the CIA had recalled me. Like us, he suspects someone at our highest level is pulling the strings."

"You mean the eight-hundred-pound gorilla in the room."

"Yes—but I'm reluctant to say what I think."

"The director?" Jay offered.

Nando nodded. "We're on the same page. But let's not discuss it here."

"All right," Jay responded. "So what's the new tack?"

"I alluded to it when we were surveying the Palo Alto and Ransom locations. Because we're all concerned about who's behind the assassination plot, we don't want to use either CIA or Israeli assets. But we need help, and Bridgette has associates in the SFPD, who she has worked with before—a behavioral analyst with twenty-five years of FBI experience, a captain, and a lieutenant in their Serious Crimes Unit. So, if they'll help us off the record, Bridgette will quarterback it from Paris, and Mal's on board."

Jay was silent for a while. "Nando, don't get pissed with me, but your plan requires sharing top secret information with people lacking such a clearance. Not to mention we don't know these folks. I appreciate that you trust Bridgette, but are you certain about this? If it blows up, our asses will be hung out to dry."

"I'm not pissed; you wouldn't be doing your job if you didn't point it out. Mal and I trust Bridgette's judgment. So you'll need to trust mine. If you can't, we'll come up with a different plan, because I want you on the team."

Jay mulled it over, finally saying, "Okay . . . I can live with it. Moving on, I'm running another search to see if anyone is accessing those building plans."

"Fine, and I think I have a solution to our hacking problems without warrants. Mal, Bridgette, and I brainstormed that too. Mal says his guy Zeb can do whatever we need from Tel Aviv. He suggests any hacks could be routed anonymously to Bridgette and then secretly rerouted to us. Zeb can set it all up. What do you think?"

"It should work; I'm fine with it."

"Okay, keep monitoring the building plans for now, and I'll make arrangements for you and Zeb to talk on a secure link. Mal says he speaks English fluently. Also, let's keep it to ourselves that Mal has located Izabella," Nando finished.

***

Tuesday evening Bridgette was back in their apartment by ten thirty. She called Nando. "Hi, I'm home. How was your flight?"

"Okay, I got to the office a little after noon."

"Did you talk to Jay yet?"

"We met at a coffee house in Falls Church earlier this afternoon. I read him in."

"Did you mention we'll be dealing with people who lack the appropriate clearances?"

"Yes, and he had our anticipated reservations—but Jay trusts me."

"These people are solid—Jay has nothing to worry about," Bridgette said. "I'm tired . . . it was a long flight. I'm turning in now, and I'll call Ellen tomorrow. Love you."

"Excellent. We'll talk afterward. Love you too."

***

On Wednesday, Bridgette waited until five o'clock in the afternoon to call Ellen Sandler.

"Hi, Ellen. It's Bridgette."

"Bridgette, this is great. Twice in such a short time."

"I know. I need your help with something serious. But you must agree to keep it confidential, because I'll be disclosing both US and Israeli top secret information. Will you agree?"

"Of course. I trust you, and I know you wouldn't make such a request frivolously."

"I'll also need Joe and Gabi's assistance," Bridgette said, and explained everything.

"Wow—that's a lot to take in," Ellen responded. "It makes sense to me, but I can't speak for Joe and Gabi. I assume they'll be under the same restrictions after I talk to them?"

"Yes."

"I'm confident they'll comply with the confidentiality no matter what they decide."

"Ellen, if this blows up, all of our asses will be in hot water."

"No shit!"

Ellen reflected for a few minutes on her approach before calling Joe Cancio. She decided to get right to the point.

"I need to see you and Gabi today but not at headquarters. Is there somewhere we can have lunch that's out of the way? No one can know we're meeting."

"Okay." Joe didn't hesitate to agree; he knew from years of experience with Ellen that this had to be important. "Do you know TIS in North Beach?"

"Yes," Ellen responded.

"One o'clock, then. Is anyone else coming?" Joe asked.

"No."

***

Gabi and Joe arrived early, and Joe spoke to Jorge Martinez, the owner, about arranging a suitable table. "If you don't mind, there's an alcove inside the kitchen with a table for four. It might be a bit noisy, but you'll be out of the way. No one will know you're here, and the kitchen crew will be too busy to pay any attention," Jorge suggested.

"Perfect."

After they were all seated and Jorge had taken their orders, Ellen disclosed what Bridgette had told her. Afterward, Joe was the first to speak. Looking at Gabi, he said, "Obviously, we'll keep this confidential no matter how it plays out."

Gabi nodded her assent, and Joe continued, "I'm unclear, though. Do you have any idea what might be expected of us?"

"I think it's mostly routine work. According to Bridgette, Nando is certain Izabella will make her hit at Holden Ransom's place. So they need lots of background information, such as who's providing the catering, bartending, security, equipment rental, additional staff, and so forth."

"And Nando is certain she'll pass up Palo Alto?" Joe asked.

"Yes, because of his background. Nando was recently reactivated by the CIA for this assignment. Even though Bridgette was reluctant to talk about him, here's what I know. He was with the CIA for around ten years and was a member of a blacker-than-black-ops unit that reported just to the director and president. He was their best sniper. After officially leaving the CIA, he was a deep-cover mercenary masquerading as a disgruntled former employee. Satie snapped him up."

"Satie. He's the guy you told us about who recently died in a Munich house fire?" Joe interrupted.

"Yes. Working for him, Nando became the top assassin in the EU. Apparently, he'd been inactive for the last couple of years; I don't know why. An assassin named Defarge—"

"Like Madame Defarge?" Gabi interjected.

"Yes, and they now know she is Izabella and that she has worked her way up to the top spot vacated by Nando."

"It makes sense to bring him back. If he's as skilled as you say he is, who better?" Joe said as he watched Gabi, who had an eidetic memory. She could absorb and assimilate large amounts of information and was onto something. "What's up, Gabi?"

"I think we may have run across Izabella already. Last week, the victim of the murder in the Tenderloin was Pedro Mahia, one of José's crew. José has been Danny's CI for years. Danny is leaning on him because we can't accept Pedro's murder as a gangland killing." Gabi went on to report about Izabella's encounter with Pedro. "She's our number-one suspect."

"What was she doing at José's?" Ellen asked.

"Well, here's where it becomes tricky for Danny," Gabi continued. "When Danny interviewed him, José put on quite a show for his crew without disclosing why Izabella was there. He just talked about her run-in with Pedro. Later, Danny met with him, and he reported she was there to buy ordnance but wouldn't say what. José is convinced she is an assassin and was uncharacteristically fearful because of how Pedro died.

All he would say was that she was 'goin' big game huntin', and it ain't for grizzlies or elephants.' That seems to tie in to information Danny had previously developed about José branching out."

"Gunrunning?" Joe asked.

"Not exactly—merely rumors that José had developed an overseas supplier for high-end items but on a limited basis. Satie was probably his contact. This is a thorny business: balancing José's value as a CI and crew chief against his illegal activities," Gabi concluded.

"So is Danny okay with this unusual relationship?" Joe asked.

"Yes, but do you have a problem, Joe?"

"Not so far. Ellen, would you tell me about Mal?"

"They think he's valuable but according to Bridgette, a bit of an enigma," Ellen chuckled. "There's one more thing she asked me to pass on. If you undertake this, you can't use any sources in the CIA, FBI, or the like. They're all paranoid that someone close to the president is involved. Anything that comes in through normal channels will probably be uncovered by that person."

"All right," Joe responded. "We need a face-to-face with Nando, Mal, and Bridgette if she can make it. And I'll need to be able to say no if what I hear doesn't make sense . . . but if it goes well, I'm in. Also, I don't see how I can expense a trip—they'll have to come here. What do you think?"

Gabi and Ellen nodded their assent, and Ellen said, "I'll call Bridgette and see to the meeting."

After lunch, as Gabi and Joe walked back to his car, Gabi remarked, "I'm nervous because nobody'll have our back, but it's important. I can't walk away."

"Me neither. And I'm not certain Palo Alto is out of the question. Dollars to doughnuts she bought a high-end sniper rifle from José."

***

It was Thursday morning the ninth, and since Luca's murder, Izabella had been nervous about a new player. *Am I on someone's radar? I traveled with fake IDs and was cautious, but I'm uncomfortable. Call it a sixth sense. I've never disregarded it before—no time to start now.* So a couple of days ago, she'd started thinking about a plan. It involved her current flirtation with Johnny, a cute nineteen-year-old who was working his way through school. He covered the registration desk and was a valet and bellhop—a jack-of-all-trades for the inn. Izabella could tell Johnny was besotted, so she acted her most alluring around him—touching and brushing up against him, all bright eyes and lots of attention. All familiar territory for her.

She had no doubt Johnny could help and facilitate her going to ground. Besides, she was beginning to think about having fun with him. So Izabella had chatted Johnny up and found out there was a simple rear exit from the inn with no CCTV. Plus she'd learned he would be working the midnight-to-eight shift Thursday morning.

Wednesday evening when Izabella returned to the inn, she had shared fake personal information with Johnny. She'd told him she was running away from an abusive boyfriend who had tracked her down once before. Izabella hinted at the debauched things he'd made her do afterward as punishment, saying she just couldn't go through it again. And that afternoon, Izabella had pretended she'd caught a glimpse of the boyfriend in Union Square. She'd alluded to what she wanted to do and finally asked

Johnny for help. *Like a deer in the headlights*, she reflected. *I didn't even have to insinuate how appreciative I could be. But why not have fun? I'll enjoy myself.*

Izabella had paid through the week's end, so she didn't have to deal with checking out this morning. She got up early and set the scene, straightening the bed and folding back the covers. Then she put out the day's clothes, making certain her laciest bra and panties were on top. Last, Izabella showered and put on a splash of subtle scent. Now she was ready to be startled by Johnny. When he knocked on the door a few minutes after eight, Izabella was combing out her wet hair while wearing only a towel. She opened the door and, acting surprised, said, "Oh, I'm not ready yet . . . must've lost track of time."

"I can wait outside."

"Don't be silly. Come on in . . . dry my back," Izabella said, handing him her towel.

Two hours later, she gave Johnny her car keys. He picked up the car, drove around to Sutter Street, parked, and returned through the inn's back door. He rode the elevator up to Izabella's floor, then carried her bag, and they left by the back stairs, the rear exit, and the alley leading to Sutter. When they reached her car, Izabella slipped him a fifty and kissed him goodbye. She felt terrific. Johnny had been better than expected . . . in every way.

Izabella was on her way to a public self-storage facility she had located earlier on Turk Street near the Tenderloin District. It was open twenty-four hours, seven days a week. She stopped there and rented the smallest locker for three months. Then Izabella was off to Stanford University near Palo Alto.

Once at Stanford, Izabella stopped at the admissions office. She had already reviewed the campus map online, but inside Izabella feigned a slightly muddled tourist mien. Greeting a middle-aged woman behind the counter, she asked, "Is this the admissions office? I think I'm terribly lost."

"Yes, ma'am, you're in the right place. How can I help you?"

"Oh, good. My sister—we're from Germany, expats—is planning on applying to Stanford. She's not with me . . . I'm on vacation. Well, she has your catalog—obviously—and thinks the pictures are neat. But my sister asked me to stop by and look around, take pictures, kind of check it out."

"That's nice. Has your sister applied yet?"

"No, I think she's just getting started. She's an excellent student, so I hope she doesn't have any trouble."

"Well, if your sister has the catalog, the requirements are in it."

"I'm positive she has looked at all that. So could you help me with a map of the campus, show me where I am, and mark any highlights I should take snaps of?"

"Certainly." The woman took a map and went over everything Izabella asked about.

"So I'm here—right?" Izabella said, pointing to the map.

"Yes."

"And what's this over here? You didn't mention it."

"That's the Memorial Auditorium."

"Oh, that sounds important. Do you think she'll—my sister—want a snap of that?"

"Well, I don't know . . . but it couldn't hurt."

"What a great idea. Thank you so much. I'm positive I would've wandered around aimlessly without your help."

Izabella started to leave but affected an afterthought, saying, "I won't have any problems with security if I take snaps, will I? I mean, I don't want to be arrested—that wouldn't do."

"Stay on the public paths and you'll be okay. If you have any problems, use my name; I'm Jane."

Izabella waved and gave a big smile. "Thanks again, Jane."

Outside Izabella, thought, *Blah, blah, blah . . . she'll remember me.*

After leaving the admissions office, Izabella took her time visiting all the sights Jane had recommended. Finally, she came to the auditorium, reconnoitered, and took photographs. Izabella was thorough, even though it took just a few minutes to determine there was only one sniping scenario that would work. And it was too low of a probability.

Nevertheless, Izabella proceeded with the less-than-thirty-minute drive to San Jose, the seat of Santa Clara County. She found the Building's Department office and repeated her befuddled performance, finally getting a look at Memorial Auditorium's plans. Izabella took her time, studied everything, photographed the plans surreptitiously, asked lots of questions, and flirted unabashedly with the middle-aged man managing the office.

No way—the university is a terrible alternative. But I made sure I'll be remembered. A little disinformation couldn't hurt if anyone is on my trail!

Then it was back to San Francisco to see José, who had called; the rifle was in. It was a repeat performance of her first arrival except that the thugs were more courteous. When they patted Izabella down, they found her handgun and took it with them as they walked her in to see José. He returned it and brought the rifle and the rest of her purchases from the storeroom. Izabella function-checked it and paid the $5,000 balance.

"Don't you want to clean it?" José asked.

"No, I'll do it later. Maybe you can help me with something else, though? I need a quiet, out-of-the-way hotel—no CCTV, no questions asked—with a nearby place to park my car."

José made a brief call. "The Hotel Royal will do. It isn't far from Union Square. It's clean and you'll stay for cash—no registration. Ask for Blake. He charges what he charges; you'll have to work that out. Arrive before eight o'clock tonight when he goes off duty. There's a parking garage across the street—down an alley."

As Izabella left, waving to the loitering thugs, she chuckled silently. *How about that . . . these hoodlums have a different attitude today.*

Izabella had stops to make before she saw Blake. First, making certain she wasn't tailed, she drove to her locker and put the rifle, ammo, and so forth inside. Then Izabella returned the rental car and had the agent call her a taxi. She asked the cabbie to take her to a different rental agency, where Izabella rented a make and model dissimilar to her previous one. Afterward, she drove to the Hotel Royal. Izabella parked on the street, spotting the garage José had mentioned. As she entered the hotel, the reception clerk looked up and asked, "Chica?"

"Yes, and you're Blake."

"Yes, ma'am. How can I help?"

"I need a room, but I'm not sure for how long—a month at least."

"The rooms are rented for a minimum of a week—cash in advance. No refunds if you leave before the week is up."

"Registration?"

"None."

"Fine." They agreed on a price. "I'll pay a month in advance."

"José said you needed parking. It's right down the alley across the street; you probably saw it when you arrived. Tell them you're with the hotel, and if you want a monthly rate, it's the same deal as here—cash in advance, no registration. We also have a coffee shop; it's open from six in the morning till midnight, and the food's pretty good," Blake said, pointing across the lobby.

"Would you like me to call you something besides Chica?"

"No, that's perfect," Izabella laughed.

She paid, left her duffel in the lobby, and parked the car. Afterward, Izabella went to her room. It was better than she'd expected: a queen bed, sitting area with a couch, and a TV. The bathroom was retro but clean—no stained porcelain or taps. Izabella freshened up and decided to eat in the coffee shop before watching TV.

This is going to work out well. I'm confident I wasn't followed. And if anyone asks around at the White Swan, Johnny will have my six.

"'I love it when a plan comes together.'"[3]

CHAPTER TWELVE

Friday, October 10, 2014
Washington, DC

Late Friday afternoon, the director met with the president, who inquired, "Nando and Jay are back from San Francisco—what can they report?"

"They reconnoitered both sites. Nando is certain Izabella will strike at the Ransom mansion. He has completely ruled out Stanford."

"Well, that helps; it narrows our scope."

"Not so fast. As recently as yesterday, Jay has reliable intelligence that Izabella visited the Santa Clara County Clerk's office to evaluate the auditorium's plans. His information is from the digital access records of the clerk's office—the only request in months."

"So what does it mean?"

"I don't know. Perhaps disinformation, perhaps not."

"Did they obtain a warrant?"

The director paused, ignoring the president's question. "Let me tell you what happened with their source."

"You didn't answer my question."

"I'm sorry, sir. I didn't hear you. I was focusing on what happened with their source."

Suppressing an ironic smile, the president replied, "All right—tell me."

"They've confirmed their source is a woman, yet they still don't know for whom she's working."

"How's that possible?"

"Apparently, she orchestrated a clandestine meeting in the garage under Union Square. She managed to conceal herself and distort her voice. The source is willing to cooperate but wants guarantees about witness protection for her family."

"We can do that, but we need to know what she has to offer first."

"Yes—I'm working on that."

"Have they located Izabella yet?"

"No, not yet. They just know she's in the area because of the trip to San Jose."

"Well, find her, for Christ's sake! Once we do that, at least we can nab her. That would foil the plot, and we could deal with the rest of the bastards later. Honestly, it doesn't seem like we're making much progress. Should I reconsider my plans to bring in other agencies?"

"It's your call, Mr. President. But I remain convinced we should keep this within the CIA because of leaks. So let's move Nando to San Francisco for the duration; he'll be more effective there."

"Agreed. Fly him on a CIA jet."

Sitting in the back of his car returning to Langley, the director ruminated. *The president is becoming impatient. That's okay if he keeps to his schedule and doesn't bring in reinforcements from other alphabet agencies.*

I'm also finding it hard to accept that Nando and Jay haven't made better progress. Perhaps they're sitting on intel; it could mean they have suspicions. Although it might simply be the way it is . . . who knows. But the plot is virtually on autopilot now. All I need to do is give Izabella the new location at the last minute.

I wonder if she's figured out who I am; I only talked with her twice on burners. I have plenty of evidence against her if necessary, though. That leaves Bruce Campbell; he doesn't know who I am. Nevertheless, he's a loose end. Perhaps it's time to call Cole. He has the skills to deal with Campbell, and Lord knows I have enough dirt to ensure his cooperation. But take your time—no rush—think it through.

***

The first thing Monday morning, the president made a call.

"'Morning, Mr. Director. Over the weekend, I thought about our conversation. Let's schedule a debrief in the Oval Office with Nando and Jay—just the four of us. Would you set that up as soon as possible?"

"Certainly, Mr. President." *Shit . . . I don't like him talking to my officers or staff directly. You never know what the hell might come out.*

***

The meeting with the president was scheduled for nine o'clock Tuesday morning. Since the director needed his car afterward, he asked Nando and Jay to join him there. Driving over, Nando said, "The director gave me a heads-up that the president is asking about warrants. I think the director is planning on handling that, but we need to follow his lead."

"Well," Jay said, "if the president persists, I'll say we've already obtained all the information we need. Namely, that we know Izabella is in the area because she has investigated San Jose, and we can assume she'll do the same at the Ransom location. There's no need to verify it further."

"I'm not convinced it'll go that far. I think the president really doesn't want to know. He's just doing his job by cautioning us."

The director had already arrived when the president's secretary ushered Nando and Jay in.

"'Morning, gentlemen. Have a seat. I'll get right to the point. I've told the director that I'm a bit frustrated with how long it's taking to pick up Izabella's trail and to verify the location she'll choose." Nando looked at the director, who nodded at him.

"Mr. President, we share your frustration. Let me answer about the location first. I'd bet the ranch that it will be at Holden—"

The president interrupted curtly. "But it isn't the ranch—it's my butt."

"I apologize. I didn't mean to sound cavalier—a bad figure of speech. May I explain why?"

"Please."

Nando went into a detailed analysis of why Palo Alto wasn't the place Izabella would choose, finishing with, "We know a lot about her, and she's simply too experienced to take that route unless she knows something we don't."

"I don't know how she could; I don't even know how I'll be entering the auditorium. What you've said makes sense. Do you need help from us to expedite finding her?"

The director chimed in. "I think it's a matter of time before we pick her up. And we have time to adjust your schedule if necessary."

"So still no additional agencies?"

"That's still my recommendation." the director replied. "Keep it within the CIA."

"But don't you think that at least the director of National Intelligence should be read in?"

"I continue to be concerned about leaks. I'm not jumping the chain of command; I'm authorized to brief you directly."

"I know. Well, all right . . . for the time being," the president responded. "Any assistance needed with expediting warrants or FISA court applications?" the president asked, looking at the director, who again nodded to Nando.

"Mr. President, we have already uncovered that Izabella is in the area. Our US source is on the verge of disclosing her bosses' identity, and afterward, we should be able to flip him. Also, in the EU, my friend Bridgette Dubois, who is an inspecteur in the Sûreté, has an extensive network with the police in most European cities, a connection at Interpol, and a contact in Tel Aviv. That's how we unearthed Izabella's identity. We are developing a lot of information. I don't think we need any warrants at this time."

The president chuckled. "Nando, perhaps another 'bad figure of speech'? Isn't Bridgette your girlfriend?"

"Yes. You're well informed."

"And is her Israeli contact Mossad?"

"Yes."

"Okay. Nando, we think you should move your base of operations to San Francisco. Any problems?"

"No, Mr. President."

Then, looking at Jay, the president said, "All right, Jay, you'll stay in Langley; it makes sense to keep you close to your resources. And Jay, forewarned is forearmed about the warrants. Thanks for coming this morning."

As they left, the director chuckled and looked at Jay. "And you thought you'd dodged a bullet."

CHAPTER THIRTEEN

Tuesday, October 14, 2014
Washington, DC

En route to his next meeting, the director pondered. *That went well with Nando and Jay, but I don't like that the president is asserting himself. Jesus, the last thing I need is him taking charge. And the director of National Intelligence won't let this play out the way I need it to.*

I probably should've paid more attention to how they identified Izabella. I'm suspicious Mossad is more involved than I thought. But I'll let it play out a bit longer. Also, it's strange they haven't mentioned Bruce Campbell's meetings. Are they withholding intel?

I need to move towards damage control. First, verify if Campbell's October 16 meeting is still on and if it's the last one. If so, will it wrap everything up? Second, send Cole to New Orleans and have him manually disable the hotel's CCTV ahead of that meeting. I can't risk having Nando and Jay identify those miscreants! Third, Campbell: I'll deal with him later.

Lastly, interview the roommate in Berlin. I need additional information about Izabella. But ever since July, after the chancellor threw out our chief of station, everything's been screwed up. She fucking totally overreacted to discovering two of our deep-cover officers. What the hell did she think we were doing in Germany anyway? I'll call the chief's number-two guy—I've known him for years. He'll do it and keep it off the record.

***

After Nando returned to Langley, he called Bridgette and caught her before she left the office.

"I just came from a meeting with the president, the director, and Jay. The president wants me to move to San Francisco for the rest of this assignment. Jay's going to remain here. I'm flying on a CIA jet, so I only need to make hotel reservations."

"I was going to call you this evening. I have an idea. Ellen and I have been planning that meeting I talked to you about. It occurred to me that it might make sense to take a two-bedroom suite with a living room. That way you and Mal could stay at the same place, and we would have somewhere to get together outside of SFPD's HQ. What do you think?" Bridgette asked.

"It's a first-rate idea—try to put it together."

"Is there anything else going on?"

"Today, our meeting was a little strange. I think the president is starting to assert himself, and the director doesn't look happy. Also, the president is concerned about Jay's hacking. He told Jay 'forewarned is forearmed' as we left. So we need to have the Jay-Zeb procedure in place quickly."

"Is he pissed? The president?"

"No. I think he doesn't want a scandal if things go wrong. His approval rating is already upside down, about forty percent."

"All right, I'll work on the suite tomorrow."

"Fine, I only need to pack. I can leave anytime—the jet's a priority."

***

When the director returned to his office, he called Cole on a burner.

"Can you go to New Orleans ASAP?"

"You're in luck. I'm blue-water fishing in the Gulf overnight." Cole chuckled.

"Gulf?"

"Of Mexico. A junket sponsored by one of your ABC cousins." Cole continued chuckling. "We're sailing about fifty miles southwest from the Mississippi/Alabama border—terrific fishing out there—and should be back in port before sunup. I'll head to New Orleans afterwards and be there before noon tomorrow."

"Excellent." Then the director explained what needed to be done ahead of Campbell's meeting on Thursday.

"It shouldn't be a problem. Give me a number for after I'm done."

"Okay, and we need to meet when you're finished; I have an important new project. Bigger payday also."

"Cool. Talk to you Thursday."

Next, the director called Berlin on a secure line. After exchanging recognition codes, he said, "I'm glad I caught you in the office. How's it going?"

"Still a bit at sixes and sevens since the July hullabaloo, but we're soldiering on."

"Hang in there. I have an assignment. Do it yourself, off the record, and report to me only."

"Sounds like old times. What do you need?"

"I need a rundown on a woman named Izabella Ricci—former Kidon Unit."

"Dangerous?"

"One of the most. She's in the US now. Here's her Berlin address. Izabella lives there with a girlfriend—don't know her name or what name Izabella's using either. I need you to find out everything you can about Izabella. But I'm particularly interested in any other residences or names she uses. I gotta be able to find this broad if she goes to ground."

"I'll get right on it. I'll print up a bogus census form, put on my nerd specs, and interview the girlfriend. I'll act confused about her houseguest's legal address because it must be correct for the census . . . you know. Germans love detail and order. She'll cooperate."

"Great, sounds like a plan."

Finally, the director called Bruce Campbell on another burner and confirmed that everything was a go for his Thursday meeting.

That's all I can do today. I have just one job left for Campbell. After that's finished, Cole could deal with him. But I'm beginning to have second thoughts about Cole. Is he the right man? Can I trust him with this? Well, I don't have to decide now. After Berlin uncovers where Izabella is likely to go to ground, I'll develop a contingency plan. I can't risk this all going to hell in a handbasket.

***

Shortly after nine o'clock on Wednesday morning, Ellen reached out to Joe Cancio. "'Morning. I just got off the phone with Bridgette. I think the plan's coming together well." Then Ellen told him about Bridgette's idea for a suite. "Nando's flying tomorrow morning, and Bridgette intends to come over on Friday, taking vacation time. She suggests you reach out to Mal. You two can work on a hotel, and then he could move in. Also, I have Mal, Nando, Jay, and Bridgette's mobile numbers for you. I'll pass Gabi's and yours on to her, if it's all right."

"That sounds fine—pass on our numbers. I'll give Mal a call, and I think the Kensington Park Hotel on Post Street would be a suitable location. I'm friends with the hotel's manager."

Joe called Mal, and they agreed to meet for lunch at a pizzeria on Bush Street. Joe easily spotted him from the description Mal had provided. Once they'd gotten to know each other and lunch was nearly over, Mal said, "I know we haven't organized yet, but I've put something in motion already. Our US source is attending a meeting of the conspirators at the Ritz-Carlton in New Orleans on the sixteenth. We need to hack the hotel's CCTV. Hopefully, we'll obtain identifiable photos of them as they enter the suite. I have my guy ready to do that and run a test first thing tomorrow."

"All right, from what I gather, our president is concerned about the CIA's hacking. So that solves the problem. Now we need to get Jay and your guy together ASAP."

"Agreed."

"Let me fill you in on the plan Bridgette came up with," Joe said, and explained her idea of a suite. "If you're on board, we can go to the hotel now and see what they have. If it looks all right, I can help you move this afternoon."

"Let's do it," Mal replied.

At the hotel, they met with the manager, John, who said, "We have the Royal Suite on the top floor. The bedroom is king-sized, and there's an attached dining-meeting room. I can furnish it any way you'd like, and it connects to another standard room. We have a secured Wi-Fi network, and there's valet parking as well. I'll work with you on the price for all of it."

After John showed them the rooms, Mal said, "I think this is excellent. Nando and Bridgette can take the larger room."

"I like the meeting room. We need it if we want to keep this confidential—there're no secrets at HQ," Joe said.

"All right. Let's get together as soon as Nando and Bridgette arrive."

"Agreed. Gabi and I are fine with a meeting over the weekend." Mal nodded his assent, and Joe continued. "Okay, now let's move you in."

"Great. I'll prepare the paperwork while you're doing that," John said.

After Mal was moved, Joe headed back to HQ and met with Gabi.

"I still haven't disclosed our tangential interest in Izabella as a suspect in Pedro's murder or my suspicion that she purchased a sniper's rifle," Joe said. "I want to do that when we meet. Plus, lean on Danny to pressure José for additional information on where Izabella went. I think he knows more but doesn't want to cross Izabella. That's odd, considering his background."

"You didn't see the savagery of her death blow," Gabi remarked.

CHAPTER FOURTEEN

Wednesday, October 15, 2014

At Sea in the Gulf of Mexico

Shortly after one a.m. CDT, the old tramp steamer *Geraldine Leigh* reduced her speed to five knots. She was en route to New Orleans and now sailed slowly toward a rendezvous at latitude 30° 04' 93" north, longitude 88° 94' 77" west. The transfer was scheduled for one thirty. The captain began scanning the horizon to the north—plenty of lights from other ships but nothing close or approaching. He wasn't concerned because he'd made similar drop-offs before.

At ten fifteen p.m. on the fourteenth, Cole had sailed from a small down-and-out deep-sea sportfishing cove. He had chartered Pap's forty-two-foot old Hatteras fishing boat, which could cruise at twenty knots. Pap's boat was ideal for Cole's purposes because it was outfitted with an up-to-date chart plotter, radar, VHF radio, and depth sounder. And Pap was always willing to captain these unusual trips because they augmented his barely profitable daytime charters.

Cole had stashed aboard a large duffel containing two automatic assault rifles, two .45 semiauto pistols, and ammo. After that, he put on his life jacket and joined Pap on the flying bridge. He and Pap talked baseball, drank coffee from a large thermos that Cole had brought along, and turned off the running lights when they were about ten miles out to sea.

Around one ten a.m., Pap pointed to the radar and then out over the starboard bow. "That should be the *Geraldine Leigh* ahead," he said.

"Okay, when you're closer, flip the spot on and off five times." Shortly thereafter they signaled, and the tramp steamer responded with a like sign. As they neared the ship, Cole said, "Approach from astern, come alongside her starboard, and when you're within a hundred yards, put on your lights." Cole went to his duffel and removed the guns, sticking one .45 in his waistband. He returned, handing Pap the other semiauto and propping the rifles in a corner.

"Expecting trouble?" Pap joked.

"No . . . but we'll keep them out for the return trip just in case anyone becomes nosy."

When Pap put on the lights, Cole went on deck and dropped the portside fenders. After they came alongside, the freighter's crane, using a lifting hook, lowered a suitcase to the fishing boat, followed by a second trip with a passenger. As the vessels separated, Cole waved and shouted to the captain, who was leaning over the railing. "See you next time, Skipper."

The return trip was uneventful. Approaching the cove before five a.m., Cole made a call on a burner and then jettisoned the guns overboard. By the time they tied up, two black SUVs with tinted windows and government plates had arrived. Their passenger was whisked away.

"Wouldn't you just love to know sometimes," Pap observed.

"Probably better not to, but at least whoever it is is on our side."

"Got time for breakfast?"

"Yeah," Cole said, looking at his watch. "I need to be in New Orleans by noon—plenty of time." Then he jumped into his red Hellcat and followed Pap's pickup to an all-night truck stop.

Cole arrived in New Orleans before noon and parked on the street. From his car's trunk, he grabbed a jacket labeled MAINTENANCE, a baseball cap, and his tool belt. He set out for the hotel, entering through the rear door. After that, he rode the service elevator up to the Ritz-Carlton Suite. On that floor there was only one standard-type CCTV camera. *It shouldn't be a problem.* Next, he found a utility closet. The door was unlocked, and inside were amenities, cleaning supplies, and so on, as well as an eight-foot stepladder. *Perfect. No need for lockpicks.* Then Cole looked at two other floors, discovering like setups. Finally, he ditched his disguise at the car before locating a lunch counter. While he waited for a server, Cole called his client.

"How'd you make out?"

"I'm in New Orleans now," Cole responded.

"And?"

"I looked it over—no problems. I'll do it around nine thirty tomorrow morning—less time for the hotel to bring in their vendor for service. I'll do two other floors as well, create a little confusion."

"Don't forget we need to meet afterwards. I'll catch up with you at the beginning of next week."

Cole returned to his car, wiping the burner and chucking it into a refuse container along the way.

***

After dinner on Wednesday, Bridgette called Nando, reaching him when he and Jay had returned from lunch.

"Bridgette, I'm glad you called. I can update you on a few things."

"What's new?"

"Zeb called Jay. They're ready to do the setup for the surveillance we need. Zeb will call you tomorrow morning to set up your link," Nando responded.

"That should work—I'm not heading to San Francisco until Friday. I'm taking a ten thirty morning flight that arrives there about one thirty in the afternoon."

"Okay. I'm flying tomorrow. I'll rent a car when I land and pick you up at the airport. Do we have the hotel suite set up?"

"Yes, Mal and Joe Cancio took care of that yesterday. Mal is all moved in, and I'll give you the address of the hotel before we hang up. They're talking about a meeting with everyone on Saturday," Bridgette reported.

"The meeting sounds fine. See you Friday."

"'Looking forward to it . . . don't like being apart!'"

"Me either."

***

Thursday morning the sixteenth, Nando flew out of Joint Base Andrews. He was the only passenger and landed about noon at SFO. Nando rented a car and headed for the Kensington Park. As he entered the room, Mal came in through the connecting doors, asking, "So what do you think of the setup?"

Nando investigated the dining-meeting room "This is great." After looking in Mal's room, he added, "Thanks for giving Bridgette and me the better room."

"No problem. I want to call Madame before she goes to bed—haven't spoken to her in a while. You can settle in; then later we'll have dinner and go over things we ought to discuss."

***

Thursday morning at eleven thirty, Orwell MegaData's corporate jet landed at the Louis Armstrong International Airport located outside of New Orleans. Bruce Campbell and his assistant, Anna, were the only passengers on the three-hour flight from San Jose International Airport.

During the flight, Bruce ruminated about what they needed to cover at the meeting. But gradually his thoughts drifted back to how their plot had developed. Like many ideas, it had started as meaningless speculation among a few businessmen with common interests—not much more than a joke. But through personal contacts, industry associations, and the like, it had grown to the present group. Ultimately, they'd met, swearing each other to secrecy. But the only thing that had resulted from the meeting was their realization that they didn't have a clue how to begin. Afterward, Bruce concluded that the plan would merely die on the vine. Then, one day at work, he'd received a call on his private mobile—an INCOMING SECURED CALL. Curious about the unusual designation, Bruce answered.

"Mr. Campbell, you need help with your project. Call André Satie in Munich," the caller said.

"Who is he?"

"Use your company's immense data-gathering capabilities to verify Satie is who you need. I'll give you his home and business addresses and phone numbers."

"Who are you? How can I reach you?"

"Never mind who I am. You can't reach me, but I'll call you if I need to. Here's the information . . ." And the line went dead.

Although Bruce had thought it was a prank, he'd eventually called his security chief and had him run down Satie. Ostensibly, it was an off-the-record search on behalf of an undisclosed law enforcement organization. Several hours later, his chief knocked on the doorjamb.

"I don't want to put this in writing; I'll do it in person." After the chief reported on Satie, he concluded by saying, "I had the IT manager wipe any record of our searches from the system."

That had set their plan in motion. The enormity of how powerful the caller had been took a while to sink in. Bruce hadn't heard from him again until he texted to arrange their meeting in Montreal at the end of September.

Bruce's musings were interrupted as the pilot announced, "We're on final approach to MSY and should be at the gate in fifteen minutes." A black car awaited them, and they checked into their suite at the Ritz-Carlton a little after noon.

Plenty of time before our two o'clock meeting, Anna thought. *Bruce will undoubtedly want to make phone calls, so I'll check on all the arrangements for refreshments and so forth while he's doing that.*

As Anna was finishing up, Bruce came in from the bedroom. "How are you getting along?"

"I'm done now."

"Let's have lunch in the coffee shop?"

"All right—I only had orange juice and half a bagel on the flight."

When they were chatting, awaiting their orders, Anna asked, "Bruce, do you think it will be a long meeting this afternoon?"

"Why? Are you worried you won't have enough time for shopping?" her boss joked.

"No. You told me this was the last meeting, so I thought if it was short, we could take a nap, then shower, dress, and celebrate tonight."

"The meeting should be brief. Your plan sounds fine, although it needs a little tweaking—I wasn't thinking about napping."

"Well, you know what I mean," Anna said, adopting a bashful giggle.

The meeting started promptly, and all the participants were there. Anna made sure the men had what they needed and went to the bedroom. Bruce updated the group. There were questions about what had happened to Satie and whether it affected their final payment.

Campbell responded, "The Munich authorities are still investigating whether it was a freak accident, arson, or arson-murder. I've talked to and met with the man who's stepping into Satie's role—call him control. I don't know who he is, because when we met, it was in a confessional, and I didn't see him. But I have no doubts that he's powerful.

"You recall that we significantly front-loaded our payment to the contractor at Satie's request. Control thinks the hit man was maximizing the up-front payment so Satie could be done away with. Apparently, it was worth it to him to forgo the remaining balance."

One of the men asked, "How much was the contractor's net after Satie's cut?"

"We believe one hundred fifteen million dollars," Bruce replied.

Another man observed, "That's an excellent payday, even at the lower amount. So the hit man murdered Satie—it makes sense to me."

"Yes," Campbell responded.

A third man said, "All right, let's sit tight for the time being but agree this afternoon that if the contractor is successful and makes a claim for the balance, we'll chip in equally and make it. But frankly, I don't think we'll ever hear from the hit man again."

The meeting broke up shortly thereafter. When Campbell went to the bedroom, Anna was already waiting in bed. It wasn't even four thirty, so she set a slow pace. They had plenty of time because they weren't leaving until tomorrow. Anna wanted Bruce relaxed and happy. *Then I ought to be able to get additional information for Jay and Nando*, she thought.

An hour and a half later, as they lazed in each other's arms, Campbell started to doze. Anna noticed and teased him. "I thought you didn't want to take a nap."

"Must be getting old—I think you wore me out!"

"Oh no, don't say that—I was just beginning."

Bruce laughed and said, "Promises, promises."

Anna continued bantering. "Okay, mister, you asked for it. But if it's too much, say *red*."

"I love it when you're playful like this."

"I don't know why I am today," Anna said. "Probably because I feel like all the pressure is off; you seem happy. That makes me relaxed and happy as well."

"You're right about the pressure—I couldn't be more pleased."

"I wish you'd share all of it with me," she said, reaching for him under the covers. "I mean, we work so closely together on everything else. It makes me feel like you don't . . . trust me."

"I trust you—of course I do."

"But not one hundred percent, I guess," Anna said, and stopped stroking him.

"No, don't say that . . . don't stop what you're doing. This conversation is going off track." Bruce hugged her closer. "Don't be upset. I'll be more forthright; what can I tell you?"

"Well, I don't know, because I know so little. I don't know what to ask." Anna said, reaching for him again.

"All right—it's all about politics. I've put this group together—powerful, wealthy businessmen, including a foreigner . . ."

"The Asian guy I saw that time when he came back for his umbrella? Is he Chinese?"

"Yes. Anyway, we're all unhappy with the political climate and policies of the administration. So we're going to do something about it.

We're forming a PAC—political action committee—to support the candidate of our choice for the next presidential election."

"Who's that?"

"The current vice president."

"Really? Isn't the vice president a bit of a putz?"

"Precisely—we'll manage and control him. So we've raised one hundred fifty million dollars with all but twenty-five mil already in hand. We're going to launch it the weekend of November seventh through ninth in San Francisco. That and who our candidate is are confidential—don't breathe a word of it."

"I'm a bit confused. How can China be involved? That's gotta be illegal."

"We've accumulated all the funds in a private bank in Switzerland. We think it'll go unnoticed, and we'll just bring it back in drips and drabs."

I think that's bullshit, Anna thought. *In fact, it's all bullshit— except that they raised the money and they want the vice president in the White House after the 2016 election!*

"So are we okay now?" Campbell asked.

Anna continued loving him, yet she was worried. *I don't think I'm going to get anything else out of him. But I've confirmed the amount and that the Chinese are involved. Also, I now know the launch date.*

***

Mal and Nando went to Scala's Bistro next to the Sir Francis Drake Hotel. While they were walking over, Mal said, "I hear this place is good—both new and classic French and Italian." They ordered wine, and after the waiter took their orders, Mal began. "Let me go over some new developments.

"First, Zeb successfully hacked into the Ritz-Carlton's CCTV system. He ran a test at five o'clock this morning, New Orleans time. Everything looked fine, and he kept it streaming. Unfortunately, the stream went dark later in the morning. Zeb called me just before we left."

"That's unsettling," Nando said. "Jay and I never passed on the New Orleans meeting to the director or president."

"Obviously, whoever is behind this isn't relying on the intelligence you pass along. They're in contact with one of the conspirators—probably Campbell," Mal said, and continued. "The second thing is that we lost Izabella. Zeb last saw her at the White Swan Wednesday evening the eighth."

"That's the evening before she went to Stanford and San Jose," Nando observed.

"Zeb has kept up the monitoring, but nada—I think Izabella is out of there."

"Well, at least now we aren't lying to the director when we tell him we don't know where she is," Nando joked.

"I'll give a complete update on these two items at our meeting. Also, I need a favor if possible. I ditched my firearm before flying from Canada. I didn't want to be busted on a gun charge. We have a consulate general in San Francisco, but I'm too deep undercover to ask for their help. Can you arrange a gun for me?"

Nando responded, "I carried my sidearm with me, but I need a sniper's rifle. So I'll ask the director to arrange that here. I'll tell him I also need a short-barrel semiauto for my ankle holster. Is a .45 okay?"

"Perfect."

As they walked back to the Kensington Park, Mal said, "Müller and Cancio will be at our hotel at ten o'clock Saturday morning. Dr. Sandler suggests we utilize her on an ad hoc basis for profiling, so she's skipping the meeting."

"Makes sense. What's your take on Cancio? You spent time with him yesterday."

"I think Joe's solid—he'll be an asset." Then Mal described Cancio's relationship with Müller. "Joe says he's the strategist and Gabi's the tactician. Apparently, she has a photographic memory and can be 'detailed to the point of frustration'—his words. Gabi likes being in the number-two role, loves to research, and is tenacious. They've been partners for almost twenty years."

"It sounds like Gabi's the kind of ground support we need. Hopefully, she'll have some ideas on how we can locate Izabella," Nando concluded.

***

As planned, Nando picked up Bridgette on Friday; then on Saturday they met with Mal, Joe, and Gabi. They chatted for a few minutes before getting down to business. Nando went first.

"All of you know why we're here and what we're up against. I would like Mal to bring us up-to-date with his investigation, after which Bridgette and I will report on our progress. After that, Joe and Gabi can give us their thoughts. Lastly, we need to talk about how we proceed—

how often we should get together, do we need any equipment or supplies, and should Jay and Zeb be conferenced in whenever we meet. Afterward, we'll assign tasks."

Mal briefly reviewed his CV, explained what the Kidon Unit was, and talked about his assignment. "There's one thing I want to stress: do not underestimate Izabella. I'm not being melodramatic when I tell you how dangerous she is. Izabella kills without hesitancy. I'm positive she did away with Satie. Here's a copy of her recent evaluation by Mossad. Return it before you leave today. Also, I'm texting you her photo, which you may keep."

Joe spoke up. "We think we have already run across her. Gabi will fill you in later, but from what we've seen, we don't doubt your assessment."

"Okay, here's where we stand." Mal updated them on Izabella's activities and concluded, "I think she has gone to ground. We need to verify that and do our best to locate her. Nando will cover it later, but we know Izabella was in San Jose on Thursday the ninth, and we need local help finding her.

"Another topic is the conspirators meeting at the New Orleans Ritz-Carlton on this past Thursday afternoon." Mal reviewed the problems with the CCTV feed. "I'm also concerned that the CIA hasn't ordered a termination or insisted the president change his schedule. It doesn't make sense to me, unless there's someone behind the scenes manipulating the president."

Nando began his report. "We've concluded that Izabella will attempt the assassination during the overnight of November seventh/eighth when the president is at Ransom's mansion. Jay and I reconnoitered both the Ransom and Stanford sites. A professional would never choose Stanford. Proceeding on that basis, we have assumed

Izabella will access the fundraising dinner as temporary waitstaff, a bartender, cleanup crew, or the like. We're going to need local help identifying those vendors as well.

"Regarding the New Orleans meeting, we have a source in Silicon Valley who works for and travels with the head of the conspirators. She is due to report on that meeting on Monday or Tuesday. We had hoped to be able to identify the conspirators through facial recognition software. Zeb's trying to sort out what happened with the CCTV.

"For security reasons, our investigation is being kept entirely within the CIA, and we only talk to two people—the director and the president. Neither Jay nor I alerted them to that meeting. So, if our CCTV feed was sabotaged, it reinforces Mal's concern about someone behind the scenes who's in touch with the conspirators directly," Nando finished.

"So it has to be the director," Gabi observed quietly.

"Yes, we think so," Bridgette admitted.

"It's a lot to take in," Gabi said.

Nando continued, "Joe, do you have anything to add?"

"Yes, we can assist with the issues you'd like help on. I'll start looking at caterers and so forth. Gabi, why don't you talk about why we think we've encountered Izabella already?"

"Sure, but before I cover that. About the White Swan, I can investigate that for you. My husband and I occasionally take R & R weekends there when we need a break from the kids. I should be able to get the name she's using. If she is parking with the hotel's valet, I'll obtain the plate of her rental car. That will lead me to the rental agency. It ought to be enough to get on her trail again. I'm in court on Monday and Tuesday, so I'll talk to the White Swan first thing Wednesday."

Gabi went on to describe Izabella's visit to José's shortly after she arrived in San Francisco, Pedro's abuse, the probable purchase of a sniper rifle, and Pedro's subsequent murder.

"Danny Wong and I are convinced José knows more than he's telling. From what I've heard this morning, I suspect José may know where she went—who better for her to ask in a strange city? Danny and I will lean on him harder. And Danny can pursue Pedro's murder investigation without knowing the full scope of what we're dealing with."

"That would be great," Bridgette said. "All of this is new to us. But if Izabella isn't doing it at Stanford, why the rifle?"

"Perhaps a contingency or additional disinformation," Mal suggested.

"Okay," Bridgette said. "So Joe will look into the vendors, Gabi will talk to the White Swan, Danny and Gabi will lean on José about Izabella's whereabouts, and Mal, Nando, and I will follow up with Jay about New Orleans."

The meeting broke up. They decided to reconvene on Friday, October 24, with Jay and Zeb on a conference call.

CHAPTER FIFTEEN

Sunday, October 19, 2014

San Francisco

Izabella had breakfast in the hotel's coffee shop and then walked over to Union Square, picking up two Sunday papers, the *Chronicle* and the *Examiner*. When she returned, she spent the rest of the morning studying their society columns and entertainment sections before developing a list of the most popular caterers and party equipment providers. Afterward, on her smartphone, Izabella researched their addresses, phone numbers, hours of operation, and so forth.

But before she was finished for the day, Izabella needed to adjust her plan. She had already determined that the Ransom mansion was the better location. Izabella reasoned, *Stanford and San Jose are useful deceptions. So is the rifle, although I don't mind having it in reserve. But Medina may figure this out. Also, my sixth sense is still bedeviling me; it's stupid to be complacent. Even though it has gone smoothly so far, I need to be cautious and go deeper to ground.*

So she continued to cogitate before returning to the papers. Then a plan formed: *Why not use San Francisco's huge LGBTQ community?* It didn't take Izabella long to discover that the El Rio on Mission Street was the premier lesbian nightclub. *And thanks to Elsa, I can take advantage of my own, more flexible sexuality. This scheme's already falling into place; it's gonna work.*

***

On Monday morning the twentieth, a man knocked on the door of an upper-floor apartment in the Mitte section of Berlin. He wore wire-rimmed glasses and was neatly dressed in a three-piece, conservative brown suit, with all the buttons of his jacket done up. He identified himself, showing appropriate credentials as a census taker for the Bundesrepublik Deutschland, and quickly gained admission.

"*Guten Tag, Fräulein,*" he began. "I'm here today because you haven't returned your completed census form yet."

The young woman replied, "Oh, I didn't know a census was being taken."

"You didn't receive a form in the post? You could have filled it out online as well."

"I'm sorry. I didn't know anything about it—am I in trouble?"

"Oh, no, no—nothing like that. I have the form right here, and we can fill it out together. Then you'll sign it and we'll be done. Fifteen minutes; that's all it takes. Would you like to do that?"

"Yes."

He fished in his briefcase for the form. "So let's start. May I have your full name, please?"

"Elsa König."

"Occupation?"

"Freelance fashion designer."

The census taker kept asking questions, such as age, birthplace, parents' names, and so forth. Finally, he got to what he was interested in. "Married?"

"No."

"Then you live alone?"

"No, I have a . . . roommate," Elsa replied, blushing a bit.

"I see. And how long has your roommate lived with you?"

"Gosh, I'm not sure—about two years, I think."

"May I have your roommate's name, please?"

"Katja Schmidt."

"Did she fill out a census form? Is this her permanent residence?"

"I guess so—about the address. Don't know about the census form."

"Well, I better take all the information about her that you know. We don't want to miss her in the census. Any other addresses you know about?"

"Well, Katja mentioned once that she had a retirement condo in Saint Martin—Grand Case. It's on the French side."

The census taker kept probing, but Elsa knew little about her roommate. She seemingly had no interest in Katja's career, yet volunteered that Katja traveled frequently and was in Canada now.

When he returned to his office, he called the director. "I didn't develop a lot of information. Elsa, the woman she's living with, is remarkably ignorant about Izabella's details. Elsa's young and incredibly hot; I'm certain those two are lovers. I determined the name Izabella uses is Katja Schmidt, and she owns a condo in Grand Case, Saint Martin. If the condo is in Katja's name also, it could be a recurring ID. Plus, from the information you gave me, I was able to confirm that Katja's height, weight, eyes, and hair color are the same as Izabella's."

The director took down the information and thanked his officer. After he hung up, he thought, *I wonder if I have enough for a warrant to go after banking information. Obviously, we have legitimate reasons. It'll probably go nowhere, though. Grand Case is still France, and the French are simply obstructionist.*

***

Monday morning, Izabella went shopping. Because she'd traveled with a limited wardrobe, she needed to buy slacks and sweaters favored by younger women. Another wig as well—auburn and longer than her own hair. Izabella had all the makeup she needed to pass as a college girl seeking part-time work. Later in the day, she would identify which vendors were supplying the fundraising dinner and begin arranging interviews.

***

Before she left for work Tuesday morning, Anna called Jay and reported on the trip to New Orleans. When she was finished, Jay said, "You've confirmed a lot."

"Yes. That's about it, though. I don't know if there's any other information to be sussed out," Anna said.

"All right, keep your eyes and ears open. Call if you have anything new, but let's talk every week—until this is over, anyway. Nando is in San Francisco now. I'll give you his mobile number; you can talk to him anytime as well."

They chatted for a few minutes. After they hung up, Jay called Nando and briefed him.

***

The first thing Wednesday morning, Gabi headed for the White Swan. When she arrived, she recognized the registration clerk. "'Mornin', Don," she greeted him.

"Hey, Gabi. I haven't seen you in a while. Do you need reservations?"

"No, I'm on the job today."

"That sounds ominous," Don joked. "What do you need?"

"We're trying to locate a missing person. We have reason to think she might have stayed here."

"That's not your usual bailiwick."

"No, we're helping Missing Persons. Can you look at her photo?" Gabi asked as she pulled the image up on her phone. "Recognize her?"

Don nodded. "Sure, she was here around the beginning of the month. She's hard to forget—that photo doesn't do her justice."

"That attractive—huh."

Don shrugged his shoulders and laughed. "One can but dream. Let me see . . ." He went to the computer. "Paola Conti—checked in on September thirtieth and out on October ninth. She used an international driver's license as ID and paid cash in advance. That's odd—we always require a credit card."

"I gather you didn't check her in. Any address?"

"No, Johnny was on that day." Don looked for an address. "Only Berlin."

"Is that odd too?"

"Not if she paid cash, I guess. She used valet parking also, so I have a license plate number."

Gabi noted all the appropriate information.

"Anything else?"

"Now that I think about it, I heard she really didn't check out. Housekeeping found her key and a tip on the pillow that morning when they went to make up the room. She was paid through the twelfth, so it wasn't a problem."

"All right, thanks. Do you mind if I walk around, check out the CCTV and such?"

"No, go ahead. Holler if you need anything."

Gabi was certain she recalled the CCTV setup and the rear exit from her previous visits. *As I thought, two CCTV cameras on this floor: one over the entrance pointing towards the registration desk, and one in the rear of the living and breakfast room area. That one is in the left-hand corner, angled diagonally. It won't pick up the door in the right-hand rear corner.* Next, Gabi left through that door and went down a hall, past the stairs, out the back door, and then along an alley to Sutter Street. When she came back inside, Gabi asked Don, "Do you have any CCTV on the other floors?"

"No, only these two down here."

"Okay, thanks. We'll need to look at the CCTV pics; I'll pick them up later on."

Gabi walked to a luncheonette on Powell Street, had coffee, and called the office to run the tag. Before she was finished, they had called back. The car was registered to Pacific Northwest Leasing. Gabi called the leasing company's number but was transferred around a bit before finally learning that the car was leased to Intra-City Car Rentals on Geary Boulevard. Gabi drove to Intra-City, and the rental agent easily recalled Paola. She had already returned the car—on the ninth—and paid cash there too.

"Isn't that unusual?"

"Yeah, but she left a two-thousand-dollar cash deposit," the agent said.

The rental information was also incomplete—no address for the international license.

"How did she leave? Did someone pick her up?"

"No, I remember we called her a cab—City Taxi. Gus, one of their longtime drivers, came by."

So Gabi headed for City Taxi next. Gus was just reporting to work and recalled Paola. Gabi learned that Paola had asked him to take her to a different car rental agency. Gus had dropped her at Bay Area Rent-a-Ride. It was the same story there as at the other agency. Cash rental, cash deposit (this time $2,500), a local address at the White Swan, an international driver's license with an incomplete address recorded. The good news was that the car was still out on rental. Gabi obtained a description of the vehicle and its plate number. Then she returned to the office and issued an APB containing Izabella's photo and the notation DO NOT APPROACH—ARMED AND DANGEROUS—CONTACT SERIOUS CRIMES.

Done before lunch—not bad for a half day's work. Izabella certainly knows how to manipulate men—each one of them bent the rules for her!

***

By Wednesday afternoon, Izabella had visited the two most likely caterers. She determined that Bay City Banquets would be providing the DNC's catering. They were happy to hire her off the books but asked her to work a couple of events beforehand. *A trial, I suppose.* So on Thursday, Izabella bought a white blouse and black slacks, their dress code. Then, on Friday morning, she set out to work a retirement luncheon at a bank on Battery Street.

***

Earlier in the week, the director had called Cole, inviting him to Thursday night's Broncos-Chargers game. Beforehand, the director wanted to try a new steakhouse, Guard and Grace on California Street in downtown Denver. Cole was a little early and sat nursing a glass of red wine while he waited. He was perturbed because their last conversation had bothered him, raising his acute sensitivity to danger. Cole had learned in his Ranger days not to dismiss these feelings. He had a niche and was well paid for what he did. But the director knew his background, and Cole reflected that he wouldn't be surprised if the man tried pushing him past his present-day boundaries.

What the hell is he up to? "An important new project . . . bigger payday also." I'm suspicious where this is going. I've stayed away from wet work. I've always made it clear I don't do that anymore, not since leaving the Army. The problem is he has enough dirt on me to make my life miserable. If he outed me, I would probably do time. And even worse, if I turn him down, he might decide I'm an unnecessary risk.

Cole had been correct about what the director intended. The director had not been subtle in trying to coerce Cole through intimidation. Cole thought he'd handled the nearly overt threats well, feigning interest in the "important new project." He'd asked questions about Campbell, the timing, and so forth. The director responded, then said, "Try to make it look like an accident if you can, but do it quickly."

"All right," Cole replied. "Give me a couple of days to do some preliminary scouting. I'll get back to you."

"Okay, but ASAP."

That evening, throughout the game and afterward, Cole continued to ruminate, but he wasn't going to overreact. He'd always known this might happen and was prepared. Cole would disappear to the south of France, where he had an alternate identity in place, owned a comfortable country cottage, and had squirreled away his considerable assets with Swiss banks and brokers. *So*, Cole finally decided, *it's time to make my way to Rennes-le-Château. I'll simply retire earlier than I expected to.*

***

On Friday morning, Nando, Bridgette, Mal, Gabi, and Joe had their next meeting; Jay and Zeb were conferenced in.

Nando began the meeting. "Why don't we take turns updating the group with what we've been doing and what we've discovered? Gabi, would you start?"

Gabi summarized what she'd learned at the White Swan, concluding with, "I issued an APB. Also, I have her international driver's license number but with only Berlin as a home address. We need to obtain her address from the Germans. Plus she's still using the White Swan as her local one. The desk clerk who checked her in, Johnny, won't be in until Sunday. I'll interview him then—maybe he knows more."

Nando suggested, "If you'd like me to come along, I will. CIA credentials sometimes loosen tongues."

"That might be helpful."

"And I can probably find that address you need in Berlin," Zeb offered.

"Thanks. One more thing, I checked out the White Swan's CCTV—only two cameras on the ground floor. She could have easily left through the rear entrance—a straight shot down the alley to Sutter Street," Gabi finished.

Joe went next. "I've started visiting caterers and other vendors. Nothing yet."

"Okay, Jay, tell us about Anna and New Orleans," Nando said.

"I spoke with Anna on Tuesday." Jay reported what she'd said. He concluded, "This was their last meeting. Anna doesn't think she'll be able to develop any additional information, but we're staying in touch."

"Okay, thanks," Nando continued. "Mal, would you and Zeb fill us in on what happened with the surveillance of the CCTV in New Orleans?"

Zeb spoke and reviewed how their feed as well as two other floors had gone dark a few hours before the meeting.

"I can't prove it, but I'm convinced it was sabotaged. I don't think it was a hack, though. It was probably low-tech disabling of the cameras. I reviewed all the tapes just beforehand, but I didn't pick up any suspicious activity around them. Whoever did it was a pro; everything is back to normal now."

Mal interjected, "As we speculated before, this supports our theory that someone high up in the White House is dealing directly with the conspirators."

Zeb continued his report. "I've been frustrated that we haven't been able to find Izabella's go-to fake identity. So I took the initiative and decided to try to trace the payment for the assassination.

"I made several assumptions. First, even if the US had legitimate reasons to subpoena overseas bank records, EU countries are all members of the Hague Service Convention. It has a complicated process, to say the least. If you think the US is difficult, the EU is a labyrinth. Also, most countries have blocking statutes, which do what the name implies. So success wouldn't be guaranteed.

"Second, I assumed the funds would run through Switzerland. It isn't part of the EU. Their reputation for being more cooperative today is a bit of a misnomer. I didn't discover any changes that would make obtaining information easier. But if the Swiss bank from whom you're seeking cooperation has branches in your country, then your country can exert pressure with local threats of investigations. Frequently, the Swiss parent is coerced into cooperation. The US is particularly successful with these tactics. An exception is if the funds run through a Swiss bank with no overseas branches; then there is no leverage and the Swiss remain intractable. So I decided to search banks with only domestic operations. There're still a handful—mostly private banks.

"Next, I established a window of between September third and twenty-second, the first date being Nando's faux death and the second date being when we had a high-probability facial recognition hit of Izabella at a departing flight from Berlin to Montreal.

"And finally, I assumed the amount I was looking for would be between one hundred million and two hundred million dollars. Without going through all the machinations, I found a one-hundred-twenty-five-million-dollar incoming transfer to an account in one of the private banks.

After that, there was an almost simultaneous one-hundred-fifteen-million outgoing transfer to another account in the same bank. Next, there was an outgoing transfer in like amount from the second account to an account in Banque des Antilles Francaises in Grand Case, Saint Martin. I was able to confirm the first account was André Satie's and that the second was Katja Schmidt's with a Berlin address. The third account was Katja Schmidt's also and had both a Saint Martin address and her Berlin address. If that Berlin address is on her international driver's license, I think we have her. I'll route this to Bridgette."

"Excellent," Mal said. "Jesus, your president would have a conniption fit if the CIA had done that hacking!"

Zeb continued, "I've already investigated that Berlin address. It's an upscale apartment in the Mitte section. The lease is in Conrad König's name. He's a wealthy German industrialist and is married with one daughter, Elsa. I'm guessing the apartment is hers. I'll try to track that down too."

Bridgette commented, "Saint Martin is probably where Izabella will hole up."

"There's one last thing," Nando said. "I think it is time to tell the director about the meeting on the sixteenth in New Orleans. I'm certain he knows about it already and must be wondering why we haven't discovered it through our source. If no one has any objection, Jay, would you fill him in on what Anna reported without disclosing her or Campbell's identities? Say our source won't disclose those until the WITSEC deal is inked."

Everyone agreed, and Mal said, "It feels like we're finally making headway."

The next meeting was set for Thursday, the thirtieth.

CHAPTER SIXTEEN

Friday, October 24, 2014
Jersey City

In the morning, a CIA jet took off from Denver for the four-hour flight to Newark. The director was having dinner with a longtime friend, a longshoremen's union organizer. His associate was also reputed to be the capo of New Jersey's DeCavalcante mob that was affiliated with the Luciano-cum-Genovese crime family. This unusual association had begun during World War II, when Lucky Luciano, who ran one of the Five Families that controlled New York City's underworld, unexpectedly partnered with several federal agencies to keep the unions in line, the ports open, and armaments and supplies flowing to Europe. This alliance had lasted through leadership and name changes—even Lucky's brusque deportation to Italy in 1946.

The taxi pulled in front of a small Italian restaurant on Terhune Avenue. There was a short waiting line spilling outside the entranceway. To disapproving looks and comments, the director bypassed all of it. His associate was waiting inside the door. They kissed each other on the cheek, and the capo said, "Our table is ready. It's in the rear—follow me." As they walked over, the mobster continued, "It's hectic here, so we won't be noticed or overheard. We'll hear each other easily, though. Go figure. It's why I like it here."

"Acoustics, I guess," the director remarked. After dinner was finished, he got down to business. "I have three pieces of work for you."

First, he described Cole and reported that there had been a tracking device in his car since September 25.

"He's in the Texas/Oklahoma area now. This needs to be done immediately. I can't trust him anymore."

"Is he one of yours?"

"A mercenary, a former Ranger. If it can't be made to look like an accident, make certain there's no evidence left behind. Capiche?"

"Capiche."

"The next, Bruce Campbell, is a priority. Do it after the twenty-eighth, though. Make it look like an accident also. The last is a contingency for the time being. A woman trained by Mossad, an assassin—you'll need a heavy hitter. This will probably be in the islands, about November eighth. I'll let you know." Then the director passed a hard-copy file across the table. "This contains information on them. Destroy it when you're finished. There's no digital footprint."

"Okay. For the first, I'll use a guy from the piers in New Orleans. He moonlights and is reliable. For the others, I'll use my best, a broad called Bermuda; she lives there. I've used her for over twenty-five years—never fucks up."

"Jesus, who would've thought you were an equal-opportunity employer!"

"Hey, I don't give a shit: gay, straight, black, white, or purple with polka dots . . . she never fuckin' misses."

***

On Friday evening, Izabella went to El Rio to see if she could hook up. She dressed carefully, not flamboyantly—striking a balance between casual and professional. Hopefully, it wouldn't take too many visits to connect with her *type*: five foot nine, 125 pounds, early thirties. Izabella's cab arrived at about nine o'clock. The place wasn't crowded yet. She avoided the patio and sat inside at the bar, where she could observe most of the club. She ordered a glass of white wine. Izabella noticed an attractive woman sitting at a table for two. *She looks about right, perhaps a few years older—no matter.* She decided to wait and see if the woman was meeting anyone. Unexpectedly, her quarry must've had the same idea, because she approached Izabella. "Hi, I'm Karen. You're not waiting for anyone, are you?"

"No, I'm alone," Izabella said, and extended her hand. "Paola."

"Would you like to join me at my table? It's more comfortable than the bar," Karen asked. As they walked over, she continued, "It's a great spot. We can still hear the band in the other room, yet it isn't so loud that we can't talk." Karen made Izabella feel relaxed, and they hit it off well. After talking for a while, Izabella began feigning an undecided, bashful manner, thinking, *Time to settle if Karen is in the market tonight. If she's as sensitive as I think, she will have picked up on my change in demeanor.*

"Paola, is everything all right?" Karen asked. "You seem . . . ill at ease now. Did I say anything to bother you?"

"Oh, no—it isn't you." Paola paused, and Karen reached out, taking her hand. "I'm mixed up, that's all . . . I don't want to mislead you."

"First time?"

"No, not exactly. I had a three-month relationship with my roommate in college. It ended badly. I walked in on her with another woman—in our room, in my bed. I couldn't move past it. I was so hurt that I had to change roommates."

"I'm not like that."

"Oh, no! I didn't mean to suggest that you were, Karen. I'm just muddled. I've been with men since. But those relationships haven't worked out either. Now I'm coming off a bad breakup. I don't mean to bore you—sorry."

"You're not boring me—I'm an excellent listener. I won't pressure you. I want you to be happy when we make love. Don't fret; you're worth waiting for."

Karen's confident. She's taking the bait; seduction isn't new to her.

They talked and held hands. Paola expanded on her faux previous relationship, which had been psychologically abusive. Karen said she was a lawyer who was changing firms and taking a two-week vacation. Paola looked at her watch. *Let's see if I can land her.* "Oh, look at the time. Do you think they'll call me a cab?"

"I'm positive they will. But before you go, would you like to see me again?"

Paola nodded.

"Wonderful—I have my car. Why don't I drive you home, or you could spend the night with me? We can simply cuddle if that's what you'd like."

When they arrived at Karen's two-bedroom high-rise apartment on Broadway between Van Ness and the Presidio, Karen showed Paola to the master bedroom, turned down the sheet, and said, "The bathroom's through there. I'll be in shortly."

When Karen returned, Paola was waiting in bed. She'd left her panties on. *Karen has gotta do a little of the work*, Izabella thought, and chuckled.

***

It was four thirty Sunday morning, and Cole was on the road. His getaway plan had come together well—at least until earlier this morning. *But it worked out anyhow, so no harm, no foul.*

On Thursday, Cole had decided to stay overnight in Denver— resist the temptation to move. He needed information, and it was too difficult to work on his smartphone while driving. Also, by the time he drove the nearly seven hundred plus miles to his home—a small rented ranch house near the Texas, Oklahoma, and Chickasaw Nation borders— everything would be closed for the weekend. So Cole stayed in his hotel room through Friday morning, making plans. He needed to choose an escape route and had several alternatives that would be easy: the southern or northern borders and one other to explore. By checkout time on Friday, Cole had the information he needed. He fueled the Hellcat and headed southeast. Even with only two quick pit stops, Cole didn't pull into his driveway until after midnight Saturday morning. He slept late and then checked and reorganized his go bag: cash, passports, credit cards, burners and satellite phones, ammo, and so forth. He took a large duffel and packed as much as he could, including personal items such as family pictures and a few favorite books. Last, Cole cleaned and function-checked his full-sized .45, sliding in a magazine before putting it aside.

He had planned on a full night's sleep Saturday and then on Sunday taking a relaxed drive for the next seven hundred miles to Pap's house. On Monday morning, they would rendezvous with the *Geraldine Leigh*, sailing from New Orleans on the nine-thirty slack tide.

So Cole had turned in early Saturday night after taking a few low-tech safeguards—*an abundance of caution*, he thought. In the living room, Cole moved his recliner into a corner on the same wall as the front door. The chair provided an unobstructed view of the only floor—the arch to the kitchen, the entranceway to the hall. After that, he made newspaper balls, putting them inside the back and front doors, under the windows, and so on. Later, he turned off the lights and settled into the chair. Cole pushed his night goggles up to his forehead and put his semiauto in his lap, the hammer cocked, safety off.

Things deteriorated early Sunday morning when Cole, a light sleeper, was awoken. He heard a car's engine shut off, then quiet noises at the front door: the lock being picked. Moving behind the recliner, Cole pulled down the goggles, braced his elbows on the back of the chair, and aimed toward the front door. The intruder came into view, holding a gun with a two-handed grip, a flashlight below the barrel. As the man skulked through the room, Cole saw an ear below the bottom fold of the trespasser's watch cap. He aimed there, tracking the man as he progressed. A newspaper rustled, and the man froze. That's when Cole put two rounds into his ear.

Cole checked for a pulse—none. Putting aside the assailant's car keys, he destroyed the man's mobile phone, stripped him, and placed his clothes and shattered phone in a lawn-and-leaf bag. Next, Cole dragged the corpse onto the front lawn before returning inside. The hollow-point cartridges hadn't exited the skull, so there was negligible blood to clean up. Nevertheless, he scoured with bleach, letting it soak while he finished up. Then Cole collected the newspaper balls, his brass, and the assailant's gun and flashlight and stuffed them into the bag also. Finally, he drove the man's car two miles to the municipal dump. It was a large excavation—an exhausted quarry. Cole hurled the bag in before driving farther along the rim to a spot where there was a steep drop to the quarry's floor. He pushed the car over the side and then flipped the keys after it.

He trotted back to his house and dragged the naked corpse across the lawn and then ten yards into the woods. *With any luck, the animals will get to it before it's discovered.* Cole cleaned up inside and stuffed the used paper towels into his jeans pocket. After that, he put the cleaning supplies away, grabbed his bags, and headed for the car.

Only one more thing to do. When he'd heard the assailant's car, it had dawned on him how the attack had been devised. Consequently, Cole started moving around the Hellcat, looking for a tracking device. He found a magnetic one in the car's passenger side, rear wheel well. *Son of a bitch. He must've planted it when I picked him up in Montreal. Sneaky bastard; I never saw him do it.*

Cole paused at the end of the driveway and tossed the device into the field across the street. He was on the road by four o'clock. Several miles later when the Hellcat was up to speed, Cole dropped the used paper towels out the car's window and headed southeast for Pap's. *No reason to wait around.*

***

On Sunday morning, Gabi stopped by Nando's hotel and picked him up on the way to the White Swan. Johnny was working at the registration desk when they arrived. As they approached, Gabi asked, "Are you Johnny?"

"Yes. How can I help you?"

"I'm Lieutenant Müller, SFPD, and this is Operations Officer Medina, CIA." They both showed their IDs, and Gabi continued, "We'd like to ask you a few questions about Paola Conti. Do you recall her?"

"Yes, Don said you were here asking about her. What can I help you with?"

Gabi asked him to identify Izabella's photograph.

"Yes—that's Paola."

"She has been reported as a missing person, but her real name is Izabella Ricci. You checked her in on September thirtieth, correct?" Gabi asked.

Johnny typed at the computer. "Yes."

Gabi asked him about the lack of a credit card number and the cash payment as well as the incomplete home address.

"Well, she wanted to pay in cash." Johnny looked at the computer again. "I don't recall about the home address—it's an oversight. I don't know how it happened."

"We saw you talking to her on the CCTV for quite a while on Wednesday night the eighth; what can you tell us about her?" Gabi asked.

Then Johnny told them about Paola running away from her former boyfriend.

"So she asked you to help her check out without going through the lobby," Nando surmised.

"Yes, she was afraid he might be watching the front entrance. I got her car from valet parking and took it around to Sutter Street."

"Then you showed her how to leave by the back stairs, back door, and alley," Gabi said.

"Yes."

"Do you have any idea where Izabella went?" Nando continued.

"No. Did I do anything wrong? She didn't stiff us on her bill. It all seemed like no harm, no foul—she was sweet."

"No, you're not in trouble," Nando said. "But Izabella isn't a missing person; she's a rogue Mossad agent—a top-notch assassin for hire—and very dangerous. Everything she told you was bullshit. If she turns up again, be careful—I can't stress that enough—and contact either of us immediately," Nando said.

They gave Johnny their cards and left. When they were out of earshot, Gabi said, "I'm positive Izabella showed him some TLC. But notwithstanding his outward composure, Johnny's rattled."

"Agreed, but I'm not convinced he knows more. Still, Johnny might be thinking he dodged a bullet!"

***

On Sunday afternoon, the director called Izabella. When she answered her burner, he said, "We need to meet ASAP—things are changing. Meet me at noon—on Tuesday the twenty-eight—at Uncle Vito's pizza joint. Do you know it?"

"I've seen it—near Bush and Powell Streets, correct?"

"Yes," the director replied.

"I'll be in disguise and arrive last. We've never met, so carry a copy of *A Tale of Two Cities*."

The director laughed. "Okay, Madame Defarge. Let's switch burners; here's my new number."

CHAPTER SEVENTEEN

Monday, October 27, 2014

San Francisco

After Joe stopped by the office on Monday morning, he set out to the next caterer on his list, Bay City Banquets. A young woman, a receptionist, got the owner. Joe showed his ID and asked, "Are you putting on any temporary staff for an upcoming DNC event?"

At first, the owner was reluctant to disclose that they were providing the catering, but eventually he cooperated.

"No, our regulars can handle it."

"Are you positive? It's a big party. Look at this photo, please. Did you hire her?" Joe said, showing him Izabella's photo.

"No. As I said, we don't need anyone."

Joe gave the man his card. When Joe was leaving the shop, the receptionist whispered, "Wait for me at the corner." A few minutes later she came out, spotted Joe, and approached him. She lit a cigarette and said, "He's lying to you. He has put on several girls."

"Why would he lie?"

"He pays them off the books—not even minimum wage. He doesn't want a hassle with the government."

"I'm not the IRS," Joe observed.

"He's just a prick."

"Is that why you're telling me?"

"Yeah, and that he's a pig."

"Anything I should know about?" Joe asked.

"Probably, but I need this job."

"All right. Call me if you want help," Joe responded, and handed her a card. "Before you go, look at this photo."

"Yeah, she's one of them—Paola. But she has dark hair. Looked a little younger too."

"You're sure?"

"Yeah. She worked a lunch the other day also."

"A trial?"

"I guess."

"Do you know her address?"

"No, it's cash. She either shows or doesn't."

As Joe walked away, he thought, *I almost hope that son of a bitch messes with Izabella. Jesus, he'd be surprised.*

***

Monday morning, Pap and Cole set out from the cove where Pap's boat was moored. Cole had arrived before supper Sunday evening. At dinner he'd handed Pap an envelope containing the signed title to his Hellcat. Pap looked confused and surprised when Cole said, "I thought you and your son might be able to put this to good use."

Pap's expression changed to sadness. "You're not coming back?"

"I don't think so—it's too dangerous."

"I'm sorry. You've been a good friend, but things never stay the same." Pap sighed. "Well, I'll be your caretaker. When it's safe to return, just holler, and I'll deliver it."

It had been foggy early in the morning, but the mist was nearly burned off by the time they sailed from the cove. The day was mild now, with temperatures in the mid to high seventies, wind from the north at less than five miles per hour, and a calm sea. They talked baseball and drank coffee from a thermos Pap had brought. About one thirty p.m., they spotted the *Geraldine Leigh* approaching the coordinates where they had previously rendezvoused. Coming alongside, Cole waved to the skipper, who was leaning over the railing. A crane lowered a lifting hook and hoisted Cole's bags aboard. Cole hugged Pap, and when the lifting hook came down again, he put his foot in the bend, grabbed the cable, and was hoisted aboard. He and the captain, leaning on the railing, watched the vessels slowly part. Pap waved, and Cole called down, "Au revoir."

Cole mulled over his upcoming voyage: sailing down the east coast of South America to Rio de Janeiro, then crossing the South Atlantic to the Port of Abidjan on the Ivory Coast, and finally heading to the Mediterranean and Marseille, where he would disembark. After that, Cole would begin making his way along the 225-mile trek to Rennes-le-Château. He continued leaning against the railing, musing until Pap's boat was barely a speck.

***

On Tuesday the twenty-eighth, Campbell was seated at a corner table in Uncle Vito's. A few minutes after noon, a middle-aged woman with straggly smoke-colored hair came in, dressed in a loose-fitting sweater and cargo pants. *Good Lord, she looks like a cross between an old hippie and a bag lady,* he thought. Unexpectedly, she approached, pointed at his copy of *A Tale of Two Cities*, and said, "It's an excellent book. Thérèse Defarge's my favorite character."

"Jesus, I never would have guessed."

"That's the idea. Are you the man I've been speaking with? You don't sound like him."

"Control? No, I'm his representative." They ordered a large thin-crust cheese pie and sodas. While they waited, Campbell spoke quietly. "Control wants to make a change in plans. You ought to have time to adjust. First, do you have a rifle? You'll need one."

"Yes."

"Excellent. Continue as if Ransom's is your plan. Here's a hard-copy file for the new one. It has everything you need. There're no indications as to its origins—no digital trail—but it goes without saying: destroy it as soon as possible."

"Of course. I'll check it out. Do I talk to you from now on?"

"No, I'm a stand-in for this meeting. In the future, use the burner number control has already given you."

They parted shortly thereafter. As Izabella returned to the Hotel Royal, her feelings about the meeting were mixed. She felt better that control was at least attempting to conceal his identity now. He never had before, not even the first time when she'd called from Berlin, after Luca's death. Maybe he'd been caught off guard because he was an emergency contact. But after that, he hadn't bothered either. Why? The incongruity must've been nettling at her, because today's meeting with his stand-in had focused her thoughts.

I'm convinced I recognize his voice from hearing him on TV. The more I think about it, control has to be the director of the CIA. And Izabella didn't like the inescapable conclusion. *The director isn't a careless man. He doesn't care. He doesn't care because he intends to terminate me! I need to deal with this: it's time to buy insurance.*

So on the way back to the hotel, she stopped at a wireless carrier, bought a new smartphone, and activated CALL RECORDING. *He'll think it's a new burner.* Then Izabella spent the afternoon reviewing the file. Later, she called him. When control answered, he asked, "How did your meeting go?"

"Fine—it looks doable. Tomorrow I'll scout the location and see if I spot any problems or need anything. Tell me, how is Medina's investigation going?" Izabella asked.

"I've a source close to the president who reports that Medina has moved to San Francisco; his team consists of his analyst, who remains in Langley, and his girlfriend, an inspecteur in Paris' Sûreté who travels back and forth. They know you're in San Francisco because they accessed the digital records of your visit to San Jose to look at Memorial Auditorium's building plans. Also, they've concluded you'll do it at Ransom's but haven't located you yet. Apparently, the president is getting antsy about that.

"They have a European source who has revealed your connection to Satie and suspects you for his murder. Then there is a local source among the conspirators who is unidentified and passes on information without disclosing the identities of the collaborators. The director of the CIA is working to secure a WITSEC deal for that source. Their plan is to arrest the source's boss and flip him. This change of plans increases our odds of success—you'll see."

"Have they issued a termination order on me yet?"

"Not as far as I know. Is this a new number?"

"Yes."

***

After the call, Izabella packed, leaving out only what she would need for later. If things went as she hoped, tomorrow she would be out of here and at Karen's. Nevertheless, Izabella decided to pay Blake for an additional two weeks—a contingency. *I'll ask him to tell anyone who might inquire about me that I checked out. Karen's guest parking will do for the time being. So I'll hold off renewing the car's parking for now; it's still good through November 8. I'll take care of all this tomorrow. But now I'll take a nap, because I need to be well rested for Karen. She's going to think she died and went to heaven tonight,* Izabella thought, chuckling inaudibly.

Izabella had a light supper in the coffee shop and began getting ready for her date. They had agreed to meet at El Rio at nine o'clock. Izabella took a taxi and intentionally arrived a half hour late. *Karen will be anxious that I'm standing her up. I'm teasing her—she'll be delighted when I finally walk in.*

Karen was noticeably relieved when Paola entered. "I'm glad you're here; I was afraid something happened."

"No . . . just running behind."

They talked, having a pleasant time, Paola touching Karen and holding her hand. *My plan is working,* she surmised. By eleven, Karen was ready and suggested calling it an early night.

"Oh no . . . not yet," Paola begged. *I'll tease her a bit more!* "The band's just getting good. Let's dance. Please?"

"All right," Karen laughed.

Paola kept her on the dance floor as long as possible, dancing sensually during the slow songs, holding Karen close while moving against her. *This is heartless.* At last, Karen faintly entreated, "Paola, we need to leave . . . now . . . please."

"Yes, let's."

In the elevator, Karen could scarcely restrain herself, and then inside the apartment, heading for the bedroom, she began undressing Paola.

"Calm down, silly. We're nearly there—let me help," Paola giggled.

They made love until they fell asleep at sunrise. Paola awoke first, looked at the bedside clock—nearly noon—and went to the bathroom. When she returned, Karen was still sleeping on her back. Slipping into bed, Paola softly loved Karen, who gradually roused, opening her eyes and climaxing. She was bewildered, and seeing Paola, she mumbled, "Was I dreaming?"

"No—just me," Paola laughed.

"Don't leave me," Karen murmured happily as Paola nuzzled her. Over coffee and toast, Karen said, "I meant it. I know your plans are unsettled, but I want you to move in for as long as you can."

Mission accomplished.

Izabella took a cab back to her hotel. She picked up her bags, made her arrangements with Blake, and stopped at a costume shop before returning to Karen's. *Halloween is right around the corner, and no one will give a second thought to purchasing a costume.*

***

In the late afternoon of October 29, Jay answered his phone. It was Anna—no greeting when he picked up. All she said was, "Did you hear?"

"What?"

"You really don't know?" Anna asked.

"No, I don't. What's happened?"

"It happened so fast; it's confusing. I thought it might be you."

"Anna, take a deep breath and tell me."

"Bruce is dead. I was on the phone with him when it happened. There was this terrible noise, and then everything went dead . . . oh God . . . I mean—"

"I know what you mean. When did all this happen?"

"About seven this morning. We're always in early. Bruce stops at a bagel shop on the way in and gets bagels and coffee to go. He always asks me the night before if I want a bagel. Bruce called me this morning because he wasn't in yesterday. He had to fly to San Francisco for a last-minute meeting."

"It's upsetting. Do you have any details?"

"Of course I'm upset. It's a shock. I know what I said before, but that was simply an idea. This is so real-world—so violent. We worked together for a long time, and I was with him three or four times a week. You understand, right?"

"Yes. It's natural that you have feelings . . . no matter what. Give me the details; it'll help calm you down."

"All right. Bruce parked on the other side of the street from the bagel shop and called me. He was run over when he crossed—a hit-and-run accident. The driver didn't stop."

"How did you find out the details?"

"The police stopped by a while ago. They have a couple of witnesses. Apparently, a Hummer ran him over. The witnesses said it was traveling at a high speed—didn't even slow down."

"Did the cops get a plate number or a description of the driver?"

"No."

"Any CCTV in the area?"

"Don't know."

"It doesn't sound like an accident to me."

Anna paused. "I know . . . I thought it was my fault. Are you certain you didn't know about it?"

Anna was crying now, and Jay thought, *So, that's why she's so upset.* "Anna, it wasn't your fault. It may not be an accident, but we knew nothing about it, honest. Give me the address of the bagel shop before you hang up. Do you know anything about the San Francisco meeting?"

"No."

"I'll call you in a few days. I'm sorry."

After they hung up, Jay thought, *No way is this an accident. A heavy, oversized vehicle traveling at high speed. If it's who I think it is, he's tidying up loose ends.*

***

After their last meeting on Friday the twenty-fourth, Mal had spoken with Gabi. "I've been thinking. It seems like José has been stonewalling you and Danny on where Izabella might have gone? It's a tricky situation all around. José must maintain his street creds, and you and Danny can only push so hard without disrupting the CI arrangement."

"You're correct. If José rats out Izabella, he'll lose credibility. And Danny thinks the relationship is too valuable to risk it. I can't disagree with him."

"Well, here's my solution. Why don't I talk to him? I'm not constrained by your rules and regulations. José will have no idea who I am. I'll act like a sinister foreign thug—mysterious and threatening. My accent helps—his imagination will fill in the blanks. What do you think?"

Gabi was quiet for a moment. "No doubt you'd be effective. Look, I'll be honest; I'm concerned about you straying outside of our boundaries. You can't use torture."

"Agreed. At least not physical . . . okay?"

Gabi laughed. "Go ahead—scare the shit out of him."

She gave him José's details. On Monday and Tuesday, using their rental car, Mal surveilled José's Mission District home as well as the Tenderloin bar. Throughout the day he photographed José's two girls on their way to and from school along with his wife doing her shopping. Then in the evening, Mal staked out the bar. It was unmistakably a smoke screen for José's real activities. Mal's plan was simple. The bar usually closed between seven and nine o'clock. After that, José saw his guys off, chatting in front of the bar for a while before he returned inside, locked up, and left by the back door, where his car was parked in the alley. So when José returned inside, Mal would be seated in José's accustomed spot, which Gabi had told him about. But this time it would be Mal's .45 on the table.

On Wednesday evening the twenty-ninth, Mal waited on a side street—down the block—near the alley. About eight fifteen, the men came out. Mal went to the alley, picked the back door's lock, and went in through the storeroom and into the bar. When José came in, Mal had his gun trained on him with a two-handed grip, elbows on the table.

"What the fuck," José snapped, beginning to reach behind his back.

"Don't even think about it," Mal said softly. "Get over here and be quiet."

José didn't move at first.

"Now."

Who the fuck is this prick? José thought, but he reluctantly complied.

As he approached, Mal said, "Before you sit, take your gun out of your waistband with two fingers, put it on the floor, and kick it away."

"Who the hell are you?"

"Don't speak—do it now." After José sat, Mal rested his gun on the table and continued. "Here's how this works. I'm going to show you photos on my phone. Look at them carefully and keep quiet. I'll ask you about the first one, and then you'll tell me everything you know about her. You'll figure out what's going to happen if you don't cooperate or give me bad information."

Mal pulled up Izabella's photo, let José take a thorough look, then slowly scrolled through the remaining ones of José's family. Mal was out of there in fifteen minutes with the information he needed about Izabella.

CHAPTER EIGHTEEN

Thursday, October 30, 2014
San Francisco

At six o'clock Thursday morning, Jay called Nando, who was just rousing and could hear Bridgette in the shower.

"Sorry to wake you so early," Jay apologized.

"It's fine. I was getting up—I'm putting you on speaker," Nando replied as Bridgette came in, wearing only a towel wrapped around her waist and combing out her wet hair. "Bridgette's here too. What's up?"

"I need to fill you in on a new development, and then I want your opinion on something I'd like to bring up at our meeting/conference call this afternoon. It's complicated and vague."

"Are you concerned about selling it to our law enforcement partners?"

"Yes. What I've discovered strays from the science of intelligence gathering into its art form."

"You don't have enough documented or confirmable evidence yet," Nando observed.

"Correct. We live in that world, but I don't know if the others will be comfortable there."

"Jay, this is why you're paid the big bucks," Nando joked. "Go ahead."

"Okay. But first, here's the development. Anna called me yesterday afternoon: Bruce Campbell was killed in a hit-and-run accident yesterday morning, around seven o'clock." Jay filled them in on what Anna had reported.

"Wow, and you assume someone's tidying up?"

"Yes—it looks professional. This afternoon, I'll ask Cancio and Müller to interface with Palo Alto's PD, requesting they share any CCTV pictures unearthed in their investigation. I want to look at it; we're better equipped to analyze it than the locals."

"All right."

"Also, we need to brainstorm how we'll report to the director so that we can take Anna out of the picture. I don't see how we identify the other conspirators now."

"Okay, let's talk about it this afternoon. What else?"

"Now, for my unscientific suppositions. The Chinese guy who's a collaborator has been bothering me. I wondered if I missed something when I concluded he was private sector. One of my buddies runs the China Desk. We used to work on *The World Factbook* together, so I reached out to him. It turns out they've had eyes on a Chinese banker who has been over here for four or five months traveling around the country, visiting China's correspondent banks. Since the financial crisis five years ago, he routinely makes these trips, supposedly shoring up those relationships. His name is Hui Wang."

"Why are we interested?"

"It seems Wang is known to us. He's a longtime friend and ally of the secretary general. They came up through the CCP together. We suspect that, at the least, he passes on any useful information he stumbles across, and at the worst is a deep-cover agent. We're concerned Wang has been wheedling sensitive information from the banks he visits. On a hunch, I had a comparison made of his travels to the meetings Anna has been attending."

"Don't tell me—" Nando interrupted.

"Yup—a direct hit each time. Wang is our guy," Jay said.

"Will your buddy on the China Desk be reporting this discovery up the chain of command?" Nando asked.

"No. He thought I should figure out what's going on first."

"That's unusual, isn't it? Normally, the director would be briefed—correct?" Bridgette said.

"He's an old friend; we'll just leave it at that."

"Anything else?" Nando inquired. "Yes, and even vaguer. I don't have a clue if it's related, yet it jumped out at me. My friend's purview includes the Koreas. Apparently, on October third, the ambassador from South Korea made an unscheduled trip home. He was cloistered with their president over the weekend. Their president doesn't usually become directly involved with ambassadors. Since then my friend has been picking up an unusual amount of chatter surrounding South Korea's consulate in San Francisco."

"And?" Nando asked.

"I'm filing it for future reference. I'm going to talk to Zeb and see if he's picking up anything about the Koreas or China. Maybe I'll have additional information by this afternoon. Could you talk to Joe and see if his guy Danny Wong has contacts inside China's consulate in San Francisco?"

"Fine. I'll call him first thing. Maybe we'll have something this afternoon too."

Nando hung up and reached for Bridgette.

"What?"

"Don't ask 'what' when you're dressed like that."

"Oh, I thought you were too wrapped up in your work to notice," Bridgette joked, tossing her towel aside and coming back to bed.

***

Later that morning, Mal went to the Hotel Royal and spoke with Blake.

"I'm looking for a woman—a missing person. I have reason to believe she might be staying here. Can you help me?" Mal asked.

"Are you a cop?"

"Consultant with SFPD's Serious Crimes Unit—I have their captain's business card. You can call him if you'd like."

"I'm okay, but a missing person doesn't seem like a serious crime," Blake opined.

"It's complicated. She's using the name Paola Conti. I'll show you her photo."

Blake looked and said, "Yeah, she was here. Checked out yesterday."

"What name?"

"I only knew her as Chica."

"No registration?"

"No, it was cash."

"Then I assume she didn't leave a forwarding address?"

"No."

"How about a car?"

"I think so. She asked about a garage," Blake said, pointing through the hotel's front window to the sign at the entranceway of the alley across the street.

"Do you have a plate number?"

"No. Check with the garage."

Undoubtedly a "no-tell hotel." Probably won't have any better luck here, Mal thought as he walked across the street. The garageman recognized Izabella's photo. He told Mal she was paid through November 8—cash in advance. He didn't know the plate number and couldn't recall the car's make, model, and so forth.

"It ain't here now," the attendant offered.

"Any CCTV?" Mal asked before leaving.

"You're kidding," the attendant joked.

Surprise, surprise, thought Mal.

***

Early Friday morning, October 31, the premier of the People's Republic of China waited patiently outside the president's Zhongnanhai office. The premier, known informally as the prime minister, was the second most powerful man in the PRC's government, surpassed only by the president, who was also the general secretary of the Chinese Communist Party. Finally, the premier was escorted into the office. The president arose from his desk, greeting him warmly.

"Mr. Prime Minister, I'm glad you were able to find time for me today. We hardly ever have quiet time anymore."

As they sat, the premier responded, "Yes, we're both busy: the fruits of success. Today is entirely my pleasure, Mr. President. How may I be of service?" The men chatted casually about family, friends, and so on. Then, at the president's suggestion, they moved to an informal seating area, where he began talking about why he had summoned his old friend.

"I know you've been wondering why I've asked you to accompany our trade delegation to San Francisco for a conference on November sixth through tenth, especially since I asked you to keep it between just the two of us."

"Yes, and of course I complied with your request for secrecy, but I am curious. This is outside of my usual purview."

The president chuckled. "Yes, your highest and best talents are not in meeting and greeting. You must have surmised that what I would like you to do while you're in San Francisco is more important. Let me explain."

Although the president's briefing was concise, it took nearly an hour. Finally, he summarized: "There are problems ahead in our relationship with the US that could interfere with our long-term goal of overtaking them militarily and economically as well as becoming the preeminent world power. Their president is in a weakening position. Next week's midterm elections will likely return the Republicans to power in the Senate while holding the House, resulting in a complete legislative impasse. He'll be reduced to using what they call executive orders. Other issues coming into play are his unfavorable poll numbers and the lack of legacy accomplishments. Frankly, since his healthcare initiative has started running into trouble, what's the president left with . . . bin Laden?

"I've concluded that the president will seize on reining us in through his executive orders—items like currency manipulation, trade imbalances, child labor, transfers of intellectual property, greenhouse gases, and so forth. Also, he's looking at domestic matters that will interfere with our trading partners. I can't let him slow us down. I don't want bringing China to heel to be his grand legacy. So I'll sidetrack him for a few years and work towards having the vice president elected in 2016—he is sympathetic to us.

"To that end, for the last several months while formal talks have been proceeding, I've been negotiating secretly with the American president to resolve our difficulties. We have produced a comprehensive, confidential document that will not be released after the conclusion of the Asia-Pacific Economic Cooperation summit. I've worked closely with our international scholars and lawyers along with our chief of the Joint Staff Department of the Central Military Commission. We've crafted a document that will give us all the flexibility we require while apparently giving the Americans a slight advantage. The American president is so eager for this legacy victory that he has indicated he'll accept our final draft.

"That's where I need your help. My stratagem is to have a top secret meeting in San Francisco on the Saturday before he leaves for China. We'll transmit the document the evening before so that he won't have too much time with it. I want you to represent me at that meeting. If the president is still in agreement, it's a no-brainer, as the Americans say, but if there's a problem, I trust you unconditionally to represent our interests and make appropriate changes. After that, you may sign the final document on behalf of China."

"It will be my honor and pleasure to represent you," the premier said. "But isn't there a protocol problem? Is it appropriate for a number two to meet with a number one?"

"Normally, it would be a problem. But I don't want to be there. I need to maintain my flexibility."

"I understand."

"Plus, I have an excellent excuse with hosting this summit. I know he doesn't trust his vice president to represent him. The president isn't comfortable with his secretary of state either, who will already be here and not available for San Francisco. So the American president feels like he needs to do this himself," the president finished.

After the premier left, the president reflected. *If necessary, this will work out well. Ironically, this stratagem has morphed into plan B. If the plot the director of the CIA is managing prevails, it won't be necessary. Sometimes it's better to be lucky than good. When our Ministry of State Security uncovered the assassination conspiracy, it made sense for us to have banker Hui Wang, who was traveling in the US, ingratiate himself to the collaborators. And presenting them with a gift of ten million US dollars was most welcome.* The president chuckled. *No need for my old ally to know.*

***

On Thursday, October 30, at five p.m., everyone was in the suite, and Jay and Zeb were conferenced into the meeting.

Jay went first, updating the group on Anna's call and Bruce Campbell's death. He reported that he was convinced it was a professional hit and the Palo Alto PD was considering it a suspicious one.

Mal interjected, "Someone's cleaning up loose ends."

"Bridgette and I agree," Nando said.

Jay asked Gabi and Joe if they would reach out to the local PD for copies of any CCTV files.

"I'll get on it; I've worked with their captain before," Gabi said.

Jay continued, "I have additional information. I identified the Chinese guy. His name is Hui Wang—he's a banker and longtime ally of the president. My friend on our China Desk has had eyes on him. He's been traveling around the US for months visiting China's correspondent banks. Wang is believed to be at least a low-level spy. We compared his travels with Anna's meetings—he was in the same city where they were held each time."

"Could you get a photo of him from your file or off the internet and send it to Anna? That would give us a first-person ID," Bridgette suggested.

"I'll do that. Also—on a hunch—I asked Zeb if he could survey the airlines for any upcoming flights Wang is making."

Zeb picked up. "The best flights are out of LAX. Earlier today, Wang took a shuttle there. He's booked to Beijing on China Southern tonight, at eleven fifty."

"Sounds like Wang's getting out of Dodge," Joe quipped.

Jay agreed. "I also have information on the South Korean consulate in San Francisco. This is a vague area—I'm not convinced it's related." Jay then reviewed what his China Desk buddy had reported. "He's following it, but nothing has taken shape yet."

Next, Joe interjected, "I turned up something on China today. I'm also not certain how or if it is related. Nando asked me to call Danny Wong to see if he had a CI he could tap about what's happening at the Chinese consulate. Danny called back before I came over. He reports that there is a lot of activity surrounding the arrival of a trade delegation on November fifth. The CI said it is odd for several reasons. First, they are sprucing up the entire consulate like a VIP is arriving. Second, they're readying the suite they have for visiting dignitaries. My source says this suite isn't used for the hoi polloi—top government officials only—and there's extra security being lined up as well. The trade delegation is staying at the Sir Francis Drake. So, who's coming?

"We don't know how all this fits together yet," Jay commented.

"Keep on it, Jay, until it becomes clear," Nando said.

Joe continued, "I also located the caterer who's doing the Ransom dinner. He's putting on extra help—cash off the books. One is Paola Conti. The woman I spoke with identified the photo as Izabella, but she said her hair is longer and auburn now. Notwithstanding that, she is certain of her ID."

Chuckling, Mal said, "With Gabi's approval, I visited José last night. He was cooperative—I don't know why you guys had such trouble."

"Oh, give me strength," Gabi muttered, rolling her eyes.

Mal continued, "Izabella/Paola went to the Hotel Royal. It's a second class no-tell hotel not far from Union Square. She stayed there after leaving the White Swan." Mal updated them on what he had learned from Blake and the garageman. "We're one day behind her now."

"Terrific," Bridgette said. "It sounds like she's becoming proactive. Why don't Mal and Gabi start staking out Ransom's? Eventually, Izabella must show herself if that's the spot."

"Okay," Nando said. "Joe, would you and Bridgette watch Stanford—just in case?"

"Sure."

"What are you going to do, Nando?" Bridgette asked.

"I'll fly to DC. Jay, would you coordinate a briefing with the director and president on the third—only the four of us? I'll be back in Palo Alto well before Friday morning the seventh. Then I'll meet up with Bridgette and Joe there. If nothing is happening, the three of us will head back to Pacific Heights and join up with Gabi and Mal."

"If she shows, do you want her arrested?" Mal asked.

"Yes, unless she attacks; then do what you have to. I'll get revised orders while I'm in DC."

CHAPTER NINETEEN

Friday, October 31, 2014
Parsippany, New Jersey

O n Thursday, October 30, Bermuda had flown out of SFO to Newark, New Jersey's Liberty International Airport. She rented a car, drove to the Sheraton Parsippany Hotel, and checked in. Bermuda frequently used this hotel as a base of operations and kept a self-storage locker in the area for the tools of her trade. Friday morning she called the capo.

"'Morning. I'm back from the West Coast."

"How'd it go?"

"Well, no problems. Do you have any other information on the next assignment?"

"No, only that it'll be around the eighth, in Saint Martin."

"All right, I'm gonna hang here, stay flexible. I'll probably go to the city a few times and maybe to Long Island. I have family there."

"Okay."

"Find something out for me. I've heard that Russia's Federal Security Service, the FSB, has a monopoly on a new top secret poison they've developed. They're not even sharing it with their military or other security services; it's supposedly painless, untraceable, and acts instantly. Have you heard anything?"

"No, it's the first I'm hearing of it. Do you want some?"

"Yeah, for this next assignment."

"All right, I'll ask around. We got connections with Bratva—that's the Russian mob. They hang in Brooklyn at Brighton Beach."

"Cool."

***

It was Friday night, and Izabella sat quietly alongside Karen, holding her lifeless hand. They had gone to dinner earlier, and afterward, Paola wanted to drive to Point Lobos, near the Cliff House, to see Seal Rock. But when they left the restaurant, Paola staggered a couple of times.

"Are you okay to drive, Paola?" Karen asked.

"I don't know . . . I only had two glasses of wine . . . they must've hit me."

"Here, give me your keys—I'll drive."

They parked apart from other cars. It was romantic with the waxing gibbous moon illuminating the surf crashing against the rocks. They started kissing, and after a while, using a small syringe, Paola injected Karen in her neck. Then, only a tiny gasp . . . nothing more and Karen was dead. Seat-belted in place, with her eyes open and lips parted,

Seal Rock

Karen didn't even look startled.

Paola caressed Karen's cheek and looked at her watch—eleven forty-five. If she wanted to make the twelve twenty-five number 38 bus, she had to get moving. After switching phones, Izabella took Karen's purse and left the car. Checking that no one was around, she popped the trunk and took out a five-gallon can of gas that she'd bought earlier. Next, she soaked Karen and splashed the rest of the accelerant over the front seat. Izabella tossed the empty can on the floor and dropped a lit match in Karen's lap. She waited until the fire was underway. Following that, Izabella walked less than a mile to Geary Boulevard and Forty-Eighth Street, where she waited a few minutes for the bus to the Union Square area to arrive.

Riding back to the square, Izabella realized how nervous she'd been about using the new, cutting-edge poison she'd bought in Berlin. It was purported to be so lethal that even a drop in an open cut was instantaneously fatal. But it was worth it, because the poison was undetectable with ordinary toxicological analysis and broke down within twenty-four hours. *Perfect.*

Izabella wasn't normally inclined to reflecting, but sitting on the bus, she mused over Karen's death. *Karen was so happy after dinner, chatting about what we could do on her vacation.* Then Izabella sighed silently. *I'm glad you never realized what was happening . . . rest in peace, my sleeping beauty. So now I have a safe place and a different car. I must put Karen behind me.*

***

On Saturday, November 1, Izabella scouted the corner of Clay and Laurel Streets, where the South Korean consulate was located. The front entrance was on Clay, with a built-in garage on Laurel. She was particularly interested in a five story prewar condo building on the opposite corner at

250 Laurel. It had twenty-four windows on the Laurel facade that had unobstructed views. The corner units on the third through fifth floors looked the best. It was a clear shot from any of those windows, and shooting from there ought not require any adjustments to her sights for either angle or distance. Also, it was a lot of windows for security to keep track of. Then Izabella walked left on Clay Street to the rear of the condo. A parking area, unloading zone, and rear entrance were located there. She watched for a while; it seemed like the residents frequently used this entrance. Izabella would be back before putting together her final plan.

So on Sunday afternoon, it was time to deal with her rifle, silencer, and scope. She took Karen's Mercedes, drove to her locker, and picked up what she needed. Following that, Izabella was off to an outdoor shooting range/gun club that was about fifty miles away, in Sonoma County. The club had shooting stations for various distances, and Izabella chose one for a hundred yards. She fired several shots to sight the rifle. Then she set a new target at thirty-five yards and took three more shots. When Izabella collected it, there was a hole the size of a quarter a tad above dead center. *No adjustments needed.*

Izabella drove back to Karen's apartment and napped. Later, she called a taxi to take her to a café at the corner of Grant Avenue and Bush Street. She had a light dinner and turned in early. *A fine day*, Izabella thought, and fell asleep.

***

Nando's United flight arrived at Dulles International Airport at four fifteen Sunday afternoon. He took a cab and before six o'clock was at Jay's house, where he was spending the night. Jay had schedule the briefing with the director and the president for ten o'clock the next morning. After Nando dropped his gear, he and Jay had a beer in the den, and Jay spoke up. "I received a call from Joe Cancio while you were en route. Quite a development. Apparently, Izabella was murdered around midnight on Saturday morning."

"No shit. What happened?"

"She was burned to death in her rental car out at Point Lobos, near the Cliff House. According to Joe, there was nothing left of her remains except for badly burned bones."

"How did they conclude it was Izabella?"

"By the license plate and a first impression from the ME. The fire marshal called in the arson unit. Eventually they checked for APBs and picked up the one Gabi initiated. That was Saturday afternoon. The remains arrived at the medical examiner's lab that evening. She took a quick look this morning but won't be able to work on the autopsy—such as it is—until tomorrow. She reports height five foot nine, estimated age thirty to forty, and probable weight one twenty-five pounds. There's nothing else until they do a DNA analysis of the bones. That's why I say 'apparently.' The medical examiner will send a sample to Quantico. We don't know how long it will take—the FBI is always backed up."

"Do we have her DNA for comparison?"

"Mal says Mossad will have it; it's standard procedure. We need to disclose all this but must craft a plausible story line on how we acquired the plate number, DNA, and so forth. I don't think we should blow Mal, Joe, and Gabi's involvement yet," Jay opined.

"Agreed. We need to think about how we present everything."

"But not until after dinner," Jay's wife quipped, poking her head into the den.

***

The next morning when they assembled, the president said, "The director tells me you're making good progress. I'm glad, because we're nearly out of time. I need to make decisions."

"Yes, Mr. President," Nando said, and continued, "Jay, why don't you go first and update us on your source and Bruce Campbell?"

"Who's Bruce Campbell?" the president asked.

"He was the head of the conspirators. The one we had hoped to flip. My source has finally identified herself. She's my cousin, Anna, who worked for him; he was the CEO of Orwell MegaData."

"*Was*?" the president asked.

"Yes, Campbell was killed by a hit-and-run driver in Palo Alto on October twenty-ninth. Anna called me about it."

"An accident?" the president said.

"The Palo Alto PD considers it a suspicious death," Jay answered.

"Probably cleaning up loose ends," the director remarked.

"Well, at least we won't have to put your cousin in WITSEC. But it shuts down identifying the others."

"Not entirely, Mr. President. I'm confirming the identity of one of the other conspirators, the Chinese man Anna saw. In coordination with our China Desk, we believe he's banker Hui Wang. For verification, I'm sending a photo to my cousin," Jay continued.

"The private sector, then," the president said.

"Not necessarily," Jay replied. "The China Desk has had eyes on him for several years. They are suspicious Wang may be an asset of the

Ministry of State Security. In any event, he left for Beijing on October thirtieth."

"Mr. President, let me review our progress tracking Izabella," Nando said, but in accordance with their plan, he didn't disclose Mal, Gabi, and Joe's involvement.

"So Izabella is changing hotels and cars," the president observed.

"Yes—but it seems to be a dead end for the time being. So I moved on to checking caterers, party equipment suppliers, and so forth. I found Bay City Banquets. They're handling the catering for the Ransom affair," Nando answered.

"Well, at least we know where she'll be."

"I think Jay and Nando have done a great job," the director interjected. "But it's time to change strategy. I want you guys to keep trying to find her, yet if you can't by tomorrow afternoon, it's time to bring in the Secret Service. We need to beef up security. We can't risk her slipping into the affair and disappearing in that huge house—just too dangerous."

"Agreed," the president said.

"Also," the director added, "I can give you additional help. Church Gagne is en route from Venezuela. He's been down there trying to appraise Maduro's mess. The dictator doesn't seem to have a clue how to straighten it out. Church is making good inroads with Maduro's opposition. We're bringing him back for a quick debrief. He'll be here this afternoon, and I can temporarily deploy him to San Francisco afterwards. The two of you could fly back tomorrow first thing. I'll arrange a CIA jet."

"I'd appreciate it, but we need to report on new information Jay and I learned last night." Nando updated them on the apparent murder of Izabella. "The problem is we may not have the DNA back from Quantico soon enough to stand down."

"Do we even have her DNA?" the director asked.

"I have it covered. Bridgette's reaching out to her Mossad contact. It's their standard procedure to keep DNA samples of their agents. She's certain they'll cooperate off the record."

"Jesus Christ," the president said. "That would be a game changer."

"I have a question, Mr. President," Nando said. "In the event she's still alive and we spot her, what are your instructions?"

The president didn't hesitate. "Bring her in if you can; otherwise, terminate her."

"I know the head of the FBI's forensics lab. I'll call and kick him in the ass," the director said as they parted. "Maybe we can resolve this quickly."

In the rear seat of his car, returning to Langley, the director thought, *I'm sure as shit glad she tipped me off on Saturday about any reports of her death being incorrect. Jesus, she's merciless. Nice move, though. Now she has an untraceable hideout, a new identity, and a different car. I'll call the FBI but not to kick ass. I don't want them discovering Izabella's victim's identity too soon.*

***

After he returned to his office, the director called the head of the FBI's forensics lab on the man's private mobile. At best they had a quarrelsome relationship—too many banged heads over demands for prompt lab results.

"Doctor, I need your help."

"We haven't talked in a while. What is it?"

"Assistance with a request for a DNA analysis from the San Francisco medical examiner's office. You'll be receiving it tomorrow or Wednesday."

"We're up to our asses in alligators right now," he snapped in response.

"Christ, you didn't even give me a chance to explain. Look, this is a little different. The sample is a badly burned bone. I would appreciate it if you would not rush the analysis—make certain it is correct. Sometime next week will be fine."

"Well, DNA isn't always retrievable from burned bones—it depends on the degree of degradation. And if it's retrievable, it takes time. So your analysis might take that long anyway."

"That isn't good enough."

"What . . . do I understand you correctly?"

"Yes."

"Really. Slow-walk it. Is that what you're asking?"

"Yes. We understand each other now."

"It isn't ethical, to say the least."

"Agreed, but I'm positive you'll want to cooperate anyway."

"Why the hell would I?"

"I'll tell you what; I'm going to text you a video. It is over an hour long, but you'll understand if you scroll through it for about fifteen minutes. Call me back at this number—it's a burner."

The doctor received the video and in a short time exclaimed, "Oh shit." It was of Luli Tang, his former mistress, with him in a hotel room. He didn't recognize which one—there had been many. Luli had been a consultant attached to a Chinese cultural NGO. They'd been together for nearly a year. That was five years ago, before she returned to mainland China. As much as he missed her, he was glad it was over. The stress of keeping such a long-running affair from his wife had been terrible. He loved his wife and kids and hadn't been looking for a change, but then he'd stumbled—one night in bed with Luli had overwhelmed him. He'd never experienced a woman like her; he couldn't stop himself. Although he'd been amazed at how talented Luli was for her young age, it had never occurred to him until this moment that she might have been professionally trained. Perhaps Luli hadn't worked for an NGO after all. *Why else would she have been on the director's radar? Shit!*

As the director answered his burner, he thought, *Message received—not even ten minutes.* "Doctor, did the file come through okay?"

"You son of a bitch."

"Be civil—it isn't personal. You were with the wrong broad at the wrong time."

"What do you want?"

"I told you."

"That's all?"

"Yes."

"And I'll get the video back?"

"No, it's a digital world. It's probably out there in the ether along with five others of Luli and you."

"Maybe. I'll tell my wife. We might be able to work our way through this. At least I won't be under your thumb then."

"Your wife is the least of your worries."

"What do you mean?"

"Luli was deep-cover: MSS."

"Ministry of State Security?"

"Yes, but don't blow this out of proportion. I've had this for five years, and this is my first ask. I'm not out to ruin your life. Just cooperate with me when I need it. Call my regular number with the results before they're sent to San Francisco. By the way, she was gorgeous."

Next, the director called Izabella. "They've provisionally taken your bait—the license plate and body type."

"That was the plan," Izabella responded. "I assumed they would eventually pick up the name I was using along with my plate number."

"They're sending a bone to Quantico for DNA analysis. It'll be there tomorrow or Wednesday. Whether the FBI is successful depends on the sample's DNA's degree of degradation. In any event, the FBI is slow-walking it for me—it'll take at least until next week. Is your DNA on file?"

"Yes, with Mossad. This will only slow them down. I know I'm just buying time. I don't have a clue if Karen's DNA is on file either."

"It doesn't matter. I assume you'll be out of the country by then."

"Yes," Izabella said, thinking, *He'd shit if he knew I've been recording his calls.*

CHAPTER TWENTY

Monday, November 3, 2014
Washington, DC

A t eleven thirty in the morning, the president's secretary rang the Oval Office.

"Mr. President, the director of the White House Military Office is here."

"Thank you. Send him in," the president replied, standing up from his desk to greet his invitee. After they were seated, the president said, "I need to change the departure of Air Force One on Saturday, November eighth."

"That's no problem, Mr. President," the director said, thinking, *Odd. Why is he making this change himself? It's clearly below his pay grade.* "What is the change you'd like?"

"It's scheduled for eleven a.m., correct?"

"Yes, sir."

"All right, please change it to twelve thirty p.m. and adjust Marine One accordingly."

"Certainly. Does the itinerary remain the same?"

"Yes. But there's something else," the president said, as he escorted the director to the door. "This is top secret. Please make the changes yourself and don't tell anyone about them."

***

Late in the afternoon, the president called the CIA director. "I've been thinking about our meeting this morning. I agree it's time to bring in the Secret Service, but it's also time to read in the director of National Intelligence. My secretary will schedule a meeting with you, the directors of the Secret Service and National Intelligence, and me."

"I agree completely, Mr. President." *Shit!*

***

Later, Nando and Jay waited for Church. He finished his debrief and came to their area about six thirty. Nando introduced Jay, and they all rode with him to his house. Church was spending the night there in the second guest room. On the drive, Jay said, "After dinner, I thought Nando could bring you up to speed on Mal. He's been a big help. Then we can watch the Colts and the Giants on *Monday Night Football.*"

"Sounds fine; I don't know Mal."

"Actually, you've seen him," Nando said.

Church thought for a minute. "At your funeral? The cleric?"

"Yes."

"I wondered about him. Can't wait to hear."

When dinner was over and Nando had completed his update on Mal, Church observed, "It seems like he and his guy Zeb are a big help. Zeb is filling a gap if you want to stick to the rules about hacking. How's

Bridgette dealing with the Luca Ricci situation? It must've been tough duty for her."

"Bridgette took it hard. It's not her world, and she made her feelings known to Mal."

"Do they get along?"

"It's an odd relationship, but they seem to like and respect each other. Yet Bridgette doesn't take any shit from him. She's been known to rip him a new one." Nando laughed.

"What about his relationship with Madame? She's a lovely woman, and I'd hate to see her hurt."

"Bridgette feels the same way . . . she's protective. I haven't talked to Madame about it because I'd already left for the States when it developed. Madame is a savvy lady; her eyes are wide open. Mal has made no secret about his loyalties being with his wife and family. I think Madame just decided to go with it, accepting whatever pain might come along."

"So we trust Mal?"

"Yes, as long has our objectives don't conflict with Israel's," Jay said.

"Fair enough," Church concluded.

"I'll brief you about everything else on the flight tomorrow. How was Venezuela?" Nando asked.

"Frankly, it's all fucked up. Maduro controls the military and has created a KGB-style secret police, both of whom effectively suppress the opposition. Inflation is out of control. He also relies more and more on Russia. I don't see how we straighten it out unless we take direct action."

"And I assume if we do that, it may well draw in the Russians," Jay observed.

"Yeah—but don't worry. This administration doesn't have the stomach for confrontation."

Church was sound asleep in his chair well before the Colts beat the Giants 40–24, and their flight out of Joint Base Andrews left the next morning at seven thirty. During the flight, Nando called John at the Kensington Park and arranged a rollaway bed for Church in Mal's room.

***

The president met with the directors at eight o'clock on the morning of the fourth. The director of National Intelligence had a conniption when he learned that an assassination attempt was possible and that he was just now finding out about it. Not known for his reticence, he vented his frustration.

"Jesus Christ, Mr. President, why the hell wasn't I informed? No offense to the CIA, but isn't this in the Secret Service or the FBI's purview? Were gonna have to really fuckin' scramble to coordinate a sufficient response. Goddammit, it's the fourth, and this shit could go down on the seventh!"

"Don't be offended, Director. The assassin is a foreign mercenary, there're other black-ops players as well, China is involved, and much of the intelligence came from overseas. I made the call that the CIA was the proper agency to run with this. Plus, using only one agency controls the possibility of leaks—that's paramount. But it's becoming an all-hands-on-deck situation now. We need your expertise—that's why you're here."

"I'm sorry if I overreacted. Look, here's what we have to do . . ."

The president suppressed a smile, thinking, *He's taking control— no surprise there. It's time for a change, but the CIA won't be happy.*

An hour later, the president had approved a plan:

- The president would not change his schedule.

- The director of National Intelligence would be in charge, and immediately:

  o confirm preparations with SFPD for traffic control, the motorcade's escort, and placing metal detectors at both venues' entrances, and

  o coordinate a thorough review by all intelligence agencies for any new data.

- The CIA officers in San Francisco would continue trying to preemptively apprehend or terminate the assassin.

- A Secret Service Counter Assault Team (CAT), including three snipers, would be deployed.

- At the entrances of Memorial Auditorium and Ransom's mansion, CCTV would be set up to stream photos of the arriving guests to the National Security Agency for facial recognition scanning.

- Air Force One would be activated as a command center, linked to the White House's situation room and the director of the CIA's office.

- Mobile command vehicles would be dispatched to both locations.

- The directors of National Intelligence and the Secret Service would accompany the president on Air Force One, and the director of the CIA would coordinate activities from Washington, DC.

As they were leaving, the director of the CIA said, "Mr. President, I'll let Nando's team know of the changes." But riding back to Langley, the director brooded and bristled. *What the fuck! Didn't see any of this coming. And the director of National Intelligence has usurped my power, thanks to the president—the prick. I gotta watch the director of the Secret Service too. Shit, how the hell am I gonna rein them in?*

***

On Tuesday morning the fourth, Izabella called Elsa, reaching her at five thirty that afternoon.

"Oh, Katja, I'm happy you called. It's been awfully long. Is everything okay?"

"Yes, fine . . . just busy. Where are you? I hear street sounds."

"Unter den Linden—I was shopping. Just heading home."

"Did you find anything?"

"Yes, a cute outfit; you'll like it. When are you returning to Berlin?"

"That's what I want to talk to you about. I'll be done here Saturday afternoon the eighth."

"Where's *here*?"

"America, the West Coast."

"Oh, I thought you were in Canada."

"I was . . . not important. I'm heading to Saint Martin. I should be in Grand Case by late afternoon on Sunday. I'll take a red-eye Saturday night to JFK and then to Saint Martin first thing the next morning. Can you come and stay with me?"

"It would be fun, but I need to be back for a show on the twenty-first."

"Fine, but I'm most likely staying in Grand Case for a long while, maybe permanently. I'm probably retiring."

Elsa paused. "Did I do anything? You didn't find someone else, did you? Are you letting me down easily? I couldn't stand . . . *sympathy* sex!"

"What's the matter? You're upset. Why?"

"You are away so much—nearly six weeks now. And you've only called once."

"Well, you didn't call either."

"I thought you were avoiding me . . . so I didn't want to find out."

"Oh, no. I just need to make a few changes. That's why I'm moving—nothing to do with you. Elsa, don't worry about it. I don't want anyone else. Think about moving to Saint Martin and living with me; we'll talk about everything in Grand Case."

"That makes me feel better. Okay, we'll talk about it then. Change is good."

"All right. In case you arrive before me, bring a spare key. It's in my dresser drawer—the one I keep my bras and panties in."

Elsa giggled. "The one with the Hitachi?"

"Yes . . . why don't you bring it along as well."

"Okay, can't wait to see you. I'll call if I have trouble arranging flights. Love you."

"Me too."

***

On the afternoon of November 4, Bermuda was shopping at FAO Schwarz in Rockefeller Center. She was looking forward to spending Christmas at her brother's in Charleston and was picking out toys for her niece and nephew—it was fun. One of her burner phones rang; it was the capo.

"I tracked down that poison," he said. "What a friggin' pain in my ass. No one was saying shit—yet it exists."

"Great. Were you able to score any?"

"Yeah . . . tomorrow. It'll be delivered to your hotel in the evening. A small amount of the shit disappeared from the FSB's HQ in Moscow; it made its way to Berlin and Brighton Beach. The FSB is trying to track it down—this stuff is like gold."

"Well, if it's too costly, I'll pass. I'm not willing to go into the red on this job."

"No worries, my guy owes me big-time—he'll work something out. He tells me it's dangerous as all hell: painless, colorless, tasteless, and odorless. It acts like a heart attack. It's so fuckin' deadly that even a drop in a cut and you're done for it. They call this shit *spyashchaya krasavitsa*, sleeping beauty. Be careful."

"Thanks. I'll head to Saint Martin on the sixth, so I'll be in place."

"That works. I'll let my client know you're heading south and call you when he gives me the go-ahead."

***

In the early afternoon on the fourth, Bridgette, Nando, Church, Mal, Gabi, and Joe met at the hotel; Jay, Zeb, and Ellen Sandler were conferenced in. Nando spoke first.

"There isn't much time left. We have new information, so let's synthesize it with what we know and make a final call on what's happening. Then we need to plan. But first, I asked Ellen to join us and share her final profile of Izabella. Why don't you start, Doctor?"

"Thanks," Ellen said. "Izabella's an interesting subject. Most of you have already heard some of this, but I'll review for the others. She also has unusual characteristics that are emerging now.

"I continue to agree with Mal that she's a most dangerous person—don't underestimate her. Here's what we're dealing with. Izabella is a high-functioning sociopath. There are numerous personality traits, but high-functioning sociopaths don't necessarily exhibit all of them. Typically they have extremely high IQs and hardly any conscience. They know right from wrong but don't care. They can be charming, clever, and their actions may seem genuine and sincere although they lack empathy. Other common personality characteristics are narcissism, manipulation, insensitivity, lying, sexual deviation, quick tempers, and cruel/violent behavior.

"So what drives them? Repressed rage, anger, and hatred. For example, childhood sexual, physical, and emotional abuse are common. But whatever the drivers are, they're always there, subconsciously stoking the sociopath's rage. They live their lives normally until pressure builds up to an intolerable level, and then a psychotic break occurs. Stressors create that pressure and can be one traumatic event or a series of smaller ones, building cumulatively over as short a period as three to six months. Think of a pressure cooker exploding. The stressors are the same as for the general population: death of a loved one, spousal infidelity, foreclosure, bankruptcy, loss of a job, and so on. When such a break with reality occurs, a high-functioning sociopath becomes dangerous—torture and murder are possible.

"I would feel much better about opining if I had talked to Izabella or witnessed an interview, but here goes. The Holocaust seems to be at the root—that's an atypical driver. It's sketchy, but she was born of Jewish parents in Italy. There's a note in her file that some of her relatives perished in Dachau. Then Izabella immigrates to Israel when she's five. Now she lives in a country where the effects of the Holocaust are still prevalent. She can't get away from it. Why Izabella feels so strongly, who knows, but there are probably things we don't know about. I think she has become obsessed. Also, Izabella uses fire, which has been long associated with the Holocaust and is becoming increasingly linked to sociopathic behavior. I wonder if she has ever gone to Dachau—perhaps when she visited Satie.

"Here's another unique characteristic. Ironically, her career choice seems to have kept the Holocaust stressor at bay, preventing a psychotic break. Her assassinations are a pressure valve. One of the reasons Izabella is so dangerous is because she's never out of control; she doesn't make mistakes. Since she started freelancing, I think it has become a game of chess with her pursuers—Izabella loves matching wits.

"Her number of kills is top secret, but if I knew how many there were during the ten years since she joined the Kidon Unit, it might support my thesis. I'm thinking between thirty and forty would be likely. Can you confirm it, Mal?"

Mal didn't respond at first, but finally he said, "Between us, that number fits, plus or minus a few—we don't have accurate information on all her freelancing."

"I'm curious," Dr. Sandler continued. "Did you test her before deploying her to the Kidon Unit?"

Again, Mal hesitated. "Let's say we weren't surprised at how well Izabella performed."

"I have a question," Bridgette said. "We know that Izabella kills without hesitancy, but is she indiscriminate?"

Ellen thought for a moment. "Without more information, it's hard to say. But I don't see evidence of psychotic breaks. She's too controlled, but that's not to say there couldn't be collateral damage. I think she would kill in situations where she was threatened, cornered, scared, and the like, but it wouldn't be personal."

"Revenge?" Bridgette probed.

"That's a tricky one. I think Satie was for protection; he simply knew too much about her. Remember, if she pulls this off, every major intelligence agency will be after her, either to help the US or to acquire a bargaining chip. She'll need to go to ground for a long time. The woman at Point Lobos—protection again—it was part of a plan to acquire a secure hiding place, a new car, and to fake her death. Pedro's the oddball. I don't see a psychotic break, though. She's still under control. In fact, her attack is precise, but I have no doubt it was personal. I would love more details about what brought it on.

"I'm not certain any of this is helpful. After all, you know who you're looking for, where Izabella is, what she's going to do, and when. I'll be in the office if you need me again," Ellen concluded.

"Ellen's the best—she is rarely wrong," Joe said. "I've new information that might be helpful in sorting this out. Danny stopped by my office after lunch today. The Chinese consulate continues to spruce up in anticipation of the trade delegation that is scheduled to arrive tomorrow afternoon. His CI is convinced a bigwig is coming. Danny's source is responsible for the consulate's vehicles—he keeps then washed, polished, and fueled as well as scheduling routine maintenance. He told Danny that he was instructed to make certain the two newest SUVs were fueled and in tip-top shape by eight o'clock Saturday morning. It becomes more interesting, though. The consulate's security guys hang out, smoking and bullshitting, in the garage where the CI works, and they don't give him a second thought. He overheard that those two cars are making a trip to Clay and Laurel Streets for a nine o'clock meeting on Saturday morning. Security will be minimal; only a few of the best guys are going."

"Do we have any idea who this bigwig is?" Bridgette asked.

"There are no official visits from China scheduled other than the trade delegation, yet that shouldn't cause all this fuss," Jay said. "So whoever it is must be high up, but it wouldn't be the president. He's tied up with preparations for the Asia-Pacific Economic Cooperation summit, and the president would never be able to sneak in. He's too recognizable. Moreover, it is too much of a security risk, but it could be his number two, the premier."

"I picked up on your comments about the South Korean ambassador after our last meeting, Jay," Zeb said. "Clay and Laurel Streets is where their San Francisco consulate is located. Then we have an asset in South Korea's National Assembly building in Seoul. I snooped about their US ambassador's visit home on October third. It's vague and hush-hush, but the rumors in Korea are that the San Francisco consulate is hosting a top secret meeting at the request of the US government. Apparently, the South Korean president is pissed because they weren't invited to the meeting. Nevertheless, they're cooperating. I can't find out anything else."

"Jay, I buy your conjecture that it is the premier," Nando responded. "The president would normally only meet with his counterpart, but I could see him agreeing to meet with a number two if it were important and the Chinese president were unavailable.

"I see a scenario that makes sense. On the morning of Saturday the eighth, we have our president, a high-ranking Chinese official, and a secret meeting site all within two miles of each other; they must be meeting. I also suspect if the Chinese are only bringing minimum security, we will be doing the same."

What the hell are they up to? Mal wondered.

"We need to survey that location and assess its feasibility for an assassination. If it's doable, I'll bet Ransom's is a subterfuge now, even if it didn't start out that way," Bridgette said.

"While you were talking, I reviewed the president's schedule," Jay continued. "As I expected, the meeting isn't listed. But I checked Air Force One's departure time on Saturday morning. Originally, it was scheduled for eleven o'clock, but yesterday the director of the White House's Military Office changed it to twelve thirty in the afternoon. I agree with your conclusion—the president is meeting there with this Chinese muckety-muck."

"Doesn't this confirm the CIA director's complicity? He must be aware of the meeting, yet he hasn't told us about it. Why? Because he wants us squandering our time on Ransom's?" Gabi observed.

"It makes sense," Mal added. "And you can bet that Izabella knows all about it; we have to assume so. Also, Nando, when you met with the president, did he give you final orders on Izabella's disposition?"

"Yes—bring her in if we can; otherwise, terminate her. I'm glad you brought it up. For planning purposes, let's assume termination is the most likely scenario. Church and I report to the president and we've received a direct order. Mal has his own orders. It makes sense to keep our law enforcement members deployed elsewhere so they aren't there if a termination goes down. I don't want to put you in a difficult position," Nando said, looking a Joe.

"Thanks," Joe responded.

"Okay," Nando continued. "We have two possibilities to cover. First, Izabella shows at Ransom's either on Thursday or Friday and tries to enter with the catering crew or others. This will be before the president arrives, and I think it's unlikely now."

"I'm betting the consulate is where Izabella will go," Bridgette said.

"Me too," Nando agreed. "But we need to cover both contingencies. So let's do this: Joe, Gabi, and Bridgette, you handle surveillance of Ransom's on those days. If Izabella enters, let Jay know. He'll notify the director of the Secret Service immediately. Then identify yourselves to the on-site officers. They'll lock down the mansion and do a person-by-person search. They ought to pick her up. If it becomes confrontational, at least the president won't be there.

"Next, Mal, Church, and I ought to scout the consulate first thing tomorrow. I also think we can't withhold what we've learned anymore; it's above our pay grade now. But I'm not sure to whom we should talk yet."

"Let's sleep on it, do the recognizance, and decide then," Mal suggested.

CHAPTER TWENTY-ONE

Wednesday, November 5, 2014

San Francisco

The first thing Wednesday morning, Nando, Church, and Mal surveyed and photographed the South Korean consulate and environs. After Nando had spent an hour walking the area, they sat in the car, talking.

"So?" Mal asked, looking at him.

"There's no CCTV to interfere. It's a suitable site for a hit if he travels with minimal security. Normally, the Secret Service would undertake set procedures for scheduled visits, such as reconnoitering the area the day before, leaving officers on site afterwards, sweeping the area again the next morning, and so on. But we know the Chinese aren't bringing much security. The distrust between these two nations is so great that a show of force on our part might spook the Chinese and break up the meeting before it starts. So I assume our security will be reduced to match theirs."

"How would you do it?" Church asked.

"Notwithstanding the limited security, I wouldn't do it from a rooftop, because it's too exposed. I would use the building across the street at the northeast corner of Laurel. I'd shoot from a window after the president exits his car and moves along the walkway towards the front door. But there's a problem. If the president enters through the consulate's built-in garage, it would stymie the shooter's plan. The assassin must neutralize that possibility."

"If Izabella is thinking along with you, it would be tantamount to a home invasion," Mal observed.

"Yes, that's the tricky part, but it's possible."

"So it's time to call in the cavalry. We don't have the manpower to cover this," Mal said.

Nando nodded, and Church added, "Let's fill Jay in and text him these photos."

As they headed back to the hotel for lunch, Nando said, "I'm still uncertain about whom to call, but whoever it is, they need to be alerted to the built-in garage. It's the solution."

***

After lunch, Izabella continued her assessment of Clay and Laurel Streets. First, she confirmed the sight lines and distances she had observed before. She looked for CCTV, discovering there wasn't anything that would cause a problem because the consulate's cameras covered only its front entrance and the built-in garage's doors. Then Izabella focused on the roofs. The building on the southwest corner wasn't conducive for sniping. But the consulate's and southeast corner's roofs were flat, and Secret Service snipers could set up on either of them. *A potential problem.* She continued scrutinizing the consulate. On the Laurel Street side but at a lower level because of the street's slope, there was an oversized, built-in two-car garage. *Another problem if it's open and the president's vehicle pulls straight in*, Izabella thought. But at the intersection—parallel to Laurel Street—was a walkway entrance, flanked with a thigh-high brick wall. It ran right up to the front door. *That's the spot if I can solve the problems of the rooftop snipers and the garage.*

Next, Izabella had to obtain the building's layout. There were six floors, including the lower level. Izabella went to the front entranceway and up the four steps to the lobby. In the middle of the rear wall were three elevators. All needed a keypad security code to call a car. To the right of the elevators was a door marked STAIRS. Also on the right-hand side of the lobby was a corridor leading to meeting rooms and a fire exit. The left-hand wall had two doors: one was probably to the manager's apartment, and the other was designated OFFICE. Izabella tapped on this door and entered when the manager called out, "Come on in."

"Hi, I'm Thérèse. I'd like information about the condos. Can you help me?"

"Well, nothing's for sale now, but I'll help you if I can. I'm Ricki Cruz."

"Do you handle any of the sales here?"

"No, we have arrangements with a local broker. I can give you their card."

Izabella flirted and chatted Ricki up. She learned much of what she needed to know. There were eight residential units, two to a floor. The B lettered apartments were further from the intersection—quieter—and usually more expensive. CCTV was going in next year. There was a lower-level parking garage for owners at the northwest corner of the building. There wasn't much turnover, yada, yada, yada.

At last, Ricki said, "The only unit that might be coming up for sale is the Rosens'—3A. They're elderly, eightyish, and he has a bad limp, uses a cane. I think they may move to a continuing-care retirement community. Check in with the broker periodically."

"I will, thanks." Izabella returned to her car and mapped out her scenario:

Finally, she tackled how to gain entry. Izabella drove the Mercedes along Clay Street; there was a street-level side door at the building's southeast corner—the fire exit. Then she pulled into one of the eight guest parking spots behind the condo. The rear doorway was at street level also. Izabella watched for several hours, observing residents returning; they seemed to use the rear entrance when they were going out again. She focused on the elevators' keypads through high-powered field glasses until she learned what she needed to know—the security code, 250. But Izabella kept watching. At last an elderly couple fitting Ricki's description of the Rosens returned, in a late-model black Lexus 350. It had to be them—he limped badly and used a cane. Afterward, Izabella headed back to Karen's apartment. Later, she called control and again recorded their conversation. "I've checked everything out. I know how I'll do it, but I have a few problems."

"What are they?"

"First, there're flat roofs at the intersection of Clay and Laurel Streets. If the Secret Service has snipers stationed on them, I can't do this without turning it into a suicide mission."

"Not to worry—no snipers. The president's entourage is in two cars: him, two drivers, one body guard, and a translator. Next."

"The consulate's built-in garage on Laurel Street could be a problem. If it's open, the president's car can pull in. A shot wouldn't be possible once he's inside."

"I'll arrange for last-minute roadwork right there. They won't be

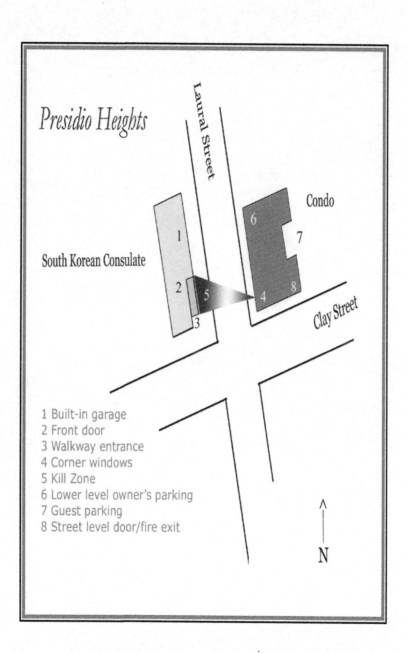

Presidio Heights

Laural Street

Condo

South Korean Consulate

Clay Street

1 Built-in garage
2 Front door
3 Walkway entrance
4 Corner windows
5 Kill Zone
6 Lower level owner's parking
7 Guest parking
8 Street level door/fire exit

N

able to use the garage. Anything else?"

"Do they know I'm aware of the meeting?"

"No. Less than five people know besides the president and me. The intelligence chatter has died down—and it never indicated where, just when."

"Okay, then it's a go," Izabella said, thinking, *Well, that doesn't leave any doubt about who you are!*

"Good luck," control said, and hung up.

After their call ended, Izabella transferred the recordings of the director's calls to a thumb drive and switched to a new phone.

***

In Beijing Thursday morning, November 6, at nine o'clock, the chief of staff called the president. "The election results are in from the US."

"Were we correct?"

"Yes, the Republicans held the House and took back the Senate. It's the biggest congressional majority for them since the Depression."

"Excellent. This is playing out as expected. The American president can't be happy, but frankly, I think he anticipated this. And about the trade delegation to San Francisco?"

"They landed three hours ago, sir."

"Thank you for calling."

"You're welcome. Have a good day."

"Yes, I will."

***

Thursday morning the sixth, Bermuda was up at four o'clock to prepare for her eight o'clock flight from Newark to Saint Martin. As she finished packing, Bermuda looked again at the carefully wrapped package containing *spyashchaya krasavitsa* along with several syringes. After the hotel's concierge had called last night, reporting that a package had been delivered for her, she'd handled it with kid gloves. And in an abundance of caution, she had wrapped it yet again in a T-shirt before placing it in her checked bag. Now Bermuda felt more comfortable, and it would be diabetic supplies if anyone asked.

Bermuda still didn't have the go-ahead but would call the capo after landing. She was a perfectionist and wanted enough time to stake out the Grand Case location before the hit. Her flight landed at one thirty, and after picking up her bag, Bermuda called the capo.

"Are you in Saint Martin?" he asked.

"Yes, I just landed. I'm renting a car and heading across the island now—staying at the Grand Case Beach Club. Do you have details yet?"

"Yes. Here's the address—an upscale condo. She should be there by the eighth. I'll text you her photo and call you later this evening with the final approval."

After they hung up, Bermuda picked up her car and headed for the French side of the island. It was slow going with traffic and school buses, but in a little over an hour, she pulled into the parking lot of the beach club on Rue de la Petite Plage. Bermuda unpacked, locking the poison and syringes in her room's security safe, then went for a swim, had a late lunch, and obtained directions to Izabella's condo. She found it easily and staked it out until after dark. No lights came on. Returning to the beach club, Bermuda changed and walked into town for dinner at a place that the concierge had recommended for local cooking. Back at the hotel, she worked out her plan. If the condo was still empty tomorrow morning, Bermuda would pick the lock and prepare everything before her mark arrived. She didn't need to be there when it went down, simply confirm the kill afterward and clean up—easy peasy.

***

On the afternoon of the sixth, the president called together the directors with whom he had met on the fourth.

"Gentlemen, I need to read you in on an upcoming event. But before we begin, my secretary will conference in the CIA's West Coast team, and would National Intelligence request an update from all the clandestine services for any new data about the assassination plot?"

After San Francisco and Jay were on the line and the director of National Intelligence was waiting for a return call, the president continued, "What we'll talk about now won't change any of the plans we've already made." Then the president spoke about the upcoming meeting with China on Saturday morning.

"I trust you completely. Perhaps my waiting until the eleventh hour to bring you on board was an excessive abundance of caution, but I'm paranoid about leaks. What I've undertaken is simply too delicate of a behind-the-scenes negotiation to be bandied about in the press—it could scuttle the talks. You see, gentlemen, this will be the foremost foreign policy initiative of my administration. It will shape our geopolitical position for the future vis-à-vis China. I've worked closely with my advisers, and we feel that—at a minimum—it will stalemate China's aggressive geopolitical strategy. The president of China and I both feel our countries are getting what we need out of our top secret agreement, which we will jointly sign before the Asia-Pacific Economic Cooperation summit. Frankly, my advisers feel we've improved our position versus theirs."

Then the president, addressing the director of the Secret Service, continued, "On Saturday morning after the fundraiser in Pacific Heights, when I'm returning to Marine One, arrange a low-security—two-car—breakaway from the motorcade. We'll drive to the Republic of South Korea's consulate at the corner of Clay and Laurel Streets; it's not far. I'll meet the premier of China there for a two-hour top secret conference. It'll just be the two of us, with translators, and two security officers guarding the conference room. If everything goes as planned, we'll sign the agreement then.

"We'll have no advance reconnoitering, no snipers, no routine security. The Chinese are insistent on a low presence. Years of distrust are hard to overcome," the president said.

"On both sides," the director of National Intelligence commented acerbically.

"Yes," the president admitted.

The director of National Intelligence's phone rang. After answering and hanging up quickly, he said, "No new intelligence, Mr. President."

The director of the CIA added, "That confirms my information. We have kept an effective lid on this. Until now, the only people who knew besides the Chinese were the president, South Korea's ambassador, probably their president, and me."

"Excellent. Nando, would you report on any new intelligence at your end?" the president asked.

"Yes, Mr. President. The timing of your call couldn't have been better. We have new information we were about to report to our director. First, we've concluded Izabella Ricci is still alive, and I don't think we'll nab her before it goes down; we still can't find her."

The president interrupted. "Then her death at Point Lobos was a deception?"

"So it would seem, at least until Quantico's DNA analysis proves otherwise."

The CIA director spoke up. "I haven't heard from them, so I called the head of the forensics lab again. He's still sticking to the beginning of next week."

Nando continued, "So then she's still in play. Second, we had already decided Izabella would do it at Ransom's mansion and had developed sufficient intelligence to support that conclusion. But once we studied the new data we just discovered, we changed our opinion— Izabella will do it at Clay and Laurel Streets on Saturday morning. That's because we uncovered the meeting you just spoke about, Mr. President."

"What exactly did you find out?" the director of National Intelligence asked.

In response, Nando reviewed all the new information they had unearthed: the increased activity at the South Korean consulate and the top secret request by the US government for a meeting there, the Chinese consulate's increased activity followed by the arrival of the Chinese premier, and the change in Air Force One's departure. "The data only leads to one conclusion," Nando said.

"How the devil did you find all that out?" the director of the Secret Service demanded.

The president interrupted, "Let's keep this on a need-to-know basis."

"Well, we sure as hell need to know if there're any leaks," the director continued.

The president addressed Nando, who responded, "There're no leaks."

"Well, that doesn't help me."

"Ease this group's concern. Is there anything we need to know about?" the president asked.

"No. Our information is from miscellaneous, unconnected bits of data along with intelligence from assets or confidential informants who are not employed by our government or their contractors.

"I have a question, though. Should we alert the Chinese?" Nando asked.

"I've thought a lot about this. If they don't know, no harm, no foul. But I'm suspicious they know. They probably didn't initiate the plot, but they're happy to take advantage of it. I think the intelligence your team and the China Desk uncovered on banker Hui Wang makes the case. And his rapid departure after Campbell's death seals it. Frankly, if you pieced it together, their Ministry of State Security could as well. No, I say leave it alone. Our negotiations are too delicate. Let's move on, Nando," the president said.

"Certainly, sir. Then this morning, we reconnoitered the Clay and Laurel Streets intersection," Nando replied, and made a report of their activities and conclusions and the photos that had been texted to Jay.

"Fine. Jay, stream those photos to the Oval Office."

"Already in process, sir."

"So are you positive Izabella knows about the meeting? And if so, how will she do it?" the director of National Intelligence asked.

"Notwithstanding the administration's successful control of leaks, the information is out there if you know how to put the pieces together. If we found out, she can also. Izabella's highly skilled and well connected. About the attack, she'll do it from one of the windows in the condo located across Laurel Street, facing the consulate's front entranceway," Nando answered.

"Then Izabella will have to take over a condo."

"Yes."

"Are you positive?" the president asked.

"Yes."

"Mal, you know her the best. Do you agree?" the president asked. Everyone in the room looked confused.

Without hesitation, Mal replied, "Yes, Mr. President."

"Who the hell is Mal?" the directors exclaimed.

"All right, Nando. What's your solution?" the president continued, disregarding the directors' query.

"We should stake out the building on Friday evening; we may be able to pick her up as she enters. If that doesn't work, on Saturday, have the consulate move their cars from the Laurel Street garage, because the president's cars can pull in there and be shielded from the shooter. Then have one sniper and spotter on the consulate's roof but deployed as inconspicuously as possible.

"There are four scenarios: first, we pick her up Friday night; second, she sees the open garage and/or sniper, aborts, and tries to escape; third, Izabella stays and the sniper picks her off. Those are our lines of defense. But there's a fourth scenario—she succeeds or fails and holes up with hostages. That's the one I'm most concerned about. The way around it is if we have the manager let us in and we go door-to-door before the president arrives. There're merely eight condos with a high probability that she's in one of the top three A units."

"In general, I agree . . . and by the way, your team has done excellent work," the president said. "That includes you as well, Bridgette."

Bridgette was surprised but managed a "Thank you, sir."

"We're going to thrash out a plan now. Your director will call back with what we decide. If you have problems, let him know," the president said, and rang off.

Bridgette looked at Mal. "How the devil did the president know about you?"

Looking less surprised than Bridgette had, Mal sat quietly. At last, she looked at him and said, "It's your boss, isn't it? The prime minister? He spoke to our president . . . right?" Mal shrugged his shoulders in reply, and Bridgette piped up, with humor in her voice this time,

"Oh, for Christ's sake, Mal. Just tell us!"

***

Riding back to Langley, the director was fuming, *What the fuck—who the hell is Mal? He rings a bell—niggling at the back of my mind. I need to take another look at Nando's Mossad file on Izabella.*

And what about the additional security Saturday morning and opening the built-in garage? It changes everything. There'll be officers on-site, and they'll certainly chase away the road crew if I go ahead with that part of the plan. I don't like the odds now. If Izabella's caught—successful or not—it's a probable death sentence. She'll flip on me to avoid it. So the gamble is that Izabella's ego will drive her to try the hit, no matter what, and die in the process. Is it a gamble I ought to take? I don't think so! And there are other possibilities as well. If she learns we know that she's aware of the meeting, Izabella could abort and escape ahead of time. Even though I have plenty of dirt on her, I'm still at risk, because Izabella has dirt on me. A tit-for-tat battle is too dangerous.

So a change in plans is required. I won't arrange for the road work, and I'll give the capo the final go-ahead.

When he returned to the office, the director called Nando. He decided not to ask him about Mal—at least not yet.

"Nando, here's the recommended plan. We've tried to balance your concerns with POTUS' need for a low-security profile:

"At seven p.m. on Friday, a Secret Service Counter Assault Team, sniper, and spotter will bivouac in the consulate's garage, and eight special officers will stake out the condo's two entrances as well as their lower-level garage. We'll try to apprehend Izabella before she enters. If it fails, security will be increased at the consulate on Saturday, and we'll have a hostage negotiator standing by. At eight o'clock that morning, we'll contact the condo's manager and arrange for entry. At the same time, Secret Service officers, including you three, will meet for a final briefing at three vans stationed near Walnut and Clay Streets. The vans will be for a command post, your team, and a CAT team. You'll be outfitted with bulletproof vests and communication devices.

"Later, at eight thirty, the sniper and spotter will move to the consulate's roof. We'll try to pick her off. Your team, consisting of a CAT officer assigned to Church, Mal and you, and two other CAT officers, will move out. You'll take up positions on the third through fifth floors, and the other CAT officers will cover the second floor. Position yourselves inside the stairs entrances, doors open. Additionally, one special officer will be stationed in the lobby and two special officers outside the rear entrance guest parking lot.

"Next, at eight fifty, the consulate's garage will be empty and opened for the president. There will be another special officer in each car who will remain in the garage after the president enters. They'll leave the garage door open and surveil the condo's windows and will be in contact with the shooter-spotter team on the roof. Then at eight fifty-five, the president will arrive ahead of the Chinese premier. The CAT team will begin moving to the condo's guest parking lot. When the premier arrives, they'll start going floor by floor, door to door, A units first. You three and the other CAT officers already inside will assist.

"Once we locate her, we'll play it by ear whether we breach or bring in the hostage negotiator. Hopefully, Izabella will come peacefully."

"Don't you think it would make better sense to start the full door-to-door search before the president arrives?" Nando said.

"I agree," the director replied, "but the president thinks that amount of activity would be noticed and spook the Chinese; he's steadfast in his resolve.

"The increased security we discussed with the president on the fourth will be in place by sunrise tomorrow at Stanford and Ransom's. If you're surveilling those locations, you can stand down but be ready for Saturday," the director finished.

The director sat at his desk, thinking about Mal. At length, he logged on to his computer. First, he reviewed Izabella's Mossad file. Then he searched through the databases. And eventually it was there: Malachi Ben-David, the shadowy, low-profile deputy director of the Central Institute for Intelligence and Special Operations—Mossad. But more important, Mal had been the trainer and commander of Mossad's top secret assassination group, the Kidon Unit. *Shit, I even had trouble locating his photograph. So is Nando running his own op? If he is, it sounds like Ben-David is helping him. Jesus, Nando even had access to Israeli intelligence. It also sounds like the president has Nando's six for whatever he's up to. I didn't see this coming.*

***

A while after hanging up with the director, Nando called Joe. "We had a conference call with the president and the directors of the National Intelligence Agency, the CIA, and Secret Service this afternoon. They're up to speed and have a plan for increased security on Saturday much as we discussed. Church, Mal, and I will be involved. I'll give you the details before we hang up. You, Gabi, and Bridgette can stand down from Ransom's tomorrow. The Secret Service will be in place by sunup."

"How's your director reacting?" Joe asked.

"He seems all in—cooperating fully."

"Maybe he has thrown Izabella to the wolves."

"Or maybe he's gambling she'll be killed in a shoot-out on Saturday," Nando postulated.

***

Later that evening, the capo called Bermuda. "I have the final go-ahead."

"Excellent. I've already located her condo. I'll set everything up first thing tomorrow. Then it's on autopilot. I'll let you know afterwards."

CHAPTER TWENTY-TWO

Friday, November 7, 2014

Berlin

Elsa was happy. Ever since Izabella had called her on the fourth, her spirits had been better. Izabella's reassurance meant a lot to her. She had to rush around to put everything together. There wasn't any nonstop service to Saint Martin. But KLM had the best flight from Berlin's Tegel Airport—ten o'clock in the morning—with one stop in Paris. It was a lot of flying—over thirteen hours—but Elsa should land in Saint Martin around six p.m. local time. Then it was about an hour by taxi to Grand Case.

The pilot announced they had reached their cruising altitude—next stop Paris. Elsa leaned back and daydreamed. *I didn't have time to shop for a new bikini . . . I want to look terrific for Katja. Or how about a monokini? They must have topless beaches on the French side. She won't be there yet, so I'll shop as soon as the stores open tomorrow morning. This is going to be so much fun.*

***

Bermuda staked out Izabella's condo in Grand Case, Saint Martin; it was before sunrise, and there were no lights or activity. She waited until ten o'clock when the shops opened and then headed out with her duffel bag. At a local market, she bought a 500 ml bottle of Evian, then drove back to the condo. Bermuda knocked on the door. If anyone answered, she'd bullshit about being from the manager's office, welcoming them, yada, yada, yada. No answer, so she put on latex gloves, picked the lock, looked for an alarm, and entered. Next, she inconspicuously mounted a miniature wireless motion detector on a picture frame, where it would cover the living area and the kitchen. Following that, Bermuda synced the device to her phone before setting her bag down on the kitchen counter.

She investigated the refrigerator. There were already two bottles of Evian inside. *I won't need the one I bought*, she thought. Bermuda placed both bottles from the fridge on the counter. Now the tricky part: handling sleeping beauty carefully. She took the vial of poison and a syringe from her bag. Bermuda held the vial firmly and inserted the needle, drawing in a small amount of liquid. Then she plunged the syringe into an Evian bottle just above its water level. It went in smoothly. Following that, Bermuda put the poisoned bottle into the refrigerator before dropping the other one into her bag. *Now there'll be only one bottle in the fridge.* Finally, she put everything in her bag and left. On the way back to the beach club, Bermuda disposed of the syringe along the roadside.

***

In San Francisco, Izabella was up early. She went to the garage and switched Karen's license plates with the front ones from two nearby cars, which were parked nose in. Then she returned to the apartment, reviewing her plan to leave for Clay and Laurel Streets around midnight. After that, she wouldn't return to Karen's apartment until Saturday morning by nine thirty. Izabella would lie low the rest of the day. She would've preferred to leave right from Clay and Laurel Streets, but flying to Saint Martin from San Francisco was a chore. Since Izabella didn't want the exposure of sitting around airports, she'd opted for nonstop flights. For that, she needed to fly to the East Coast, and JFK's flights were the best. There she could catch its only daily nonstop to Saint Martin at seven thirty in the morning. So Izabella would hang out for the JFK red-eye to New York that arrived at six on Sunday morning. *That's plenty of time to connect to the Saint Martin flight.*

***

Around noon in Washington, DC, the director called Nando. "Air Force One took off on time. They're scheduled to land at SFO at ten thirty your time—with an ETA at Stanford of eleven fifteen. The security precautions and extra officers are already in place. All the other security preparations at Ransom's are nearly finished."

"It sounds like everything is going according to plan," Nando observed.

"Yes, and we have no new intelligence."

"Same here."

"The director of National Intelligence will be calling the shots from now on. Here're both his and the director of the Secret Service's mobile numbers. I've given them yours and Church's numbers. Stay safe."

"Thanks. I'll let you know as soon as I can what goes down."

***

Air Force One had landed at SFO on time. The president and his immediate entourage transferred to Marine One, landing on the Stanford campus as scheduled. By eleven twenty, the president was in Memorial Auditorium meeting with the university's president and other dignitaries.

***

Elsa's flight was tiring, but she finally arrived in Saint Martin at six that evening. Around seven, she reached Izabella's condo, which was located on a hillside overlooking the Anguilla Channel and the island. She settled with the cabbie and entered the condo. It was after sunset, so she flipped on the lights. Elsa put her bags down beside the door, went to the bathroom, then kicked off her shoes and relaxed on the couch, putting her feet up on the coffee table. She closed her eyes for a few minutes, glad for the tranquility. But the condo was warm, so Elsa located the central air and switched it on. It was the first time she'd been there. She started exploring: two bedrooms, two baths, a decent-sized kitchen, dining area, large living room with a view of the ocean, and an attached patio. She brought her bags in to the master bedroom before going to the refrigerator. There wasn't much inside. *I'll go shopping tomorrow morning when I'm in town buying a bathing suit.* Elsa reached in, removed the bottle of Evian, and closed the refrigerator. She leaned her back against the counter, unscrewed the bottle's cap, and took a swig. Then, collapsing and scattering the bottle and its cap, Elsa crumpled to the tile floor: dead.

***

The president and his entourage lifted off in Marine One from the Stanford campus. His forty-five minute talk on global warming, which had focused on vehicular emissions such as carbon dioxide, methane, and nitrous oxide and the need for tighter standards, had gone over well with the academic community. The luncheon had been excellent, but the president had picked politely at all the courses. *Tonight's fundraiser will be lavish also. I'll eat lightly there*, he thought as his helicopter headed for the Presidio Golf Course. The short flight went as planned, and his four-car motorcade arrived at Ransom's home at three thirty.

***

Bermuda had spent the day at her hotel in Grand Case. After a morning swim and reading on the beach, she had a late lunch at the club's Sunset

Café. After that, she took a long nap. When she woke up, Bermuda checked her motion detector's app—nada, but it was early. Back to the beach for another swim and late-afternoon sunbathing. Around seven, after a piña colada and watching the sunset from the café's bar, when Bermuda was returning to her room, the detector's app beeped. She dressed and continued monitoring the app. There was sporadic motion for over a half hour—then nothing. Bermuda watched, waited, and at seven fifty, grabbed her duffel and headed for the condo.

She was inside by eight o'clock. The lights were on and the mark was lying on the kitchen floor near the refrigerator. First, Bermuda put on gloves, bent over the prone body, and checked for a pulse—none. Then she removed the motion detector. *It's too easy to forget*, Bermuda thought. Afterward, she went back to the body. *I'm not going to check IDs or luggage tags. My boss says it's pointless because this woman travels under various false identities, wearing wigs and colored contact lenses, and she's a makeup artist as well. But I have her height, weight, natural hair color, age, and a texted photo—it ought to be enough.*

The dead woman's cheek was resting on the floor, her arms splayed away from her body, her legs together. The height, weight, and hair color were correct. Bermuda moved the corpse's head enough to compare her face with the photo. She looked younger—*perhaps makeup?* The photo was like a mug shot, and the victim's face was beginning to distort with a developing bruise where she'd thwacked the floor. *Not easy to compare, but I'm convinced it's my mark.*

Then Bermuda began to police the condo. She picked up the nearly empty water bottle and rinsed it, then dropped it into a four-gallon garbage bag from her duffel, adding the bottle's cap from the floor. Next, using paper towels, she wiped up any water that had spilled on the floor around the remains, putting them into the garbage bag also. *It looks like the poor woman died from a sudden heart attack.* Bermuda did a final walk-through, turned out the lights, and left. She drove back to her hotel, disposing of the garbage in a roadside refuse container.

She'd have tomorrow morning on the beach, because her flight to Miami left at one thirty. Then, finally, it was on to Bermuda with the first available flight—easy peasy.

***

Now it was time. Originally, Izabella had intended to commandeer unit 3A when everyone was asleep after one o'clock Saturday morning. But something had been bothering her about her plan. Finally, she realized what it was. *Even though control assures me no one knows about this meeting, what if Medina has figured it out? What if he's onto my plan? Once he sees the site, it isn't rocket science. He'll understand the garage's significance. I can't underestimate him. If Medina reports that up the chain of command, control might not be able to line up the road crew. And what about additional security? I could be walking into a trap tonight. I ought to go much earlier than one in the morning. But I still think there will be lower security; I'll take my chances with those odds. And I have the Rosens as insurance if necessary, not to mention my disguise,* she thought.

So Izabella had changed her timetable to four thirty in the afternoon. She double-checked her thirty-six-inch canvas duffel bag, paying particular attention to her Steyr rifle, which had been broken down into two parts. Izabella confirmed that the scope was firmly mounted and the nail polish dots she'd applied to the scope and its elevation and windage adjustments were properly aligned. Then she rolled both assemblies in bubble wrap. After that, ammo, silencers, magazines, an adjustable tabletop bipod all went in. They were followed by assembly screws, a set of Allen wrenches, zip ties, blindfolds, and so on. Izabella packed a toothbrush, a change of underwear, a six-pack of bottled water, and a handful of protein bars. Following that, she drove to the garage across from the Hotel Royal. As she entered, the garageman said, "Hey, how you doin'? A cop was here last week asking about you. I told him you'd picked up your car and I hadn't seen you since."

"What'd he want?"

"Routine stuff . . . name, address, car make and model, and a plate number. I told him we don't keep records of that shit and couldn't remember anything about your car." He looked at the Mercedes and said, "It was a different one, anyway."

"Yeah, it's a new ride."

"You're coming up on the end of your rental—wanna renew?"

"No, I should be out of here tomorrow. Call me a taxi."

"All right."

Izabella waited with the parking attendant, slipping him a fifty-dollar bill.

"Thanks, lady. You're the best," he said as the cab arrived.

She gave the driver the address of a nail salon on Sacramento Street, where she got out and walked to the intersection of Walnut Street and Clay. Izabella turned left, and three-quarters of a block farther along, she came to the condo's guest parking lot. The Rosens' black Lexus was there. *Won't have to pick their condo's lock. So far, so good—four thirty, right on time.*

Izabella had become ambivalent about how to enter the building. Initially, she'd planned on the rear entranceway from the guest parking lot. But now she thought it might have too many people coming and going. Explanations from a stranger carrying a large duffel might prove troublesome. So she'd opted for the first floor's fire exit. Izabella had given it a quick once-over as she'd driven by on Wednesday. *Probably a blind spot if a sniper sets up on the consulate's roof.* She went straight to the door—a simple slam lock—and picked it. Izabella checked for an alarm—none. *This door is a security weakness—not my problem. It's the best way out too. Even if the sniper spots me, my disguise ought to buy me extra time while he gets approval to shoot.* Once inside, she took her semiauto, attached its silencer, and returned the gun beneath her jacket. Then, looking along the corridor, she saw through to the elevators where Ricki's office was. Next, Izabella surveyed the empty lobby, went to the keypad, and entered *250*. The piston-hydraulic powered elevator was noisy and slow. Finally, approaching 3A, Izabella checked to see if anyone was around. Nobody. She dropped her duffel, drew her gun, and stood aside from the peephole. Then Izabella rang the bell—at first, nothing. She rang it again, and finally, a faint male voice called out, "Coming." Eventually, he asked, "Who is it?"

"Hi, Mr. Rosen. I'm Kathy. My dad's the plumber. Schultz and Daughter, that's me—the daughter, I mean. Unit 2A is complaining of a leak in their ceiling, so Ricki called us. May I come in and look around?" Izabella used her cheeriest *bright young thing* voice.

"Well, Ricki never called—he usually does."

"Oh, I'm certain it's merely an oversight. I don't think he's in the office now. I won't be a minute . . . won't have to disturb you again. Please?"

Izabella heard the man unlocking the door. When he opened it, she stepped inside, putting her thigh against the door while pointing the gun at his chest.

"Step back slowly, Mr. Rosen . . . take your time. Do as I ask, and you and your wife won't be harmed—promise. Please cooperate."

Izabella picked up her duffel, then closed and locked the door. The man looked bewildered.

"I don't understand; what do you want? I'll give you all the cash we have . . . don't have any jewelry; it's in the bank."

"I don't want anything from you except your cooperation." They'd moved inside the apartment now. "Why don't I put the gun in my waistband . . . is that better? Where's your wife?"

"She's in the bedroom, taking a nap."

"All right, let's get her. We'll sit in the kitchen, have a glass of water, and talk, okay?"

As they moved to the bedroom, Mr. Rosen leading and leaning on his cane, Izabella thought, *This should be easy.* Mrs. Rosen was even more confused than her husband. In the kitchen, Izabella had them sit at the table. She checked the refrigerator and took three bottles of water out.

"Where are your glasses, Mrs. Rosen?" Izabella asked. She wanted to engage the lady and settle her down. Mr. Rosen was doing fine now.

"Over there," Mrs. Rosen said, pointing to a cabinet. Izabella brought glasses to the table, poured, and sat down with the Rosens.

When they were settled, Mr. Rosen asked again, "What do you want?"

"Honestly, just your cooperation. Let me explain. I'm going to spend the night here. I should be gone by nine fifteen tomorrow morning." The Rosens still looked confused. "Let me ask you a few questions, then I'll tell you how we'll proceed. Please be truthful, okay? I'm Izabella, by the way."

They nodded yes.

"Do you have any weapons in the apartment, like guns or hunting knives?"

"No," they said in unison.

"Mobile telephones?"

"We have two," Mrs. Rosen answered.

"Fine. How about landlines and extensions?"

Mr. Rosen responded. "One line—three extensions. An extension here," he said, pointing to the kitchen's wall phone, "and one each in the living room and our bedroom."

"What time do you have dinner, Mrs. Rosen?"

"Usually between five and five thirty."

Izabella looked at her watch and said, "Why don't you start dinner while your husband and I take care of the phones." Izabella removed the connecting cable from the kitchen's wall phone. Mr. Rosen showed her the other two extensions. While she removed those connecting cables, he brought their mobile phones. "Do you text, Mr. Rosen?" she asked.

"Yes, to our grandchildren."

Izabella took his phone, called her number, and hung up when the phone rang. *I'll text him his car's location after I'm out of here.* Then she turned off their mobiles and put everything in her duffel, saying, "I'll return all this tomorrow when I leave. You know how to reconnect the landlines, correct?"

Mr. Rosen nodded yes, and they returned to the kitchen. Mrs. Rosen was warming pasta sauce, and a box of angel hair pasta sat on the counter.

"It smells wonderful," Izabella said. "Like my mother's Sunday gravy."

"You're Italian, then?"

"Well, sort of. I was born in Italy, but my parents immigrated to Israel when I was five. We're Italian Jews."

"We have something in common. I was born here, but my family is Italian, and Saul is from Germany—he's Jewish. We met when he immigrated after the war. You're welcome to join us. I have plenty."

Izabella was bewildered. *I'm holding this woman at gunpoint, and she's being hospitable.* "No, I couldn't. I have water and protein bars."

"Well, I'll set you a place, in case you change your mind."

Izabella finally acquiesced; it smelled too good to pass up. They settled into a restrained conversation. Izabella told them to go about their normal routine. Then, after dinner, they did the dishes by hand. Mrs. Rosen commented, "It isn't worth using the dishwasher for the two of us." Mr. Rosen had rolled up his shirtsleeves before dinner. When he'd dried the dishes and was reaching up to put bowls in the cupboard, his shirtsleeves slid up. Izabella spotted a number tattooed on his left forearm. When he noticed, all Mr. Rosen said was, "Auschwitz."

"Is that where you injured your leg?"

"Yes."

They sat and watched TV. Around nine thirty, Mr. Rosen excused himself and went to bed. A few minutes later, Mrs. Rosen said, "If you hear anything in the night, it's probably Saul. He occasionally has terrible nightmares. Sometimes if I wake him, he's all right, but other times I need to hold him until he's cried out."

"Auschwitz."

Mrs. Rosen nodded yes, and Izabella began choking up.

"Oh, I didn't mean to upset you. I simply didn't want you to be startled in the night. After all, you're carrying a loaded gun."

"I lost family in Dachau," Izabella said.

"You look too young."

"Well, not my immediate family. But I've lived in Israel since I was little. You can't avoid the Holocaust there. It's all around you: in survivors' eyes, faces, recorded on their arms. It's relentless, building up in me. Sometimes I feel like screaming."

"It's okay to scream—just as it's all right to cry."

"I went to Dachau in September. I don't know why, but I felt I had to."

"Did it help?" Mrs. Rosen asked.

"Not really."

"Izabella, you need to talk about it. It can't be exorcised or purged otherwise."

"Does Saul?"

"I asked him once."

"What did he say?"

"It's hard for me to talk about. He was nineteen and had two younger sisters, sixteen and thirteen, who were at the camp as well. They were pretty. Saul still has a crumpled old photo he carried in his shoe throughout the war. You know the Nazis had rape dogs?" Mrs. Rosen asked, looking at Izabella.

"Yes."

"The concentration camp guards thought it would be fun to throw the girls to the dogs. So his sisters were dragged into the woods and stripped. Then, while Saul was forced to watch, the guards stood around laughing and egging the dogs on. It was entertainment and went on for weeks. Finally, the girls couldn't stand the bestiality any longer and refused. They were shot dead on the spot. Afterward, another woman in the camp slipped Saul a note from his sisters telling him what they were going to do. They begged Saul to forgive them for leaving him alone. He's never forgiven himself for not protecting them."

"He couldn't have done anything."

"In his mind, Saul knows it, but emotionally, he feels responsible. I've never asked again . . . I don't want to hear any more. Don't let it build up within you like that. Talk to someone."

***

Bridgette and Nando returned to the hotel by nine thirty that evening. They had tried to have a relaxing dinner but were on edge about tomorrow. Nando had been through it many times when he was on the job, so this anxiety was unexpected. But he understood why. It was different this time because he cared about someone: he cared about Bridgette. And even though she was putting on a happy face, Nando was positive Bridgette felt anxious also.

"I think I should turn in early," Nando said.

"Should I come?" Bridgette asked.

"What do you mean?"

"If you need a good night's sleep, I can read in the other room. Let you fall asleep first."

"No, I want you to come to bed—I need you."

"I don't know if I'll be much fun. I'm so worried—you could be shot."

"We'll worry together, all right?"

"All right. I'm going to say good-night to Church and Mal now."

Nando undressed, and Bridgette was back in a few minutes. "Church is reading, and Mal is talking with Madame; she says, 'Hi and *bonne chance.*'"

"It's a little after six in the morning Paris time—that's early for Madame."

"I don't think she minds. Maybe Mal's lonely."

"Maybe. Let's cuddle for a while," Nando said.

After a bit, Bridgette said, "I've been avoiding thinking about something else."

"What?"

"I need to be back at work Monday morning. They've been understanding about my time—hard to believe it's three weeks already."

"Even if everything goes perfectly, I don't think I can travel with you," Nando told her.

"Debriefings?"

"Yes, but it should only be a few days."

Bridgette was quiet for a while. "If Izabella is cornered, I'm afraid her hostages will be killed—one way or another."

"I don't think friendly fire is a big risk; we're all pros. Are you afraid Izabella will 'let slip the dogs of war'[4] if she can't escape?"

"Yes."

"I've thought a lot about what your friend Ellen said. I have no doubt Izabella kills unhesitatingly, yet I'm not certain about indiscriminately. I'm not leaning towards that."

"I hope so."

"Me too."

Bridgette responded by sliding over and taking Nando in her arms, whispering, "Be safe," as she started kissing him.

***

"Saul, are you awake?" Angie Rosen asked as she slipped into bed.

"Yes."

"How do you feel."

"Scared."

"Me too."

"You were talking to her. Did you find out what she's up to?" Saul asked.

"No . . . but I don't think it's about us. It's the apartment; we're in the wrong place at the wrong time."

"I agree. The one reason I can think of is that it's about the consulate across the street. Is anything going on over there?" Saul continued.

"Not that I know of. They're usually reliable with notifying us about events, crowds, and so on," Angie said. "It's so odd Izabella seems nice, friendly. It's confusing because I understand we're hostages. And it bothers me she doesn't care we can identify her . . . I think she gave us her real name also."

"Don't be fooled by her. Don't trust her. I saw commanders like her in the camps: a friendly facade, charming, as if they cared, but they would just as soon slit your throat. They were cruel. It's an act, a performance."

"Is she going to kill us, Saul?"

"Not if she needs us for hostages."

CHAPTER TWENTY-THREE

Saturday, November 8, 2014

San Francisco

I zabella was awake; the chair she'd slept in hadn't been too uncomfortable. Taking her toothbrush and her change of underwear, she went to the bathroom, quietly opening the Rosens' bedroom door along the way. They were still sleeping soundly. After a spit bath, Izabella brushed her teeth and changed. *Six fifteen—I'll set up before I rouse the Rosens.* She checked the weather on her phone: *Cloudy, fifty-seven degrees, high in the midsixties, no wind—perfect.*

Unpacking her duffel, Izabella assembled the Steyr and checked the scope's alignment. Then Izabella went to the window and drew open the vertical blinds. The dining room's window had a large fixed center panel with a narrow casement window on either side—no screens. She opened both windows fully. *I don't want any movement later that might draw attention. The left side is the window to use, because the opened right one will interfere with my arc of motion.* Next, Izabella focused the scope and propped her rifle in a corner. Afterward, she set up the bipod on a small table she'd brought from the living room, mounted the rifle, and adjusted the table's location so that barely an inch of the muzzle protruded past the windowsill. Last, Izabella checked her range of motion and loaded the magazine. *All set. I'll make coffee and wake up the Rosens.*

***

Bridgette, Mal, Church, and Nando had been up early also. After showering and dressing, the men checked their sidearms, loaded spare magazines, and along with Bridgette left the hotel and drove to Sears. The restaurant wasn't busy at that time on a Saturday morning. The men were cheerful, but Bridgette wondered if it was a pretense, covering up anxiety.

"I think it's a doable plan, notwithstanding the president's limitations," Church said.

"It should work; we have a lot of firepower," Nando agreed.

Bridgette didn't say anything but noticed that Mal was concentrating too hard on his eggs Benedict. *I'm not convinced. The man who knows her best—trained her—is awfully quiet. Mal doesn't agree with them. That doesn't make me feel secure. I've waited a long time for Nando; I couldn't stand it if something happened to him*, Bridgette thought, but kept her counsel.

"I think this will be over quickly," Nando continued. "I feel much better now that the Counter Assault Team is in place."

"Yeah, they have the tactical know-how. It would've been a fool's errand to try to go it alone. The director must be going nuts," Church remarked.

"I'm not so sure. I think he has already cut her loose. The director didn't get where he is without covering his ass."

"Nonetheless, I'd like to be a fly on the wall when Izabella catches on."

Mal had finished his eggs and finally chimed in. "So, Bridgette, what are you going to do while we're playing war games?"

"Gabi and Joe are coming over to the suite. We thought we'd hang together while we wait."

"Terrific idea," Mal said. "On Sunday, we should all go to dinner. Before you know it, we'll be going our separate ways. What do you think?"

Everyone agreed. Mal looked at his watch. "We better get moving." They drove back to the hotel, went to the suite, picked up their guns and ammo, and headed for Walnut and Clay Streets. Bridgette held Nando for a long time before letting go and was still sniffling when Gabi and Joe arrived.

***

At seven thirty a.m., the president met in his suite at Holden Ransom's estate with the director of the Secret Service. They conferenced in the director of the CIA in Langley and the director of National Intelligence aboard Air Force One.

"'Morning, gentlemen. Update me before I head down to breakfast with Holden."

The director of National Intelligence spoke first. "Everything's a go on Air Force One. We're already patched into Langley as well as the White House's situation room."

"Is anyone standing by there?"

"No, sir, but the link is hot."

"All right, let's hope we don't need it. How about the vice president and the Presidential Emergency Operations Center under the East Wing?"

"The center is in the same status as the situation room. We're moving the vice president in there as soon as you're on the move. He is standing by but doesn't know why."

"Fine. Keep it that way."

"As soon as the Secret Service's command post is in place, we'll make that patch. Also, we have no new intelligence," the director of National Intelligence concluded.

"Thanks. How's everything at Langley, Director?" the president asked, turning his attention to the CIA.

"Everything's in order. No new intelligence either. I read Nando in last night. He called; Church, Mal, and he are on the way to Walnut and Clay now."

"All right, what's the Secret Service's status?" the president asked, addressing their director.

"We're nearly up to full speed. The vans and the CAT are arriving now. You should be able to patch in momentarily," the director said, addressing Air Force One. "Also, there haven't been any sightings of her or other anomalies noted by our special officer since they went on duty last evening."

"And I haven't heard anything from the Chinese . . . it looks like a go. Thank you all. I can enjoy my breakfast with Holden now," the president said. After hanging up, he said to the Secret Service director, "I need to go over numbers with Holden, but ride with me in my car when we leave."

***

Izabella had made coffee and went to wake up the Rosens. "'Morning," she said as she opened their door. "I have coffee in the kitchen. Go to the bathroom and then come in. We need to get started." Izabella noticed that the Rosens acted apprehensively. "Don't worry. Everything is fine. I still ought to be out of here by nine fifteen, and then you can have your life back—promise."

On the way to the kitchen, the Rosens came through the living room and then into the dining room. The rifle setup alarmed them; they exchanged glances but didn't say anything. Izabella poured coffee and they all sat down. "I'm not going to explain anything—you're smart people, you've figured it out. If everything goes according to plan, I'll take one shot at a few minutes before nine o'clock. After that, I'll take your car keys and go. I'll leave your car near Union Square and text you its location. That's it.

"But I need to take precautions. I'm sorry you'll be inconvenienced for a half an hour or so. About eight thirty, you'll have to go to your bedroom. I'll blindfold you and zip-tie your hands. If you're quiet, I won't gag you. I'll put your phones and the connecting cables on the kitchen table when I go. After I depart, wait five minutes before leaving your room."

***

In the mansion's country kitchen, the president and Holden Ransom finished breakfast. They'd been friends for years, and the president enjoyed having quiet time with him. They chatted about personal and family issues until Ransom said, "Mr. President, we haven't put all the numbers together yet, but last night's take is going to be over five million dollars."

"That's terrific."

"Yes, an excellent addition to the DNC's coffers."

"I appreciate all your efforts on our behalf. You've been a good friend."

"Thank you. I'm sorry you'll have to step down after the 2016 election."

"Well, those are the rules. Honestly, between us, I'm concerned about the upcoming presidential. Everything is so unsettled. You know I'm not comfortable with either of our two probable finalists for the nomination. And the Republicans are at odds with themselves too. I don't see them fielding a sound candidate yet. They're ripe for a dark horse to steal the nomination. Politics aside, we need a strong leader. We have plenty of challenges ahead.

"After the Asia-Pacific Economic Cooperation summit when history has been written, I think it will show that relative to the Chinese, we've improved our position."

"That would be wonderful—a fine legacy."

"Yes, it will be. I need to shake a leg now. I hate these long hauls, even though Air Force One is great. Thanks again, Holden."

***

Mal, Church, and Nando arrived a few minutes ahead of time at Walnut and Clay Streets. The Secret Service director was conferenced in, and the CAT commander began the briefing. After the layout and tactical plans were presented, the director came on.

"The sniper and spotter are ready to move to the roof, and we have an officer speaking with the manager about entry—he's cooperating.

"The tricky part of this op is the low profile the president wants and the timing. So our sniper and spotter will stay low—keeping out of sight as much as possible. Then, as soon as the president arrives, the CAT team will begin moving their van slowly along Clay Street. Once the premier is here, move quickly to the guest parking area, enter, and begin the floor-by-floor, door-to-door search. I haven't been in on this op from the beginning, but everything I've heard tells me you're dealing with a consummate pro. Don't underestimate her, and let's hope she doesn't take hostages.

"I'll be in the president's car and then in the garage after we arrive. Stay safe."

Nando's team was outfitted with vests and communication devices and met the five CAT officers who would be deployed with them, along with the special officer who would be on lobby duty. They went to a second van, tested their communication devices, and waited to move out at eight thirty.

***

It was time to move the Rosens to their room.

"Let's go to your bedroom now," Izabella said. The Rosens stood up from the kitchen table and led the way. She had them sit on the edge of their bed. "I'm going to zip-tie your hands in front of you. After I leave, you ought to be able to help each other out of them with a sharp knife. I'll put one on the table next to your phones. Mr. Rosen, let me have your hands first."

Saul extended his hands, and Izabella put the ties on gently, just enough to hold his wrists together. She turned to his wife. When Mrs. Rosen extended her hands, they were trembling, and she started sobbing. "You're lying to us—you're going to kill us." Then Mrs. Rosen started crying irrepressibly. "Don't kill us—please."

Izabella sat beside the woman and took her hand. "Angie, I'm not going—"

"*Gottverdammter* Nazi—don't touch her!" Saul snapped, and shoved Izabella's hands away. "And don't call her Angie."

Izabella jumped up.

"I'm not a Nazi. Don't say that. It's awful."

Repressing a snivel, she shouted, "Don't call me that again," and stormed out of the room. Izabella was bewildered when she reached the hall.

Why do I feel like this? Hurt! For Christ's sake, it's a job. I'm not a fuckin' Nazi . . . not a psychopath. What's the matter with him!

Izabella had to work on calming down by regulating her breathing. At length, she stopped snuffling and went back inside. "I'm sorry I upset you."

They still seemed agitated, although Mrs. Rosen had stopped crying. "Mr. Rosen, I need your wife's hands to put on the zip ties." She turned to the woman, who extended her hands. Izabella was as gentle as possible. Now they seemed to be calming down. "I'll put your blindfolds on; please leave them in place." *I can't risk them seeing my disguise.* "Now, lie back and be quiet," Izabella said and left, closing the door behind her.

I'm not a goddamn Nazi!

***

The CAT sniper and spotter took their positions on the consulate's roof, prone and close enough to the Laurel Street edge of the roof that they could still see all the windows in the building across the street. After surveying the frontage, they reported to the command post that all was clear.

Mal, Church, Nando, the CAT officers, and the officers for lobby and rear entrance duty were dropped off at guest parking. Ricki, the condo's manager, let them in while their van returned to Walnut and Clay Streets. By eight thirty-five, all had taken up their positions and reported an all clear to the command post.

***

It was eight thirty-five a.m. now, and Izabella went through the Rosens' living room to the dining room, looking out the windows as she went. All appeared normal. She had a cup of coffee, then went to her duffel and took out a box containing the costume she'd purchased before Halloween. It was a nun's habit with a wimple and a long-sleeved, floor-length tunic. Izabella donned it over her street clothes, putting her silenced handgun and the Rosens' car keys into the habit's deep right-hand pocket. Following that, she placed two magazines and her clutch into its left-hand one. Finally, Izabella moved into position, sitting at the table, rechecking the rifle, inserting the magazine, chambering a round, refocusing the scope—waiting and watching with her field glasses.

The garage was still closed, but no road crew had shown up yet. This was cutting it close. Izabella was beginning to grow uneasy. She hadn't expected to hear from control after their last call. *So it's my decision.* Out of the corner of her eye, Izabella thought she'd spotted movement on the consulate's roof. She trained the binoculars there—nothing. But it was a concern, because Izabella wasn't predisposed to figments of her imagination. She'd give it more time—*just a little.* The road crew was the deciding factor. *If that doesn't happen, I'm blown, and the director has abandoned me!*

***

By eight forty-five a.m., the president's motorcade had been formed and began moving from Ransom's estate sans its SFPD escort. The Secret Service director issued orders, dispatching the first and fourth cars to Air Force One at SFO. They were to await the president, who would arrive later. Reluctantly, those cars obeyed their orders, and the two remaining cars were directed to Clay and Laurel Streets.

The director said, "Drive to the South Korean consulate; it's located there on the right-hand side. There is a built-in two-car garage shortly before the intersection. It'll be open; pull in. The president, his translator, and bodyguard will then enter the consulate. The rest of us will remain in the garage. I'll issue additional orders after we arrive." Then, turning to the president, he said, "All positions have reported in with all clears. They're opening the garage now."

"Excellent. Let's do it."

***

Izabella didn't bother with the consulate's roof anymore—she hadn't seen anything else and it had become irrelevant. Izabella focused on the garage, checking her watch intermittently. Finally, the door started opening and no road crew was in sight. *Shit—I need to decide now. Whatever decision I make, it's irrevocable. What about Angie Rosen? A shield? A hostage?* These thoughts went through her mind in a second. *No, she'll slow me down. Gotta go—right now!*

Izabella stood up, patting her pockets, taking inventory, and putting on her nonprescription granny glasses. She called out, "I'm leaving . . . remember, five minutes," and headed for the apartment's door. She opened it a crack, scanning the floor. The door to the stairs was open. Izabella watched, detected movement, and saw Medina move to surveil the floor.

Assessment: bulletproof vests, arms exposed; 10-mm's knockdown power is sufficient. They'll be down long enough to enter the stairwell.

After he retreated, Izabella took her clutch from her left-hand pocket and stepped out. Then, under her tunic, quickly positioning her feet in a shooting stance and bending her knees a little, she closed the door loudly enough to be heard. Next, she began fumbling in her right-hand pocket while muttering something about her car keys.

Nando and his CAT partner stepped out from the stairwell. His partner was out the door first, announcing, "Federal agents . . . Sister."

They saw a nun looking down, rummaging in her habit, still muttering something about car keys.

"Don't move. Hands on top of your head. Kneel."

The nun looked up, surprised.

"Sister—do it now!"

Even though what followed burst forth instantly, it seemed like slow motion to Nando. The nun exclaimed, "Oh Lord, you startled me."

She looked confused, dropping her clutch, then raised her left palm to her chest and said, "Dear me—my bag."

Following that, she appeared to begin leaning over for her bag. But instead, Izabella had drawn her handgun and was in a shooter's combat crouch, holding a two-handed grip on them. She had barely come to rest when two practically concurrent shots slammed into the CAT officer's chest. Dropping his gun, he fell backward, almost knocking Nando over. Then three more shots. Nando felt the first rip through his right bicep, followed by two more to the center of his chest. Nando was down, in shock, struggling to stay conscious so he could find his gun. Before blacking out, Nando disjointedly recalled the nun grabbing her clutch, punching a code into an elevator's keypad, and darting downstairs.

Now, down the stairs to the second floor, she counted—*five rounds left*. Izabella moved cautiously to the landing. The stairs door was open. The noise from the elevator had drawn those officers into the hall, as she'd hoped. Ignoring them, she continued down to the first floor. That officer was moving toward the lobby, reacting to the elevator's noise also. No other officers were in sight. As he walked away, Izabella cleared her throat.

"Ahem . . . excuse me."

He spun around, took two shots to his chest, and collapsed. Turning left, Izabella was quickly down the corridor to the fire exit. She drew a deep breath, slowing her heart rate—*three rounds left*. Izabella ejected the nearly spent magazine, replacing it with a full one before putting her gun back into her right-hand pocket. She straightened her garments and left the condo. *One last step*, she thought. *So far, so good.*

Izabella walked normally to the guest parking lot, holding the Rosens' car keys in her left hand. Two officers were standing by the rear elevators, watching a door close and holstering their sidearms. When they saw her, they commanded, "Federal officers, Sister. The lot's closed. You can't come in here now."

Izabella spotted the Rosens' car and continued moving toward it.

"Sister, please—stop."

"I'm sorry. I know I shouldn't have parked here. But it was only for a while—couldn't find a spot. I'm not in trouble, am I?"

The officers started approaching her. *They look bulky—vests underneath*, Izabella thought.

"Sister, you can't be here. If you don't stop, we'll have to detain you."

"Oh, no—my sister; that's who I was visiting—said I would get in trouble." Izabella kept up an addlebrained chatter—*blah, blah, blah*—while concentrating on the officers' hands.

Finally, one started to move toward his gun. Izabella reacted instantaneously—four rapid shots, two each at close range. As the officers toppled backward, Izabella got in the car and left the lot. She turned in to Clay Street, driving toward Laurel, where she turned left. Then Izabella headed toward Bush Street, turning left again, and drove to the Hotel Royal's parking garage.

***

A little before nine o'clock in the morning, two SUVs left the Chinese consulate with the premier and a small entourage. At the same time, the president's motorcade pulled into the South Korean consulate's garage. The command post requested updates from all stations.

The Secret Service director responded, "All clear."

The sniper replied, "All clear."

The second, fourth, and fifth floors' teams responded, "All clear."

"What the fuck," the commander snapped. "All stations report. Jesus, what's happened to floor three, the lobby, and the rear entrance?" Then, addressing the team leader in the CAT van, he barked, "Go now—move it. Go, go, go."

***

The CAT team had reached the condo and was deployed on all floors now. Ambulances were on the way. Nando was sitting up, and a QuikClot gauze patch had been applied to his wound. All the other officers who had been shot were up, moving, and slowly recovering from the shock. The CAT commander had been able to debrief those officers sufficiently to make an initial report to the Secret Service director. His call was patched to Air Force One and the director of the CIA in Langley.

"POTUS and the premier are safe and in their meeting. Our sniper remains in position. Medina is wounded—shot in the arm—doesn't look too serious. Four others are recovering from shock—two shots each to their chests. It looks like the shots were dead nuts over their hearts."

"Christ," the Secret Service director replied. "It would have been a slaughter without those vests."

"Copy that. They took a wallop. I'm guessing ten-millimeter at practically point-blank range. They're going to be sore as hell tomorrow."

"How the hell did that happen?" the director of National Intelligence asked.

"Apparently, she was disguised as a nun. I'm guessing that bought her a second or two—all she needed."

"How'd she escape?" the director of the CIA said.

"She took over unit 3A—the Rosens'. They're okay—shook up. The assassin took their car when she left. The Rosens had already called SFPD by the time we arrived. According to Mr. Rosen, the locals have already issued an APB. Their Serious Crimes Unit is responding."

"How the hell did she even make it to their car?" the Secret Service director snapped.

"A blind spot, sir—a side door, a fire exit."

"And the sniper couldn't take her out?"

"No, the door was out of sight."

Meanwhile, Mal had been kneeling next to Nando. "Do you feel like calling Bridgette now, or do you want me to talk for you?"

"You call, Mal—it's too hard for me."

"Mal, is everything all right?" Bridgette asked. "Joe's dispatcher has him on the phone now."

"It's okay. Nando was shot—in the arm—looks like a flesh wound. They've stopped the bleeding, and an ambulance is on the way. He's right here but says it's too hard to talk."

"Mal, hold the phone so he can hear. Love you, Nando."

"He's nodding and whispering, 'I love you too.'" Mal said.

"Okay. Are you all right, Mal? And what about Church?"

"We're okay—just along for the ride."

"I'm glad. Joe and Gabi just left for the crime scene. Call me when you know more."

CHAPTER TWENTY-FOUR

Saturday, November 8, 2014, cont.

San Francisco

A t nine ten a.m., Izabella pulled into the garage across from the Hotel Royal. As the parking attendant handed her a ticket, she joked, "Forget me already?" and pushed back her wimple.

"Jesus, Sister . . . lady . . . I didn't recognize you."

"That's the idea. I'm exchanging cars. I'll leave these keys with you. My friends—the Rosens—will pick them up later, okay?"

"Sure."

Izabella parked next to Karen's car. She put the parking ticket and a twenty on the front seat before popping the trunk. Then she stripped off her clerical garb and left it in the boot. After that, she drove the Mercedes to the exit and handed the garageman the Rosens' keys and another fifty. As Izabella pulled away, he called after her.

"Thanks, lady—you're a class act."

Before leaving the alley, Izabella texted Saul: PARKING GARAGE— ALLEY ACROSS FROM HOTEL ROYAL. *Now, off to Karen's.* A block from the garage, Izabella dropped her phone's SIM card out the window and later discarded her phone similarly. *Time for a new one.*

***

The director sat quietly in his Langley office, processing what he had learned on the call with the CAT commander and the directors of National Intelligence and the Secret Service.

What a fuckup. How the hell did two CIA officers, a probable Mossad agent, and who knows how many Secret Service officers miss a blind spot? Jesus, in five minutes she disabled five skilled officers and got away scot-free. This is the worst outcome for me. After a while, the director concluded there was nothing to do because he had already activated damage control. *I ought to be fine after I hear from the capo. In the meantime, I'll follow up on Nando. It's the normal thing to do.*

He called Church. "How's Nando doing?"

"He's on the way to hospital. I don't think it's too serious."

"And you and Mal?"

"We're fine."

"Excellent—glad you guys are okay. I'll give it a couple of hours before I call Nando."

"Do you have any orders for us?"

"Let's see how long Nando will be in hospital. We'll bring you back here ASAP for debriefings and to regroup. In the meantime, cooperate with the other agencies and the locals."

"Okay, talk to you later."

***

The meeting at the South Korean consulate had been cordial. The president said there were no changes to the document he had received the day before. The Chinese had already agreed to English being the lingua franca as well as to the proposed signing procedures. So it had gone smoothly, albeit slowly. The president's copy was xeroxed. Then the men dated the documents, initialed each page, and signed a copy. Subsequently, the documents were exchanged and the initialing-and-signing process was repeated before being sealed and witnessed by their translators and security guards. The president and the South Korean consul general walked the premier to the front door. When the president returned to his car, the director of the Secret Service greeted him.

"You seem pleased, sir. Everything went well?"

Smiling, the president said, "Yes. Did you have any problems? We didn't hear anything from outside during the meeting."

"A mixed bag," the director said, and reported on the op.

"Nando was correct, then; the garage was a game changer. How's he doing?" the president asked.

"He's at San Francisco General now—it doesn't look too serious."

"Fine. I'll call him later from Air Force One. I must tell you, though, I find it hard to accept she escaped so easily."

"Well, we were warned about her."

"That's not good enough. Jesus, we had the CIA, National Intelligence Agency, and Secret Service working on it. Is this the best result we could pull off? It's simply not good enough. When I return, dealing with her will be a top priority for all our clandestine services."

Later, Air Force One was airborne on time, and before the president met with his advisers to prepare for their China meetings, he called Nando.

***

Mal and Church had returned to the Kensington Park before noon. They picked up Bridgette, had lunch, and headed for San Francisco General. When they arrived, Nando was sitting up in bed with his right arm in a sling. Straightaway, Bridgette went over and kissed him.

"Are you really okay?" she asked.

"Yes. The bullet tore my muscle but only grazed the bone, but my chest is badly bruised. It hurts like hell now. They'll keep me overnight for observation."

"Will you need physical therapy?"

"Yes."

"Well, I'm just glad she missed . . . didn't hit you in the head."

Mal smiled, and Bridgette asked, "What?"

"The CAT commander told me Izabella made ten perfect shots on center mass. She placed that shot exactly where she wanted to, Bridgette," Mal replied.

"So Izabella shot Nando in the arm on purpose. Why?"

"Professional courtesy? Or reminding Nando who's number one—a stronger message next time . . ." Mal quipped.

"What a bitch," Bridgette snapped.

"Well, nobody ever accused her of being one of God's noblest creatures," Church joked.

"Anyway, I was on the phone with the director," Nando said. "He's pissing and moaning about Izabella's escape. I think he was hoping for a different outcome."

"I'll bet," Church said, "she's a threat to him."

"I don't think the director is the kind of man that can live with the threat of mutual destruction as a stalemate," Mal noted.

"So this isn't over," Bridgette observed.

No way, Mal thought. *For one thing, I'm positive my previous orders will be reinstated.*

"Right, but I'm uncertain how our director will play this out. Will he keep trying to bring her in?" Church asked.

"It strikes me that he'll continue going through those motions. But he'll do something else, and we know what that is. Plus, he won't use us for that," Bridgette surmised.

"That could be a problem for him," Nando said, "because the director of National Intelligence is in charge now."

"He must have plenty of underworld contacts—I don't think he'll be at a loss." Mal added.

"So it sounds like we ought to keep Jay and Zeb involved and continue working behind the scenes," Church concluded.

***

Although Izabella had aborted, everything else worked out, and she returned to Karen's apartment by nine thirty. She hadn't slept well at the Rosens'. So Izabella took a nap, woke up about two that afternoon, and had a snack. Now it was seven o'clock in Saint Martin, not too early to call Elsa. If her flights were on time, she ought to be at the condo already. *No luck. I'll try her from the airport.*

Later, Izabella called a taxi for a five o'clock pickup. The cabbie dropped her at the corner of Bush and Taylor Streets. She walked along Bush toward Grant Avenue and on the way disposed of the gun's parts in several waste receptacles. Izabella had an early dinner at the Café de la Presse and afterward had the bistro call her a taxi. By seven fifteen, using a new false identity, she was checked in for her nine-thirty flight. Izabella rang Elsa again. *No luck this time either. Maybe she's taking Sunday flights. But why wouldn't she have called if that were happening?*

At last, Izabella enplaned, settled in, and took a sleeping pill. Her flight to JFK arrived on time Sunday morning, and by six thirty she was waiting in the boarding area for her flight to Saint Martin. Izabella had booked this part of the flight as Katja Schmidt because she thought it made sense for her flight to sync with her Saint Martin identity. Elsa still wasn't picking up her phone. *Even if she missed her flights, why isn't she answering? Maybe it's her battery? I'm trying not to worry.*

Izabella landed after noon, rented a car, and started across the island to Grand Case.

***

Later that afternoon in San Francisco, the premier called Beijing. "Good morning, Mr. President. I can report on our meeting now if you would like."

"'Afternoon, Mr. Premier. Please, I'm looking forward to hearing."

302

"Everything went well. The document was signed without any changes."

"Any observations?"

"The American president seemed pleased."

"Good. Any disruptions at or before the meeting?"

The premier thought it was an odd question but responded, "No, sir. Everything was quiet. I'll be flying home later this evening, bringing the executed agreement with me."

"Excellent, and thank you for a fine job."

After the president rang off, he thought, *I wonder what happened to the other plan. I'm not entirely surprised, though. Ever since Campbell's death and Hui Wang's hasty return home, the director seems to have been moving to damage control. I've been suspicious that their plan might have been in trouble. Eventually, the Ministry of State Security will sort it out for me.*

CHAPTER TWENTY-FIVE

Sunday, November 9, 2014

Saint Martin

A t four thirty p.m., Inspecteur Albert Baudin of France's National Police Force was en route to a condo in Grand Case. He was on call this weekend, and the dispatcher in Marigot had reached him earlier. The local gendarmes had been called to a death in a condo complex. Baudin didn't have any details other than that the owner, when returning from the States, had discovered the body of a young woman, who was apparently the owner's houseguest. The gendarme he had spoken with said that at first look, the death appeared to be from natural causes, with no signs of foul play.

The inspecteur had recently arrived in Saint Martin to begin a routine six-month rotation. He was looking forward to it, especially now that fall was settling into Paris. Baudin hadn't had any interesting cases since arriving, and his first impression was that this would be no different. It seemed like the locals were simply adhering to procedures because the deceased was a foreigner, had died without a doctor in attendance, and had no apparent cause of death. Routine—shouldn't take too long. The gendarme introduced himself and said, "The owner is the woman who found her. She's sitting on the patio—I'll introduce you to her."

"Let's wait a minute, Officer. Is that the police doctor?" Baudin asked, pointing to a man bending over the body.

"Yes, sir, and the other gendarme is my partner."

Baudin saw a young woman taking photos. "Okay, take me to the doctor first." After they were introduced, the doctor said, "I can't tell you a lot until I have her on the table, but there are no signs of foul play. No wounds, defensive or otherwise, except for a bruise on the left side of her cheek where it hit the floor. It seems like she simply died. A shame; she was pretty."

"Yes, it's a pity—any time of death yet?"

"Based on body temp and the lack of rigor, I'd say between six p.m. and midnight on Friday. I might fine-tune it back at the morgue."

Turning to the gendarme, Baudin asked, "Do we have an ID and travel documents?"

"Yes, Elsa König, a Berlin address, and she arrived on a KLM flight from Paris Friday afternoon around six o'clock. The documents were in her purse—it's on the table." Baudin looked over and saw it on the dining area's table, with its contents displayed thereon.

"Did you touch or move anything else?"

"Nothing except opening the patio slider for ventilation. We didn't know if you wanted to treat this like a crime scene or not."

"Fine—and the owner's name and address?"

"Katja Schmidt, same address in Berlin; she landed from JFK— New York City—at twelve thirty this afternoon, rented a car, and came here. She arrived about two. I think they were a couple."

"Thank you. Very thorough—and I do know where JFK is. Take me to her now, please."

As Albert approached Katja, he thought, *She's probably ten years older than Elsa was. They would've been a striking couple.* He introduced himself, asked if he could call her Katja, and sat on a chair across from her.

"I'm sorry for your loss. Was Elsa your partner?"

"Yes."

"How long had you been together?"

"About two years."

"So you're familiar with her health?"

"Yes. Elsa was healthy, ate right, exercised, and didn't have any chronic conditions." The woman's voice broke, repressing a sob. "For Christ's sake, she was scarcely out of her early twenties."

Albert picked up on her last comment. "So you think her death isn't natural. Why?"

"Well, I don't know . . . don't know what I mean. It's strange, that's all."

"It is, but it happens. We will know more after the autopsy. I'll ask the medical examiner to expand the toxicology analysis to put your mind at ease."

"Thanks."

"Do you know if Elsa had any enemies, anyone who might wish to do her harm? Any problems with former lovers, friends, or disputes related to her employment?"

"None."

"All right, tell me how it is you're on the island and traveling separately."

Using a story she had prepared while waiting for the police, Katja explained how she was a self-employed security consultant. She'd finished a three-month assignment stateside. Elsa was a freelance fashion designer who'd recently completed preparations for a big show later this month. They needed R & R. Plus they were considering moving here permanently because they could work anywhere, yada, yada, yada.

"Originally, we were both supposed to arrive yesterday, but I was delayed, and Elsa must've come early. I was becoming worried because she wasn't answering her phone."

"May I see your phone's call history?"

"It's in my bag on the couch."

"You can show me before I leave. Did anyone else know Elsa was joining you?"

"No—well, maybe her parents. I don't know."

"Do you think Elsa could have been mistaken for you? You look alike?"

"No, of course not—who'd want to hurt me? Are you treating this like a crime now?"

"I don't know yet. You said it yourself: it's strange. Did you touch or move anything?"

"Well, I opened the door, checked for a pulse, went to the bathroom, had a glass of water there, and called the police."

"But not right away. Why did you wait before calling us?"

"I couldn't think; I was in shock." *Paralyzed. I've never been like this before. Screw him if he doesn't believe me.*

"Well . . . all right . . . did you move around the apartment?"

"No, I only sat on the couch."

"Thank you. Have you notified Elsa's family yet?"

"No."

"If you'd like me to do it, I will."

"Please. Her father is Conrad König; he's a big shot in Berlin. I don't know him or his address."

"I'll locate him." The inspecteur went to the gendarme who had been assisting him and talked for a few minutes. When he returned to Katja, he said, "I'm treating this like a crime scene now. We're arranging for you to stay at a nearby hotel. I'd like you to come to headquarters tomorrow, make a formal statement, and be fingerprinted. It's routine."

"I can come about four thirty. I have a meeting with my banker, then we'll have a late lunch afterwards."

"Where's your appointment?"

"It's at Banque des Antilles Francaises—here in Grand Case."

"Okay. Don't leave Saint Martin without asking me. Please show me your phone now." Baudin confirmed Izabella's unanswered calls to Elsa.

A few minutes later, driving to the Grand Case Beach Club, the hotel where the gendarme had made arrangements for her to stay, Izabella thought, *Baudin is no fool. I need to deal with the bank first thing before he confirms that I don't really have an appointment. I may have misjudged the situation. But I couldn't just walk away, leaving Elsa lying there—she deserves better than that.*

Baudin investigated the unit thoroughly while he waited for the crime scene officers. Later, as he was driving home, he thought, *Well, everything looks like natural causes, and Katja appears to be straightforward. But it seems like she took her time calling the police. And notwithstanding her denial of mistaken identity, I'm suspicious Elsa might've been in the wrong place at the wrong time.* Baudin shook his head. *I don't like unexplained deaths, especially of young, healthy people—no, I don't like them at all. Maybe the medical examiner will help me out. Something isn't right here—I feel it.*

***

In the evening, Izabella sat in her hotel room; she felt powerless. It all kept running through her mind.

She recalled parking; how it had been cool when she entered. Izabella couldn't remember if she'd noticed the slight odor. Then being in the living room, where she'd dropped her purse on the couch. And afterward, looking through the dining area and freezing when she saw Elsa's body on the kitchen floor. Next, rushing to her and feeling for a pulse—none. She remembered trembling, fighting back tears, and staring. Elsa was prone, head resting on the left side of her face, arms splayed; she hadn't even broken her fall! Following that, Izabella knelt beside Elsa's body. And for the first time she could recollect, she began sobbing and repeating her lover's name. In the end, she sighed.

"You were already dead, dead when I was calling you. I was supposed to be here . . . not you . . . you died for me!"

Izabella needed to sort out her emotions but stay calm also. She should leave directly, because Baudin wasn't about to let this go. So, at last, Izabella checked flights. Air France had a Paris nonstop tomorrow afternoon at five o'clock.

I'll take that. I ought to be outbound before the inspecteur catches on. I'll think this through on the flight.

***

Nando had been released before noon and was sitting in their dining-meeting room with Bridgette. His right arm was in a sling, and his chest ached. While Nando had been in hospital, a goodbye dinner had been hastily arranged for that night at Scoma's.

"Are you certain you're all right with tonight's dinner?" Bridgette asked.

"I'm fine—can't laugh too much, though."

"I meant . . . emotionally."

"I'm better than I was yesterday. Ellen stopped by this morning. We talked for nearly an hour."

"We talked also. I called her last night and told her what happened to you," Bridgette said.

"Did you feel better after talking with her?" Nando asked.

"Yes, but tell me. What did you two talk about?"

"Ellen correctly suspected I was struggling," Nando said. "I wasn't worried about my wounds; they'll heal, but I was beating myself up."

"Because Izabella got away?"

"Yes, but she didn't simply escape. Izabella cleaned our clocks."

"Well, you prevented the assassination. That's no small accomplishment."

"I know, but I was holding myself accountable; I couldn't get it out of my head."

"What did she say?"

"She asked me whether I had adhered to my training. And were there any breakdowns or deviations from protocol. I said that we did everything properly. So she told me to put it out of my mind, because our superiors would deal with any needed changes they discovered during our debriefings."

"Did you feel responsible, that you ought to have done something differently?" Bridgette asked.

"Yes, and more. I told her I was having trouble with being bested by Izabella. I felt like I'd lost my self-confidence and was questioning my competencies and abilities. Possibly my identity as well—maybe I'm not the man I thought I was."

"It's a lot to process, isn't it?" Bridgette admitted.

"Ellen told me to *keep it simple, stupid* and not overlook the obvious. She pointed out that despite Mal's warnings about Izabella, perhaps even he had underestimated her. She reminded me that physical and mental capacities diminish over time. 'You're at an age where even highly trained, greatest-of-all-time professional athletes must accept they've lost a step.'"

"It makes sense," Bridgette said.

"Ellen didn't pull any punches. Maybe I'm not the fastest gun in the West anymore. Izabella might simply be better. I'm glad I talked with her, though. It's helping me put it into perspective."

"That's right. Now you're merely a sedentary art dealer and academician," Bridgette joked.

***

Mal had been a prime mover in arranging the dinner because their window of opportunity was closing. Bridgette had called her boss last evening, explaining that Nando was in hospital but should be released today. He had agreed she could fly back Monday and report to work on Tuesday morning. Tel Aviv wanted Mal back at Mossad headquarters on Monday, November 17. Then the director had called. He wanted Church and Nando back in Langley on Thursday, November 13: Nando to begin his debriefing and Church for a debriefing and immediate redeployment to Venezuela. Gabi and Joe had no upcoming conflicts, but Ellen Sandler couldn't make it.

So, that evening, dinner conversation eventually centered around how to proceed. "By the end of next week, we'll all be back to our regular jobs. The question is, how do we keep in touch and resolve the Izabella situation?" Nando asked.

"I'm going to be out of the loop. I'll probably be on assignment for three months, and communicating without tipping my hand may be too difficult," Church said.

"Sorry you can't help. I'll coordinate if you'd like. Nando can keep in touch with Jay, and Mal, you can do the same with Zeb, because we're going to need intelligence," Bridgette said.

"I think we all agree she probably headed for Saint Martin, so that's a suitable starting point," Mal commented.

"If it's true, I can liaise with Marigot. The major crimes on the island are under the jurisdiction of France's National Police Force. In fact, inspecteurs from France are routinely rotated there for three to six months to maintain quality control and professional standards. Izabella is now one of the most-wanted criminals in the world. I won't have any trouble with top secret clearances and such."

"Let's not get ahead of ourselves," Joe interjected. "I have no doubt it was Izabella yesterday, but we need the FBI's DNA analysis before going too much further. I'll follow up with Quantico tomorrow. Maybe Jay could pressure the forensics lab from Langley."

"Okay, and if we haven't heard by the time I arrive there, I'll pressure the director as well," Nando said.

"Let's assume she's alive. We need to verify Izabella went to Saint Martin. We'll keep Jay honest. I'll have Zeb try to locate her on flights from the East Coast. It seems to me she might travel from there under her Katja Schmidt ID, syncing her flight with her local identity. It would avoid questions if anyone was looking at her. If that doesn't work, we can use facial recognition as a fallback," Mal observed.

"Fine, let's do that," Nando said.

"And if the director is obstructionist . . . what then?" Gabi asked.

"Church and I ought to be able to get a read on that when we're in Langley. We might need to go around him to the director of National Intelligence," Nando admitted.

***

Izabella had had a miserable night. She'd tried to focus on her troubles, but the pain kept pushing through. Eventually, she'd fallen asleep, albeit fitfully. It was nine o'clock now, and while having breakfast in her hotel's

Sunset Café, she made her plans for the day. First, she called her bank in Grand Case and, after giving her password and answering several security questions, transferred most of the $115 million she'd received from Satie to her Swiss account. Then she headed to Marigot and parked in a public lot. Her first stop was to find a phone shop, where she bought a new smartphone. Izabella arranged for the merchant to charge it so she could pick it up after lunch. Then, since she'd traveled light from San Francisco and her crime scene condo was off-limits, Izabella needed to buy clothes. She looked for a women's shop and spotted Caribbean Casuals on a side street.

"'Mornin', Mademoiselle," the sales clerk greeted her as she entered.

"Good morning. I hope you can help me—I'm in a muddle."

"What's the matter?"

"Well, the airline lost my baggage; I checked with them this morning—they still haven't found it. It's such a bother. So I need some clothes. All I have is what was in my carry-on: a change of underwear. I always travel like that—this happened before. I learned the hard way . . ." Soon Izabella had three sets of underwear and two skirts, two T-shirts, and two pairs of anklet socks.

"This is great," she said. "Do you know a decent place for a local lunch?"

"We like Bateau Lavoir—terrific native food."

"Excellent, thanks."

Izabella paid cash, started to leave, then feigned an afterthought. *Might as well keep up the pretense.* "Oh, I didn't think; I'll need a bathing suit."

"Would you like a one-piece or a bikini?" the clerk asked as she showed Izabella to the suits.

"Oh, I think a bikini—don't you?"

Next, Izabella went to her bank's Marigot office, where she had a large safe-deposit box. She removed several sets of fake identification and €10,000 in small bills, putting all of it in her shopping bag. Then, returning to the parking lot, she packed everything in her duffel bag—it just fit. When she was finished, Izabella left, abandoning her car and discarding her empty shopping bag, receipts, and old smartphone's SIM card in a refuse receptacle. She walked to Bateau Lavoir and then, following a leisurely lunch, during which she watched a tiny old man roll large Cuban cigars for the restaurant's patrons, she walked around town and disposed of her old phone. Later, Izabella picked up her new burner before hailing a cabbie, who was grateful for an airport run.

***

It was late Monday afternoon at France's National Police HQ in Marigot. Inspecteur Baudin had spent the day working on the Elsa König death. He'd contacted Elsa's father, who was shocked, having had no idea Elsa was in Saint Martin. He and his wife were flying from Berlin to the island the following day on their private jet. Baudin agreed to pick them up and bring them to headquarters to identify Elsa's body. *A formality*, he thought. *I'm certain the Schmidt woman's ID was accurate.* The medical examiner had met with him after three o'clock. His findings shed no light on the cause of death. Elsa had been a perfectly healthy young woman.

"It seems like her heart just stopped. It happens."

"Did you notice any skin pricks like an injection might leave?" Baudin asked.

"No. You're thinking she was injected with something that killed her?"

"I may be grasping at straws."

"I'll take another look—won't miss a centimeter. The blood is going out to Quantico via DHL tonight. I'll request their most sophisticated screening. If there's anything, they'll find it. But it will take a little longer than normal."

"Fine."

The inspecteur returned to his office. He reviewed his notes and couldn't dismiss the incongruities. He looked at his watch. Katja Schmidt had been due at four thirty; it was four forty-five now. Without wasting time, he called the manager of the Banque des Antilles Francaises branch in Grand Case. It took a bit of persuading, but the inspecteur eventually confirmed that Schmidt had no appointment that day. But more important, she'd transferred a sizable sum abroad. They wouldn't disclose the amount, but the manager reported that the transfer had left little in her account. Next, Baudin called the Grand Case Beach Club. Katja Schmidt wasn't there, and the receptionist reported that she'd seen her leave about nine thirty that morning. Then Baudin had one of his investigators request outbound flight manifests. This would be a slow process, because the airlines were reluctant to cooperate without a court order. But it didn't matter—he was suspicious Katja would be traveling under another name. Baudin sat back in his chair, reflecting.

I was correct. Something's wrong; this isn't a death by natural causes. And now Katja Schmidt has vanished.

CHAPTER TWENTY-SIX

Tuesday, November 11, 2014

Paris

Notwithstanding the morning rush hour traffic, Bridgette arrived at police headquarters, on the Île de la Cité, a few minutes after nine o'clock. She checked in with her captain before heading to her desk. The accumulated paperwork was daunting, but by lunch, Bridgette had made a substantial dent in it. After a salad, she called Madame.

"'Afternoon. It's Bridgette. I landed this morning—I'm at work now. How are you?"

"Fine. It's wonderful to hear from you. I'm glad you're home safely."

"Me too. I have news for you—a little bad but mostly good. The good is that Nando's recall is over. He's flying to Washington tomorrow for a debriefing, and then he ought to be home by Friday."

"Wonderful; I've missed him. Was he successful?"

"Mostly."

"So what's the bad news?"

"He was shot—only a flesh wound. They kept him in hospital overnight for observation. His arm is in a sling, and he'll need physical therapy; otherwise, Nando is fine."

"And Mal?"

"Unscathed. He has to report to Tel Aviv by Monday the seventeenth." Mal had sworn Bridgette to secrecy; he was actually flying to Paris to surprise Madame.

"I'm happy he wasn't injured. Is he going straight to Tel Aviv?"

"As far as I know. I have a lot of calls to return, but I wanted to check in. Maybe we can have dinner this week." Bridgette rang off quickly. She had heard the disappointment in Madame's voice and knew that if she stayed on, she would give away Mal's surprise.

Next, Bridgette called National Police headquarters in Marigot to enlist their help in investigating Katja Schmidt and her condo in Grand Case. She asked to speak to the inspecteur who covered that area. Bridgette was put on hold, and in a few minutes, her call was answered.

"Baudin."

"Albert . . . it's Bridgette, in Paris. I didn't know you were in Saint Martin."

"This is a pleasant surprise. I haven't been here too long—I'm on a six-month deployment. What can I help you with?"

Bridgette went on to tell him she'd been consulting with the CIA on a top secret case. They had been tracking an international assassin, who they now believed might be hiding out under the name of Katja Schmidt at her condo in Grand Case.

"Is this your NoMO Killer?"

"Oh, please—no. That turned out to be nothing. You guys were right."

"Well, you know I never teased you. I thought you were onto something.

"You're in luck. Here's the thirty-second version. Her lover and Berlin flat mate—Elsa König—arrived at Schmidt's condo Friday evening, about seven o'clock. She appears to have died almost immediately of natural causes." Baudin went on to explain the circumstances surrounding Elsa's death and his investigation. "If there's foul play, I suspect mistaken identity. Also, Schmidt was supposed to meet me at HQ late yesterday afternoon for fingerprinting and a formal statement. But instead she did a runner after transferring 'a sizable sum abroad,' as her local bank manager described it. I've reached out to Germany's Federal Criminal Police Office, requesting surveillance of her Berlin address."

They chatted for a few minutes, then Bridgette rang off, saying, "That's helpful. Let's keep in touch. Enjoy the warm weather, Albert."

Bridgette worked until about seven o'clock that evening. Her accumulated paperwork was nearly finished. After she returned to the apartment, Bridgette unpacked and changed before calling Nando.

"Did you have an easy trip?" he asked when she answered.

"Yes, I made it to work on time, and I'm nearly caught up. I called Madame, told her about your wound, and that you would probably be home by the end of the week."

"Did you tell her Mal is coming to Paris?"

"No, he swore me to secrecy." Bridgette snickered.

"He has a nonstop tomorrow at three and ought to land around eleven Thursday morning."

"She'll be happy. Do you know your schedule yet?"

"Church and I are flying to DC at eight thirty tomorrow morning; we'll land about five p.m. I figure we'll be in meetings all day Thursday. There's an Air France nonstop from Dulles at six thirty in the evening, which arrives in Paris at eight o'clock Friday morning. I'll try for that flight. Church doesn't know anything yet except that he's heading for Venezuela ASAP."

"Nando, are you going to the apartment first thing when you get home?"

"Yes. I'll clean up and walk over to La Galerie after lunch, but I'll be back before you're home. We can go to a bistro if you'd like."

"Okay, let's do that. I called down to Saint Martin. I spoke with Inspecteur Albert Baudin. I knew him in Paris, although I never worked with him." Bridgette filled Nando in on what Baudin had learned.

"Well, there doesn't seem to be much doubt Saint Martin is where Izabella went," Nando said. "It's too bad about Elsa. I agree with Baudin; it sounds like a colossal screwup. Mal has Zeb trying to confirm her flight to the island, although I think it's academic now. I'll talk to Mal before he leaves and see if he can redirect Zeb onto picking up her trail—maybe he can follow the money."

"This confirms the director was behind the attempt on Izabella's life, doesn't it?"

"Yes, he'd counted on Izabella being killed. But when everything went from bad to worse, he cut his losses and threw Izabella to the wolves. That's why Elsa died before Izabella aborted. He had already ordered Izabella's hit," Nando responded.

"This also explains his change in attitude."

"It does. I wonder if he knows about the mistaken identity yet."

"Me too . . ."

"I'll see you Friday evening. Love you," Bridgette said.

***

After their arrival Wednesday afternoon, Church went to his local apartment to prepare for his upcoming deployment, and Nando took a hotel room. That evening they called Jay and agreed to meet at Langley at seven o'clock the next morning. After that, Nando, Church, and Jay would join a secure conference call with the directors of the National Intelligence and CIA agencies and the president, who was still in Beijing. Following that, Church and Nando would be debriefed.

At the first meeting, Nando started in. "We need to talk about any new developments before our call. Also, because the director of National Intelligence will be there, I think we should disclose everything we know. It's a perfect work-around our director." Church and Jay agreed, and Nando continued, "Jay, why don't you go first."

"I have two things. First, I spoke to Anna. Her employer promoted one of the men in the executive suite to CEO. Anna knows him, and he wants her to stay on as his assistant. So I think it's working out for her."

"Will she have the same duties?" Church asked.

"I don't know. I didn't ask, and she didn't offer," Jay responded.

"Well," Nando commented, "let's hope her new boss doesn't take advantage of her."

"Anna's canny—she'll land on her feet, however it shakes out."

"Next, and this is a bit odd, I have an identification of the woman who burned at Point Lobos. A friend in the FBI's forensic lab sent it to me yesterday."

"Why odd?" Nando asked.

"My friend thought the entire San Francisco request was handled strangely. First, our director was involved. He called their lab's director and asked him to report the results to the CIA director's office before sending it back to San Francisco. Also, the lab's director said to take their time and make certain there were no mistakes. My friend wonders if something is going on, so he sent it to me in case the analysis goes astray."

"It sounds like our director was slow-walking it and trying to control the results," Nando opined. "He probably intended to keep the charade of Izabella's death going for as long as possible."

"Why would the lab's director agree to that?" Church asked.

"Who knows, but I think our director has a lot of dirt on a lot of people," Nando replied, and asked, "Who is she?"

"I dug a little on her antecedents," Jay continued. "This is all public information. I pieced it together from the internet. Her name was Karen Axelsson. She was thirty-seven, single, the same height and weight as Izabella. I have her picture from the net. She was a San Francisco lawyer. No missing persons report was filed. Apparently, Karen was in the process of changing firms and was supposed to report to her new job yesterday after the Veterans Day holiday. It seems like she'd been on vacation for two weeks beforehand; that's why no one missed her."

"Why was Karen put in the database?" Nando asked.

"There was an after-hours assault last year at her old firm's office. A lawyer was badly beaten and subsequently died. Elimination fingerprints and DNA were taken from all employees who were working late that night, including Karen. SFPD cleared her of any involvement. They caught the unsub later—a disgruntled client."

"Let's see how the director deals with this at our meeting. I'll send it to Gabi—one way or another—so she can run down next of kin, do a notification, and revise their case file," Jay concluded.

The men went to the office of the director of National Intelligence. The CIA director was already there when they were ushered in. A video call to Beijing was online. "Good evening, Mr. President," the director of National Intelligence began.

"'Morning, gentlemen," the president said. "Before we start, Nando, how are you and the rest of your team doing?"

"I'm fine, Mr. President. The arm isn't too sore, but the bruise I took to my chest is a bitch. Pardon my language."

"Understood . . . it'll pass. You were fortunate. No one else from your group was injured, correct?"

"That's right, sir. Bridgette returned to work in Paris Tuesday morning; Mal is flying there this afternoon and then on to Tel Aviv Sunday evening. I'm leaving for Paris tonight."

"Excellent, and how about you, Church?"

"I'm awaiting deployment, sir."

The director of the CIA spoke up. "I'm meeting with him after his debriefing. He'll probably be airborne tomorrow morning."

"Okay. Let's talk about the debriefings for a minute. Then I'll move on to what I want to talk about. I've instructed the debriefers to concentrate on operations and tactics—particularly on how we missed the fire exit and whether we need revisions to our procedures. Any problems with that?" He waited a beat. "Good. Now moving on, do we have any updates?"

The director of the CIA spoke up. "Mr. President, we've identified the woman who was killed at Point Lobos. Quantico matched her bone's DNA; she was Karen Axelsson. I received the results yesterday. It was a slow go because the FBI wanted to be certain and Veterans Day cost us a little time." The director turned to Jay and said, "I'll send it to you after this call. Research her as best you can and send the DNA profile as well as what you find out to San Francisco by the end of the day. If there's anything you discover that we ought to know about, call me."

Nando and Jay exchanged unnoticed glances as the analyst replied, "Certainly, sir."

"Also, Jay, anything on your cousin?" the president inquired.

"Yes, Anna seems to have landed on her feet."

"All right. We don't need WITSEC then?"

"No, sir. Thank you for asking."

"Okay. Anything to report, Nando?"

"Yes, I spoke with Bridgette. She contacted an inspecteur, Albert Baudin, whom she knows in Saint Martin. Elsa König, Izabella's Berlin roommate, died under mysterious circumstances. The local inspecteur suspects a possible case of mistaken identity for Izabella." Nando then reviewed what Bridgette had discovered. "It seems likely that Izabella will go to Berlin, probably sooner rather than later."

"Excellent job. Unfortunately, she's in the wind again, correct?"

"Yes. When I see Bridgette tomorrow, I hope to have additional information. I'll call Jay if I do."

"Fine . . . but I hope the Germans aren't too damn plodding about this. Izabella doesn't let any grass grow under her feet," the president observed, before moving on. "Nando, you and Church are returning to your regular jobs now, but I'd like to tell you how I'm proceeding. This will be a top priority for all our clandestine services, and National Intelligence will quarterback. My orders will be simple: bring her in alive. Unless it's self-defense, no termination without a direct order from me. I'll make that clear."

"Yes, sir. It makes sense."

"But I have a concern—Mal," the president continued. "I'm convinced his orders will be reinstated and that they'll conflict with mine. I'll probably call his prime minister about it.

"Nando, I'm sorry to lose you. If you ever want to come back full-time, let me know. There will always be a place for you in one of our clandestine services.

"All right. I think we're done here. First-class work, gentlemen."

***

Jay returned to his office while Nando and Church went to their debriefings. The director of the CIA returned to his office also. When he walked in, he said to his secretary, "No calls. I don't want to be disturbed." He walked over to a window, clasping his hands behind his back. The director stood there looking out over the campus for a long time. At length, he returned to his desk.

Jesus Christ—Nando dropped a bombshell. He has no fuckin' idea. What Bridgette discovered is a catastrophe. How the hell did the capo's contractor kill the wrong woman? That's bad enough, but now all our clandestine services are after Izabella—not to mention Interpol, the French, and the Germans. And with instructions to bring her in alive! Shit, and I'm not pulling the strings anymore!

Hopefully, Israel won't screw with Mal's orders, because the Kidon Unit doesn't take prisoners. They may be my salvation if the capo can't straighten out this mess. But I'm not gonna talk about it on the phone; I'm flyin' to Newark to see the capo.

***

Later that afternoon, the director's CIA jet landed at Newark's Liberty International Airport. Then he took a taxi, and in less than an hour it pulled up in front of the Italian restaurant on Terhune Avenue where they had previously dined. The capo was waiting. They sat at the same table, and over a glass of wine, the capo said, "I haven't check with Bermuda yet. I need all the facts first; tell me what happened."

"We didn't know her girlfriend was going to be there. Also, they switched their travel plans around. Consequently, the girlfriend arrived first, ahead of time. Moreover, they could pass for sisters. So I guess I understand the fuckup. But now every major intelligence service is looking for Izabella with instructions to bring her in alive. I can't have that. Jesus—I thought you understood."

"I did; I'm not fuckin' happy either. But let's relax. There's nothing time and money can't solve."

"Easy for you to say. You gotta fix this!"

"Think about it. You have history's most powerful intelligence gathering agency, and we got guys everywhere—all over the world. We'll figure it out together. Any idea where this broad went?"

"Just conjecture. She was born in Italy but emigrated from there to Israel when she was five. Izabella probably went to Germany but just for a quick in-and-out. She had a cousin in Rome, Lucca Ricci—I heard he was executed a while ago. Izabella thought he was mobbed up."

"I'll start in Rome, then. We got a lotta people there."

"Okay, but I need proof positive this time. Send me her thumb."

***

Mal's taxi dropped him in front of La Galerie at noon on Thursday. He walked in, the little bell on the door jingled, and Madame called out from her office, "I'm in back—be out in a sec. Have a look around."

Mal stood by the door, put his valise down, smiled, and waited quietly. Madame came in, perusing the papers she'd been working on, looked up, and dropped them before rushing to Mal, throwing her arms around his neck. After Madame stopped kissing him, she said, "I'm so glad you're here. I was disappointed when Bridgette told me you were going straight to Tel Aviv. She knew you were coming here, didn't she?"

"I wanted to surprise you."

"That wasn't fair."

Mal kissed her again, changed the door sign to FERMÉ, and took Madame to her office. They made love, and afterward, as Madame was straightening her clothing, she asked, "Will you stay with me?"

"Naturally, but I'll be leaving on Sunday evening. Might I have your apartment keys, please? I'd like to shower and change." Madame handed them over. "Would you like to go to a bistro for dinner, or shall I cook?"

"I'd love it if you'd cook."

"Excellent. I'll shop this afternoon. What time will you be home?"

"Around seven thirty," she replied. Madame walked Mal to the front door, kissed him, and changed the sign. When she returned to her desk, she called Bridgette.

"You've been a naughty girl! Why didn't you tell me!"

"I wanted to. I knew you were disappointed, but Mal wished to surprise you. Did he stop by? Did Mal apologize?"

"Oh yes," Madame giggled. "More than once. We're staying in tonight. Mal is cooking, so if you need to stop by in the morning, don't make it too early."

"Perish the thought," Bridgette joked.

***

In Beijing on Friday morning the fourteenth, after the end of the Asia-Pacific Economic Cooperation summit, the presidents of the United States and China held a joint announcement before a brief press conference. The summit had been productive for US and China relations. The presidents jointly announced commitments to cut carbon emissions and agreed to reduce tariffs, strengthen communication between their militaries in the Pacific, and extend the duration of visas.

A droll ol' China hand, a stringer for the *South China Morning Post*, reported that although these insubstantial agreements were a welcome change from years of bollixed up relationships, the countries' fundamentally different visions hadn't been reconciled. Skeptically, he wondered if there were an undisclosed addendum, because both men looked like the proverbial cat that had swallowed the canary.

CHAPTER TWENTY-SEVEN

Midfall through Year End 2014
Paris

Bridgette and Nando were happy as the rest of fall slowly unfolded. They quickly settled into a comfortable routine. His arm, with the aid of physical therapy, had quickly healed. Nando returned to his regular schedule at La Galerie, but so that he could spend extra time with Bridgette, he cut back on teaching, especially the late-afternoon or evening classes. It never crossed his mind to take the president up on his offer.

Bridgette was enjoying work more. She suspected that Albert Baudin had passed on her comment about the NoMO Killer to his Paris colleagues. The result was that she wasn't teased anymore. Nevertheless, a few associates occasionally asked earnestly if anything new had turned up. Bridgette always responded as if laughing at herself. "Oh, it was nothing. I was being foolish." There was no need for them to know Bridgette was laughing at them with an imaginary fist pump and a silent *Yes—I was right.*

Madame seemed to be handling her intermittent long-distance affair with Mal well. He made her happy and gave her something to look forward to. Bridgette and Nando knew that Mal and Madame loved each other, but life, chiefly Mal's, simply got in their way.

***

Bridgette took it upon herself to keep in touch with everyone. Ellen told her that Gabi was able to locate Karen's parents in less than a week after her DNA analysis had been sent to San Francisco.

"With the research that had been included, Gabi contacted the law firm that Karen was due to start at. Karen's employment application contained her parents' phone number and address for contact in case of emergency," Ellen reported.

"That turned out to be easy. Where did they live?"

"In Ogunquit, on the southern coast of Maine. They were originally from upstate New York but retired down east. Karen went to Stanford Law—that's the connection with San Francisco. Apparently, she loved it out here."

"Did her parents fly out?" Bridgette asked.

"Yes. They had Karen's remains cremated and her ashes shipped back east. But before that, they arranged for a small memorial at the crematorium's chapel. There were a few mourners from her old law firm, the managing partner from her new one, and several friends. Gabi and Joe went as well."

"That was thoughtful. Her death is one of the saddest parts of this affair. Karen was in the wrong place at the wrong time."

"I know. Unfortunately, her death will remain open on our books until Izabella is returned to California for trial," Ellen said.

Sometime later, Albert Baudin called from Marigot. "I wanted to bring you up-to-date. Unfortunately, we haven't made a lot of progress."

"Tell me," Bridgette responded.

"The blood work came back from Quantico. Nothing. Nonetheless, I'm still not convinced that Elsa's death was from natural causes. I was able to track Katja around Marigot before she left for the airport. She left Grand Case about nine thirty and parked at a public lot in Marigot. Afterward, Katja goes to a ladies' apparel shop and later lunch. Following that, she abandons her car and disappears. What's odd is that Katja has nearly an hour of missing time between when she leaves the women's shop and goes to Bateau Lavoir for lunch."

"Did you check for safe-deposit boxes at Marigot's main office of her Grand Case bank? It makes sense that she might have gone there."

"No—that's a terrific idea, thanks. I will."

"Also, I'm having trouble with a court order for the airlines' manifests and their CCTV. The blood analysis is causing the problem."

"Did the Germans set up a stakeout?"

"Yes, but they didn't put it in place until the thirteenth. Then they only kept it up during the day and just for a week—nothing."

"How about Elsa's parents?"

"They arrived on November eleventh and identified her. I was able to release the body on the fourteenth, and they left for Berlin the same day. They aren't buying natural causes either. They say she was a health nut and will be talking to her doctor in Berlin. I gave them a copy of the autopsy and blood work."

"Albert, it sounds like you've done everything you can. Let's keep in touch," Bridgette said in closing.

At length, the holidays were fast approaching. Bridgette and Nando were looking forward to their first Christmas living together. She noticed that he was relaxing; he seemed to be enjoying his new life more and more as the days went buy. Bridgette felt blessed that everything had worked out. She knew how horribly wrong it could've gone.

*****

On Tuesday morning, December 30, Mal Ben-David sat in the prime minister's outer office in Jerusalem. He had arrived early for his meeting and was greeted by the prime minister's secretary. "Good morning, Deputy Director. It's nice to see you again. You don't usually visit us in Jerusalem."

"'Morning. It's nice to see you as well." Chuckling, he said, "It's less than fifty miles from Tel Aviv, but it seems like it's a continent away."

"Well, we're glad you made the sacrifice. He's just finishing up a call—shouldn't be long."

Shortly thereafter, Mal was ushered into the office. "Good morning, Mr. Prime Minister."

"'Morning. How's the family, Mal?"

"Well, I was able to take time at Hanukkah. Thank you for asking. And your family, sir?"

"Well also. It has been a while—I thought we should talk. I know you were thoroughly debriefed at Mossad headquarters. I read the report, but I would like to hear what you have to say—off the record. I know you're unhappy with the outcome, so I want to stress how you helped the Americans and, in so doing, achieved our primary goal. The American president was grateful. He says the CIA operations officers spoke highly of you."

"Thank you, but there are still loose ends that need tidying up: the CIA director and Izabella."

"Well, let's talk about those. For one thing, you were circumspect in your debrief about the CIA director. Do you think he was complicit?"

"Yes, but unless the US captures Izabella and makes a deal, it may never come out."

"I was thinking of another scenario. How would you feel about killing two birds with one stone?"

"How so, Mr. Prime Minister?"

"Well, think this through with me. This is more your area than mine. Let's say you resume your prior task. Track Izabella down, but with a change I'd like to suggest—don't terminate her. I'm guessing she has hard intelligence on the director, so we'll make a deal for it and keep the entire scenario to ourselves. What the Americans don't know won't hurt them. Then Izabella goes to jail for life. That's the first bird.

"After that, we flip the director with her intel. He'll be ours for as long as he's in this administration or another. A source of inestimable information, don't you think? That's the second bird."

By the time the prime minister was finished, Mal was nodding. "I don't see a flaw. Zeb is continuing to scour our intelligence for any clues of her whereabouts."

"What's the matter, Mal? It's a decent plan. You should be happier."

"It's a first-rate plan—it's not that. I'm having trouble dealing with my performance in the Izabella case."

"How so?"

"It was an excellent chess match, but Izabella and I each made a mistake. At some time in the past, she told her cousin about her address in Berlin. She forgot about it, and that led us to Grand Case. Izabella had no idea we were onto that location."

"So she never expected the director to strike there."

"Correct."

"Well, what was your mistake? I assume it's the crux of your unhappiness."

"Yes, but it's more than simple unhappiness."

"Is it so bad that you can't continue?"

"I wouldn't say that—I'm just off my game."

"All right, Mal, what was your mistake?"

"I didn't take the shot, the shot in Saint Sulpice. I had her dead bang. I was selfish, thinking of my escape. If I had taken that shot, none of this would've happened. All that collateral damage, all those deaths, would have been avoided."

"It's a lot of responsibility to take upon yourself, Mal. Think about it: the conspirators, the director—all powerful people. They would have found someone else, someone we might not have known about. We wouldn't have been able to help. The US might not have even uncovered the plot."

"But the *innocents*, Karen and Elsa; they weren't even in the game. If I'd simply taken that shot!"

"Things happen for a reason, Mal. We don't always know why."

The men sat quietly. Mal struggled for a while, then sighed. "I have an idea about how to make it right. How about I take Madame on vacation towards the end of January? She doesn't get away much. I'll take her to Saint Martin for ten days; Madame would love it. And while I'm there, I'll start from scratch; I'll try to pick up Izabella's trail. But I'll need more vacation time, and you'll have to cover my butt with my wife."

"Are you certain this isn't a boondoggle, as the Americans say?" The prime minister chuckled.

"No, sir. Zeb and I will work the hell out of it. We'll bring her back."

"Okay, let's do it. Consider your ass covered."

When the prime minister walked Mal to the door, he thought, *I guess he doesn't consider Luca and his mistress innocents, or maybe he's just lost count.* Then he put his arm around his favorite agent's shoulders and said quietly,

"Remember, Malachi, our Lord works in mysterious ways, and with the most unlikely people."

EPILOGUE

Friday, February 13, 2015

Rome

On November 11, Izabella's flight from Saint Martin to Paris had landed at seven in the morning. Because of less security, she intended to travel by trains for the remainder of her trip. So, she took a taxi to Paris' Gare de l'Est and caught a nine o'clock train to Berlin's Hauptbahnhof, which arrived at six that evening. Izabella located a second class, railroad hotel and checked in for one night. Afterward, she left the hotel and took a fifteen minute tram ride to their Mitte district apartment. Izabella waited across the street, observing for fifteen minutes—no apparent stakeout. She was in and out in ten minutes and back on a tram to her hotel. Then, at eight thirty the next morning, Izabella entrained, arriving at Rome's Termini station fourteen hours later.

Izabella had realized it would be a risk returning to Berlin yet gambled it would take a day or two for Baudin to enlist international surveillance. Izabella returned to clean out her stash of several additional IDs, more euros, and most important, a Beretta 9-mm with magazines and ammo. Her hideaway was in her closet, underneath a floorboard. But while she was there, she felt a myriad of unexpected emotions—nostalgia, wistfulness, but also foreboding. Mostly new territory for her, especially the sense of an impending calamity. But those feelings began to die down as Izabella went about settling into Rome, and her attitude was changing. Izabella had stopped routinely carrying a gun, although she couldn't

341

forsake her knife yet. Also, since Berlin, she hadn't any interest in a new lover. Izabella continued to be unsettled about herself and her future.

Mostly she continued to lie low, yet today Izabella had been shopping all afternoon along Rome's Via del Corso and Via dei Condotti. She hailed a taxi as the sun was setting and was looking forward to returning to the apartment she had rented three months ago in the Hotel dei Mellini on the Via Muzio Clementi. The eighty-room boutique-style hotel—on a quiet street within walking distance of most of Rome's main sights—was housed in a nineteenth-century building a block from the Tiber River, in the west bank's art nouveau Prati District. Off the beaten path, it was favored by couples looking for a quiet escape. Izabella knew she wanted to settle in Rome. So while she decided on her final plan, this area with its boulevards, al fresco wine bars, and gourmet restaurants was perfect.

When she arrived at the hotel, her apartment was dark, so putting her shopping bags down, she turned, flipping on the lights. As Izabella retrieved her packages and looked up, she froze, holding her breath. Izabella recognized that this was the threat she'd been fearing and said, "I've been expecting you."

Sitting in a chair across the room, wearing gloves, and aiming a silenced .22 semiautomatic at her was Bermuda. While holding up Izabella's 9-mm, she said, "I found your gun. Are you otherwise armed?"

"Just a knife, in my boot."

"Remove it with two fingers and gently toss it to your right."

Izabella complied, and the assassin motioned her to a chair. They sat for a short time, sizing each other up. Eventually, Izabella asked, "Did you kill Elsa?"

"Yes. Was she your lover?"

"Yes. We lived together in Berlin."

"I'm sorry for that: I was given bad information. It was the first mistake I've ever made. She died instantly—no pain. She never knew what happened."

"*Spyashchaya krasavitsa?*"

"Yes."

"So you're putting it right tonight?"

"Yes."

They sat for a short time again. "I have a last request," Izabella said.

"What?"

"I have a thumb drive and a padded mailing envelope in the desk. Let me address it and put the drive inside. Afterward, would you mail it for me?"

The assassin motioned Izabella to the desk, saying, "I'll be five feet behind. If you make a false move—"

"I won't."

When Izabella was finished, Bermuda said, "Go to the middle of the room and kneel." As Izabella did, the assassin looked at the envelope. It had a Tel Aviv address:

MALACHI BEN-DAVID, DEPUTY DIRECTOR

CENTRAL INSTITUTE FOR INTELLIGENCE AND SPECIAL OPERATIONS

Kneeling, Izabella said, "I don't have any stamps."

Bermuda approached from the rear saying, "I'll take care of it for you." Izabella continued to kneel as Bermuda aimed her gun.

Memories of Elsa, warm and hazy, flooded her mind but were quickly replaced, overthrown by a kaleidoscope of terrifying, hellish images, cold and crystal clear—

THE END

NOTES

1. Adapted from a recurring quote in the *Mission: Impossible* TV series, produced by Bruce Geller, Desilu Productions, 1966–1973.

2. *The Third Man*, written by Graham Greene and directed by Carol Reed, London Films, 1949.

3. Adapted from a recurring quote in *The A-Team*, created by Frank Lupo and Stephen J, Cannell, Universal Television, 1983–1987.

4. William Shakespeare, *The Tragedy of Julius Caesar*, play, First Folio, 1623 (3:1:273).

ACKNOWLEDGMENTS

Thanks to my wife, Ann, for her encouragement, support, and tolerating my terrible spelling, numerous typos, and frequently humorous homonyms; my sister, Pamela H. Rappolt; and my friend Michael F. Shepherd, who encourages me and is always my first beta reader. And a special thanks to Rachel Keith for her first-rate copyediting combined with excellent comments and suggestions.

ABOUT THE AUTHOR

Joe Hodgkins and his wife of over fifty years, Ann, live in Morris County, northern New Jersey.

He graduated from Fordham University's Rose Hill Campus in the Bronx and is a member of the Fordham Alumni Support Team, FAST, representing the university at college fairs and nights held by local high schools. After attaining his undergraduate degree in liberal arts, he attended New York University's Graduate School of Business Administration in Manhattan.

Hodgkins was a senior manager in both commercial banking and corporate finance. He was a member of the Commercial Finance Association, now known as the Secured Finance Network, and was a frequent presenter at continuing education seminars for the New Jersey Society of CPAs and the New Jersey Institute for Continuing Legal Education on topics such as crisis management, asset recovery, and secured lending. He took early retirement in 2002.

He is currently a eucharistic minister at his local Episcopal church, where he also served as treasurer and chairman of the finance committee. Hodgkins has been active in Freemasonry for nearly forty years and has been an Officer or Grand Officer in all bodies of the York Rite. In 2015 he received the First Masonic District of New Jersey's Distinguished White Apron Award for his service and contributions to the Craft.

Other interests include traveling with Ann, reading, and handgun target shooting.

Made in the USA
Coppell, TX
09 June 2022